The Re-Creation of Roach

Acknowledgements:

The author wishes to thank all those believed in her and who helped bring this second edition to print.

Special thanks to these professionals:

Cover art by Korey Scott, Denton, TX.
Cover design by Ira VanScoyoc, Emerald Phoenix Media, Manvel, TX

Introduction:
The Beginning:

as revealed to Daeira Dairier in dreams and meditation

In the beginning, Essence roamed the skies looking for the right place to start a world. She saw that our planet already had cycles of day and night, water and air. It had a set path around its sun so its cycles could be numbered, but it had no life.

"I will see what can live and grow here," she said, and joined herself with it. The Creative Life Force of Essence endowed the waters with miniscule plants and creatures and the cycle of life began.

Essence cherished this new life, but was tired from her journey across the cosmos, so she entered the earth and went to sleep.

Eons later, when she awoke, the planet was filled with life forms. The water and land and air teemed with a great variety of plants and creatures. Some were tiny and frail, others huge and fierce. There was great variety even in their coverings—smooth, hard, scaly, furry. The large, scaly ones dominated at that time.

Essence watched her world. The sun fed the plants, which fed the moving creatures, who then were eaten by larger ones, and on and on. They grew, propagated, and returned to feed the earth when their time was over. Some creatures failed and disappeared, but new ones evolved to take their place.

And ants were there.

Essence, satisfied with the balance and cycles, cradled her world, and went to sleep again.

The pain of many shocks woke Essence. Chunks of matter hurled through the cosmos and struck the planet, killing millions of life forms and knocking the planet in its cosmic path. The dust from their impact screened the sun's light, denying life-giving energy to plants. Essence watched in dismay as thousands of species disappeared from her cherished world. In her grief, she shook. Hills tumbled. Mountains sent forth liquid fire from within.

But even in grief, Essence's Creative Life Force found its way again. An infinite variety of flowering plants came to be. A few species of the scaly creatures and the small ones with fur and feathers survived.

And ants were still there.

Essence watched for many eons as the fur creatures increased in size and began to dominate. "What would happen," Essence said, "if I interfered and gave one life form an advantage? If I gave a tad of my intelligence to a creature, could it create something original, as I have?"

Essence looked closely at each species and finally chose one that seemed different from others. This species was not entirely covered with fur, stood on only two appendages, and had a well developed nervous system. She infused them with more intelligence and waited to see what would happen.

Season cycles passed. Generations of Duo Pods came and went. Essence saw that they made tools, built things, and developed the planet. Their machines grew ever more complex. Satisfied, Essence took a nap.

Essence awoke with a fever. The planet's surface was a shambles. The air and the water were fouled. All the Duo Pods, all of the feathered creatures, and most of the furry ones were dead forever.

"What has happened to my world?" Essence cried.

Grief for her failed experiment and illness consumed Essence. The earth shook. Storms raged. Her tears covered many lands. Then slowly, the earth healed itself. Although it would take many more eons for all of the Duo Pod creations to return to the earth, the world looked new and fresh once more. Essence found that one substance the Duo Pods had made would not break itself down and feed the earth. They had indeed created something original. Her experiment had not been a total failure.

She looked around hopefully and found that ants, roaches and other insects were not only still there, but had grown greatly in size and changed in other ways.

"Ah, my faithful ants," she said. "You have been with me from the earliest days and have always been civilized. Perhaps the intelligence I gave the Duo Pods was not enough, I will try again. I will give you not only the gift of knowledge, but my compassion as well. And this time I will not sleep, but will watch over my world. I will be available to my creatures, speaking to their minds when they seek me. When each one's time on earth is done, the part of me that is in them will return to me in unity forever. Eat then, my ants, of the lasting creation of the Duo Pods—plastic—and receive my gifts. Cherish my world and seek to understand its mysteries."

And so we are.

While Essence was speaking, a group of roaches approached. They took the gift of intelligence, but ran away before the more important gift of compassion and inner essence was given. Thus they received no more of Essence than had the extinct Duo Pods.

Bemused, Essence observed the roaches as they ran from her. "I must watch and see what comes of this development.

Looking Back:

In To Build a Tunnel, the first book of the trilogy, Henry narrated the story of his great-grandfather, and ant who, along with two other ants, was tricked by roaches into building better tunnels in Roacherian plastic mines. The ant colony realized too late that its members were forced into slavery. They preferred to solve the matter diplomatically, but were prepared for war.
ISBN 0-9753410-1-4

New South Dairy Colony 50, the second book of the trilogy, opened with Henry as a nymph, in a coma after accidentally ingesting a bad combination of medicines in his physician father's lab. His ant grandfather, Antony Dairier, decided it was time to straighten out his grandson. He revealed to Henry the details of his own life: the war and the emotional pain which resulted in his dedication to the ideal of the experimental ant/roach colony, New South Dairy 50.
ISBN 0-9753410-2-2

Wise saying from a Duo Pod book of Spiritual Philosophy:

Idler, go to the ant. Ponder its ways and grow wise. No one gives her orders, no overseer, no master, yet all through the summer she makes sure of her food, and gathers her supplies at harvest time. Proverbs 6: 6-8

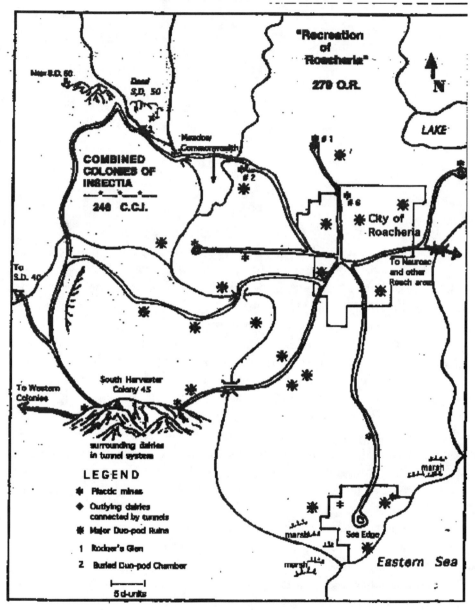

Forward:
Gabrielle Roach

With a shriek, my brother Ronald's youngest nymph scooted, his six legs a blur, out of the sleep chamber where he'd been playing with my oldest nymph. He ran past his mother and the others in the parlor, straight to Ronald squealing, "Daaaaad, Henry says if I'm not good, fire ants will tunnel under my sleep cushion and come up and sting me!"

I stormed out of the kitchen, where my father and I had been putting our Last Day feast on the dining surface, into the parlor to confront my son. "Young Henry! Shame on you! Only this morning you made your pledge to care for and cherish everyone. Now here you are frightening your little cousin with foolishness. Apologize this instant."

My son stopped and faced me and everyone else in the chamber. "I was only teasing. He sees ant larvae and roaches together every day in the nursery. I didn't think he would start crying."

My mate interceded. "Gabrielle, nymphs have been telling each other that silliness for ages."

"But Henry's nearly an adult and should know better."

Embarrassed, Henry put his pods around his cousin. "I'm sorry. I didn't mean to scare you."

In the silence that followed, my father walked slowly over to his namesake, put one pod on the back of his thorax and said, "There was a time long ago in Roacheria when roach parents used that old line on their nymphs to frighten them into proper behavior. The story had a basis in fact. What you and I know, that your cousin doesn't, is that the last violent conflict between ants and roaches was in Roacherian season cycle 219, and hatred finally died here in Meadow Commonwealth in 281. Come, let's all eat before the food grows cold."

My father took my mother's pod in his and led his three adult offspring, our mates, and seven grandnymphs to a table filled with the best of two cultures: roasted grasshopper, fungus muffins, fried bee's wings, shredded plastic salad, fried fly eggs, grassfrond seeds, honey dew and honey cake.

My father raised his pods. "We celebrate with joy the end of the 319th season cycle of Organized Roacheria, but may we never forget the past. Let us strive to build an even better future for our young."

As we began to eat, Ronald's mate asked, "Henry, what did you mean when you said that old line about fire ants had a basis in fact?"

"Have you forgotten your basic training?" my father countered.

"I wasn't trained here, remember?"

We all looked at him expectantly. My father enjoyed relating the past, and he was an expert. The way he told things made those listening feel as though they were part of it.

"Roaches formed Organized Roacheria thirty-three season cycles before the ant colonies combined. That's why in The Colonies this is the 286th season cycle. Then they set about to take over nearby ant colonies which were rich in plastic. A dairying colony, later named South Dairy 1, was the first to fall," he said, passing the sliced grasshopper around.

"They enslaved the colony to produce plastic for them and discovered a taste for grasshopper meat and honey dew. Dairying ants were the only ones at that time who knew how to milk aphids for this deliciously sweet and refreshing drink. Gabrielle, would you please refill my mug?"

We sat silently, waiting for him to continue after downing the mug and eating a slice of roast grasshopper. "They gave the ants barely enough food to survive and no plastic. Since most colonies did not communicate with each other in those days, many season cycles passed before anyone knew of their plight.

"When the first severely plastic deprived young who managed to live, emerged from pupation horribly deformed and with no intelligence, the ants knew they must get help or perish. Secretly, a few began to dig an escape tunnel. When it was ready, one named Duncan offered to break the surface."

My father paused and chewed half a muffin. Even the youngest nymph did not interrupt. All the nymphs' eyes were fixed on their grandfather.

"Duncan ran westward toward another dairying colony, later known as South Dairy 50. On the way, he made a wide circle around a fire ant colony. I've often wondered if that was when he got the idea about how to save his colony. Surface workers recognized him as a dairying ant when he reached the colony and took him to their Council Chief. 'That makes two colonies they've taken,' the Council Chief said after Duncan told what had happened, 'We've been trading with a harvester colony half a day's journey from here, getting plastic from them since our mine ran out. The roaches took over their colony only ten days ago. We were going to approach your colony for a new supply.'

"The whole council grew more anxious, realizing they had no plastic to nourish their young and unsure that the colony would continue to thrive. 'Perhaps we could ask the fire ants to help us fight,' Duncan proposed.

"'We've never gone there. As long as nobody goes near their surface, they don't make war,' he was told.

"Duncan persisted, 'We either ask their help or perish one colony at a time.' Filled with fear, he and the Dairy Council Chief set out, bearing baskets filled with honey dew, grasshopper meat, and the last of the harvester ants' seeds as gifts. Fortunately, for all of us ever since, the fire ants' Council Chief, Fredrika, was a female of great wisdom, and all of that colony's members revered her in the manner of the ancient queens."

He stopped to drink more honey dew.

"'Here in my colony,' Fredrika said, 'we protect even our weakest members. Why shouldn't we extend that to other kinds of ants? Our ways of hunting are not sufficient any more. If you will share your crops and knowledge of managing herds with us, so we may have a better life, we will give to you our protection. We should not let the roaches enslave any of us. The roaches know better than to attack us, but they watch constantly. They will see if a force of us sets out to free your colony.'"

My mother and Ronald quietly rose and cleared the soiled bowls and mugs and empty serving containers. Then Ronald cut the honey cake and passed the pieces around.

"So they set about a plan to build a tunnel from their colony to the free dairying colony, and from there to the harvester colony and Duncan's. They also sent explorers to seek out other colonies. By the end of that season cycle, the Combined Colonies of Insectia had been established. The invasions were successful, of course. The roaches didn't have time to react to a sudden, underground attack. They quickly retreated from both colonies. I suppose many of them had nightmares of fire ants popping up from the ground all around them long afterward. The strangest part is that, season cycles later, while they still feared tunnels under their surface, they never figured out that all the colonies were connected underground."

He laughed and all of us joined him. "And that is the origin of your silly story, my precious namesake. Now, let me eat my honey cake."

Later, as the others cleaned up the remains of our feast, I sat near my father while my mother massaged his painful joints. In spite of the fact that most roaches could expect to live many season cycles longer than his sixty-two, his health was failing and his joints had stiffened. Movement was quite painful for him. I feared losing him, and with him all his wisdom.

He had done so much in his early adult years to break down the hatred most roaches had for ants. His published writings of the lives of his antcestors helped both cultures understand the mistakes of the past. His life was an important part of Antstory, yet he was reluctant to reveal it. So often, when I was young, he would tell me a bit, and then stop.

"Dad," I said quietly, "there are so many things about you these little ones need to know. Please, tell it to them."

"The facts are in official records. Anyone can look them up."

"The records don't tell it with feeling," I said reaching out to stroke him.

"I don't think I want to relive that. No one needs to know what your mother and I went through."

"Forgive my rudeness, but we do need to know. What if your grandfather had not shared his life with you? You learned from his pain, and that made it better for everyone. We mustn't lose that. You stand with them: with Fredrika, Duncan, your great-grandfather, your grandfather, my name sake."

He turned and put his pods around my mother. "Regina?"

She nodded.

He looked deeply into my eyes and said slowly, "It will take more than one afternoon."

"I'll bring all the little ones to you each seventhday for an h-unit, for as many quarter time frames as it takes. Will you allow me to use a voice imager? My memory is not like yours, and I can't write as fast as you can speak."

After another long silence, he nodded.

The following seventhday, my father, Henry Roach-Dairier, son of a roach who was adopted by ants, began to reveal the chapters of his life to his grandnymphs. Sometimes my mother joined him, adding her perspective as well. I also spoke with his brothers, his ant cousins, and the other original members of Meadow Commonwealth for a broader view. I give you his story, as he gave us *To Build A Tunnel* and *New South Dairy Colony 50.*

1.

*H*enry, a roach nymph of ten season cycles, sat at the slanted work surface in New South Dairy Colony 50's training center. He stared at the list of reading symbols again, then off into space, wishing he were out in a meadow somewhere. A pod touched his solid brown thorax, bringing his mind back to the plain earthen walls of the training chamber.

"Henry, you can't learn if you don't concentrate on the task. Name the thirty symbols in order for me," the training ant said, taking the list from him.

Henry named only the first five. "Why do I have to learn these anyway? I can already read in Ant."

"You can barely read in Ant. You know we live and work together in this colony. You must know both if you are to learn about yourself. Your grandfather and all of us here have spent most of our lives trying to show others that ants and roaches can live together in harmony instead of hatred and distrust. You are named for your grandmother, Henrietta, who helped prove that the ancient Duo Pods caused their own extinction. The Combined Colonies count on us to set the example for others. You must live up to your family's expectations."

Roacheria. Why did everyone, or so it seemed to Henry, dislike it so much? His older brothers, David and Arthur, had both spent a long time there. David had been back for a season cycle. He refused to speak of it, saying the only good thing that ever came from there was his mother and the thin, young female he'd brought back with him. Their mating ceremony took place a time frame later and they now had a nymph. Arthur's communications spoke only of how he longed to come home.

Henry sighed and turned back to the list of symbols. The trainer moved on to help someone else. Henry concentrated for a short time, thinking if he learned to read, he could find out about the mysterious Roacheria. He'd be happy to go there, if it meant no training. His mind wandered back to the meadow.

An idea came to him. He squirmed at his bench, dropped the list, squirmed again. "I need to be excused."

The trainer nodded.

Henry slipped quietly out of the chamber and headed down a side tunnel that led to a little-used entrance to the mound. In a few moments, he had left the colony and scuttled across the small stream that flowed near it.

He wandered through the meadows, farther and farther from the mound, and wished he were older, like his brothers and sister, so he wouldn't have to go to training. David worked with the grasshopper herds and his mate helped in the nursery while trying to learn to speak Ant. Arthur was in Roacheria hoping to find a mate and learning to manage the plastic trade. His sister, Dorothy, had just begun a mentorship with a chemist in near-by South Harvester Colony 45. Drew, six season cycles older than Henry and closest in age, had completed his basics long ago and was almost finished exploring jobs in the colony. He worked with others in different areas each time frame to see what he might like for his life's work. Then he would enter a mentorship.

Henry came upon a path and followed it. It led to a lower part of the stream that passed by the colony to a synthetic stone chamber. He crossed the stream and entered the chamber. A lightning bug lamp sat on the floor near the portal. He turned it on and looked around. Murals covered the smooth walls, depicting life thousands and thousands of season cycles ago.

"This is the place my grandparents found," he said to himself. He looked at the images the extinct Duo Pods had made of themselves and many other creatures that no longer lived. So many varieties, so many shades of their soft outer covering. How had these creatures kept from hurting themselves with their skeleton on the inside? He looked at how they stood erect on only two pods and realized that was why they were named "Duo Pod Erectus."

He compared himself in size. "I'll be almost that big when I'm grown," he said to no one. "My father is much bigger. Oh, who cares about them any way? Studying them is stupid. I'd rather be outside."

Henry returned to the stream and spent a pleasant afternoon watching tiny aquatic creatures swim. He dipped one pod in the water and listened to the sounds around him. He lifted his antennae when it suddenly grew silent. Something grabbed his back leg. He cried out, then turned to see Gerry, an old reformed roach criminal.

Gerry didn't give him a chance to relax. "If I'd been a mantis, you'd be dead. About twenty ants and roaches are out looking for you. You'd better get back where you belong, or you'll end up like me."

"Leave me alone, you ugly old half-face! You can't tell me what to do."

Gerry's outer mandibles had been cut off, Roacherian justice for violent crime. He had mated Henry's aunt, Rayanne, late in life. Henry disliked him and felt it odd that his aunt would be a companion to someone old enough to be her father. He'd always refused to call him Uncle Gerry, even for his cousin's sake, because Gerry was not his cousin's father.

Gerry said nothing as he took a firm hold of Henry, picked him up, and roughly carried him home.

Henry's mother was pacing about when Gerry entered their domicile. "Henry, where have you been? Why did you leave training? We've been frantic!"

Gerry let go of Henry. "I found him playing in the stream that flows by the Duo Pod chamber, daydreaming. Young fool could have got himself killed. And he had the nerve to insult me. He needs a good stepping on."

Genny put her front pods around her son and embraced him. "Thank you for finding him," she said to Gerry. "You know we don't believe in stepping on anyone, especially nymphs. Rodger was raised with better ways and I agree with my mate. We've never done that to any of our young."

"The others didn't need it. This one does. I only had to step on Rayanne's nymph once, and he never needed it again. He laughs about it now and he works hard on our council. I'm proud of him."

Henry moved quietly behind his mother as she spoke.

"Gerry, please don't misunderstand me. I've always admired the change you made in your life and the way you've cherished my sister. I'm not trying to be rude, and I don't expect an answer to what I am about to say. How many times were you stepped on and abused as a nymph? Did it make you choose the right path or did it only serve to make you more bitter and rebellious? There are other ways to help a nymph learn to make good choices."

Gerry sighed. "I'll go tell the others he's been found." He started toward the portal but stopped and turned. "I got stepped on plenty, and I deserved it, too. No, it didn't make me any more bitter and rebellious than I already was. I'd hate to see Henry waste half his life like I did, or end up dead." He walked out and closed the portal before Henry's mother could respond.

Genny faced Henry squarely. "You left the training center without permission. Come with me right now and apologize to your trainer."

Henry ran behind his mother, barely able to keep up. She was of the small, thin roach variety, but she ran faster than anyone Henry knew. The discussion between his mother and his uncle and the run gave him time to think. He was out of breath but calm when they arrived at the training center. Since it was late in the day, everyone else had left.

Henry looked up at his trainer with wide-eyed innocence. "Why is everyone mad at me? What did I do?"

His trainer's voice was stern. "You asked if you could go to the sanitation area and you never came back."

"No, I didn't," Henry persisted. "I said I needed to be excused and you nodded, so I thought I was done for the day."

His mother and the trainer stared at him. Henry took advantage of the bewildered look in their eyes. He looked steadily at both of them, as if the whole thing were their fault.

"We were worried because we didn't know where you were," the trainer said. "From now on you are not to leave this chamber during training hours unless I have verbally given you permission."

Henry nodded and let his antennae droop.

"I'm sorry he troubled you. I'll talk to him some more at home," Genny said.

Later, Henry pretended to read while his mother explained the situation to his grandfather, Antony, who lived with them, and everyone who stopped by, relieved to see him safe.

Antony wrapped his appendages around Henry and held him close. The brace he wore on his mid-right appendage rubbed the back of Henry's thorax. Henry squirmed. His grandfather shifted himself, knowing his brace was rough. "While the others were searching for you, I went to meditate." He continued to stroke Henry, sliding one front pod to the very tip of Henry's antennae. "I couldn't stand the thought that anything might take you from me."

Henry basked in his grandfather's caresses. He liked the contrast of his dark brown outer covering against the deep black of his ant grandfather's exoskeleton. He was still smaller than Antony but Henry knew that would change when he made his final molt into adulthood. He didn't understand why, but no one else had ever been able to make him feel completely accepted.

Antony moved back and looked into Henry's eyes. "You may be able to front innocence to others, but you can't hide anything from me. Why did you leave training with such a sneaky trick?"

Henry's antennae drooped even lower. He could not stand the penetrating look in his grandfather's eyes. He stared at the floor and said honestly, "I don't like being underground. I don't like training."

"I may be an ant, while you are a roach, but you and I are more alike than you might think. Just because ants linger long as larvae and sleep seven season cycles as pupas, missing nymphhood as such, doesn't mean we don't go through the same feelings. Do you remember the day you hatched?"

Henry hesitated. So many times he had heard his siblings and other roaches recall their hatching. Henry could remember nothing. He secretly feared there was something wrong with him. He thought about making up something, but once again, the look on his grandfather's face prevented it. He shook his head.

Antony sighed and caressed him again. "Perhaps that's just as well. I was with you that day, grieving for your grandmother while your father took care of all the sick of the colony, including your mother. I said many things without thinking. You're too young to understand, but I believe the day will come when you will remember. In the meantime, try to have a little more respect for others. You may not like training, but it's a necessary part of your life. See if you can't be a little less like me and a little more like your namesake. Now come eat your dinner."

*   *   *   *

Over the next several time frames, Henry found many ways to slip away from training. He would claim to be sick, then tell his mother he felt better and go off into the meadows instead of to training. He would ask to go to the research center to get a book and not return. He would write notes to his trainer excusing himself and sign his mother's name. Each time he got caught, he would manage to turn things around and make his parents or his trainer think it was their fault.

At one point the trainer said, "Henry, if you would put half the effort into your lessons that you put into thinking up ways to trick me, you would be my best trainee."

*   *   *   *

One seventhday during the summer, Henry watched his uncle, Gerry, wander off into the meadows. Gerry always seemed to be the one to catch Henry when he slipped off somewhere. This time, Henry would follow him.

Gerry crossed the stream and worked his way along the opposite bank, looking up into the wood plants that lined it. About two d-units down stream, Gerry climbed a wood plant nearly overgrown with vines. Henry watched as the old renegade picked several bright red berries from the top vines and began to eat them.

"What are you doing, you stupid old fool," Henry yelled. "Those are poison! That's the first thing I was taught when I was allowed to leave the mound!"

His shouting startled Gerry. The old roach lost his grip and fell from the wood plant into the stream, groaning in pain.

Henry ran to him.

Gerry looked at him in anger. "Look what you've done! You've ruined everything. I've broken two legs! Why were you following me?"

Henry stood, staring at the fractures. Gerry's back legs had snapped like dry branches. In spite if his dislike for his uncle, Henry reached out his pod and tried to drag him from the shallow water.

Gerry howled and yelled at him. "Leave me alone! You're making things worse. Get out of here you little..." he stopped.

Henry backed off. To his surprise, Gerry picked up a rock from the bottom of the stream and threw it at him.

"Go!"

Afraid and confused, Henry ran. Anger replaced confusion. How dare his uncle throw a rock at him! He was trying to help. Let him lie there then. Henry went on down the stream, muttering insults. "I don't care about you," he said as though Gerry could still hear. A giant butterfly caught his attention. He sat down on the edge of the stream and watched as it perched in a near-by wood plant and began to lay its eggs. Henry forgot about his uncle, enthralled by the beauty and grace of the golden creature.

It flew off suddenly. Henry looked across the stream to see a mantis. He rose to run, but the mantis did not move. It was not interested in Henry. It had already eaten. In its mandibles, hung a piece of Gerry's head. With a shriek, Henry scuttled away from the stream back toward the colony.

"Gerry! A mantis!" he screamed over and over to the first creature he saw.

*   *   *   *

During fall harvest, when training was suspended so more colony members could help cut the grassfronds and gather the seed, Henry was assigned to help his brother, David.

"Would you like me to go for water?" Henry offered.

"No, because I know you'll disappear again. I need help with this section more than I need water."

"I'll come back," Henry reassured him.

"No you won't, and you'll have some wild excuse. When are you going to grow up and honor your namesake?"

"Maybe if someone would tell me more about my grandmother I could."

David swung the cutting tool and toppled another twenty-five f-unit stalk. "Maybe if you'd stay in training, you could find about her for yourself. Now get busy and gather the seed. This crop is our most important. The seed, its oil, the stems—every part of this plant is used. I thought I'd say that just in case you sneaked away the day that lesson was taught."

Henry glared at his brother and did his part that day. David's words bothered him enough that for a few time frames he concentrated on improving his reading. He read about his grandmother. She had learned to read the Duo Pod manuscripts found with many other perfectly preserved artifacts in the chamber he had seen. The toxins they left behind had probably begun the evolutionary process that increased the size of the insect world, resulting in their present state of civilization.

"So what?" he thought, but he made himself read on:

> "After Master Antony's leadership established peace with Roacheria, he and Master Henrietta established New South Dairy Colony 50. The colony thrives as a place where ants and roaches work together. The Intercolonial Council decreed that the Duo Pod manuscripts would be placed there permanently for study. Master Henrietta continued to translate the works and train both roach and ant archaeologists until her death in the 224th season cycle of the Combined Colonies."

Promising to return in an h-unit, Henry went to the records chamber of his colony. There he learned that his grandmother was the first to contract an infection that swept through the colony shortly before his own hatching. His father, the colony's physician, had been able to save everyone else with infection-fighting molds. She had not responded to treatment.

Henry glanced at the time piece on the chamber wall. His h-unit was nearly up. He returned to training and read the rest of the chapter in the Antstory manuscript about his grandfather's family and the establishment of his colony.

David had said he should honor his namesake. David's namesake, his grandfather's father, had been a dairier. David was a dairier. His sister Dorothy, named for his great-grandmother, had taken up chemistry as her life's work, just as her namesake had before Old South Dairy 50 died. Was he supposed to spend his life underground reading boring manuscripts?

2.

*M*ost roaches made their final molt into an adult body at twelve season cycles, but Henry passed that mark showing no signs of it. His mother worried.

"Rodger, shouldn't Henry have begun his final molt by now?" she asked her mate.

"He'll get there. You keep forgetting he's been late with every stage of his life," Henry's father replied.

"Maybe something is wrong with him. I mean, he's had so many other problems," Genny persisted.

Rodger put his front pods around his petite mate and stroked her. His huge frame surrounded her like a nymph. "The reason there is an average age is that some nymphs molt early and some late. Henry causes his own problems and they aren't medical," he reassured her.

"Isn't there something we can do? He slips away from training about every third day. Yesterday, your father caught him down by the stream again. All he did was hand him a book and say, 'If you'd rather study here, at least bring your work with you.' He'll have to repeat all the second level materials."

Rodger sighed. "When I try to talk to him, we end up yelling at each other. It only makes me angrier. I'm very disappointed at the way he's turning out, but he has to make up his own mind or live with the consequences."

He looked up. There stood Henry, his eyes full of anger, having heard the whole conversation.

Rodger gave his mate one last caress. "I've got to go back to the clinic. Renae' isn't doing well." He glared at Henry, "So you've been listening again. Truth hits hard, doesn't it?" He opened the portal at one side of their parlor, where a passage led directly to the colony's clinic, walked out and closed it behind him.

Henry picked up a book from a shelf near him and threw it at the portal. "You're always in that cursed clinic! Renae', this, somebody else that!" Before his mother could respond, he ran out the front portal, down the tunnel, out of the mound, and up the closest wood plant, where he sat, brooding.

Sometime later, he heard his grandfather's voice below him. "Henry, you know I can't climb up there. Please, come down and talk to me."

Longing for affection, Henry climbed down. Antony waved away another concerned colony member and wrapped himself around his grandson. They sat in silence for several minutes while Antony comforted Henry.

"Try to understand," Antony finally said. "Your grandmother and I knew nothing about raising a roach when we adopted your father. Renae' was one of the few roaches living here then. He helped your father a lot when he was about your age. Your father feels very close to him. It is difficult for him to watch Renae' die slowly and know that, even as a physician, there's nothing he can do except try to relieve the pain. Your father cherishes you, Henry. He simply forgets to say it sometimes."

Henry wanted to ask a million questions, all of them deeply personal. In the ant world, it was considered very rude to ask personal questions about someone else's past. He had violated a lot of other codes, but never that one. He looked at his grandfather, hoping for more, but Antony remained silent as he stroked away Henry's anger.

Late that night, while his family slept, Henry slipped into the clinic. He looked at Renae'. A hollow reed in Renae's mouth dripped some liquid from a glass bottle above. The reed was fixed in place with binding material, since Renae', like Gerry, had no outer mandibles. Plaster covered his body, as if he had multiple fractures in his exoskeleton, but Henry knew he had not had any accident. The parchment beside him read, "Chritinomalacia—Maximum pain potion constantly, monitor closely."

Hearing a sound, he scuttled around the bed and flattened himself against the floor. His father entered, checked the glass bottle and added more liquid to it. Henry looked up carefully from where he hid and saw his father gently stroke Renae'. He thought he heard his father crying as he left.

Henry slipped out and went to the chamber where his father kept all his medical books. He closed the portal carefully and turned on one lightning bug lamp, adjusting the shade to keep it dim. He flipped through several manuscripts until he found what he was looking for:

> "Critinomalacia: A disease of the exoskeleton related to improper nutrition, thought by some to be a physical manifestation of Plastic Deprivation. Most common among the poor in Roacheria, when nymphs might not eat a balanced diet between the third and fourth molts. This is also a time when some roach parents think they have had enough plastic to be intelligent and give them less plastic, in favor of more to younger siblings. Thus, it is hard to determine whether the cause is Mild Plastic Deprivation or generally poor nutrition. What appears to be a strong exoskeleton in young adulthood, begins to weaken after age fifty. Fractures occur at the slightest injury and do not heal. Cure: none known. Death usually occurs with a head fracture. Treatment: body casts and pain relief. The disease is practically unknown in ants, due to the fact that proper nutrition and sufficient plastic for all young have traditionally been a high priority in all ant colonies."

Henry closed the book, turned off the lamp, and went back home to bed.

*   *   *   *

Henry avoided everyone for the next few time frames. If he felt like it, he took his books and studied alone. If he wanted to know something, he looked it up for himself. When he began to feel the tightness throughout his body that signaled he'd outgrown his exoskeleton, he went to his father's books again and looked up molting.

On sixth and seventhdays when there was no training, he went to the dispensary and watched his father's assistant, Allie, grind and mix the plant parts that went into various medicines. Allie was an ant a few season cycles older than his grandfather. She didn't mind.

"Your father watched me the same way in his youth. So did your brother, Drew," she said. She encouraged him to stay and offered explanations of what she was doing.

*   *   *   *

His thirteenth summer began and the tightness in his body turned to pain. Allie retired for health reasons, which kept Henry's father away from home even more. His mother and his grandfather spent many h-units with Renée's mate, trying to help her cope with his illness. No one seemed to notice whether Henry was around or not. He struggled through each day. He began sneaking into the dispensary at night, making his own pain potion to relieve the discomfort of molting.

His father caught him the third time. "What are you doing in here by yourself at this h-unit?"

Henry twitched his antennae and said nothing. Rodger strode toward him, his eyes filled with exhaustion and irritation. He reached out with one front pod to take the bottle of herbs Henry held in his pod.

"Don't touch me," Henry said, stepping back.

His father looked at him closely. "So, you're finally breaking into adulthood." He reached up and took down a container. "Here. This is pre-mixed. Two scoops in honey when you need it. Now go home. Don't ever come in here again. There are too many things you don't know about. What heals one ailment can kill in another situation."

The container lasted ten days, but Henry's body seemed unable to break out of the ever tightening grip of his too-small outer covering. He went to his father's sleep chamber, but only his mother was there, sleeping soundly. He headed for the clinic dispensary. On the way down the passage, he saw his father asleep over a book. He went on without waking him.

Crazed with pain, he picked up one herb after another, without even looking at the names. He ground them all together, dumped the mixture into a mug of honey dew and drank it.

Euphoria swept over him. He felt light as an autumn leaf. Laughing, he climbed to the top shelf. A leaf should float gently to the ground. The shelves gave way. Henry crashed his way to the floor. Glass, powders, and piles of herbs flew everywhere. He landed with a loud thud while containers continued to fall around him.

Henry tried to move and found he couldn't. Terror seized him. He saw his father appear at the portal. Rodger reached out to turn on the main lamp. Henry tried to cry for help, but no sound came from his mouth. The room spun around him and went black.

*   *   *   *

For four days Henry wavered on the brink of death, deep in a coma. Sometimes his mind reached out to reality and he heard bits of conversations: Will he be all right? ... Don't know ... Hard to know what antidote to give ... Not sure what he took. ... His father crying, his grandfather comforting him ... Working too hard ... Time for everyone except those who need you most ... You had problems ...

The blackness grew thicker. Loneliness swept in. He longed for comfort. A voice again, his father's. "Why wasn't I listening? ... Why didn't you come to me? ... I'm sorry I left you alone ... I know you can hear me. Fight your way back. I don't want to lose you. I've lost too many I couldn't help. You came as a surprise, brought all of us new life in the midst of grief. You are so special to me. Your grandfather is right. I have not told you often enough."

Henry's sense of touch returned. He felt his father's pods, something he had not known in a long time, softly stroking his antennae. The peaceful sensation dulled the painful tightness in his thorax and abdomen. He began to cry. His father sighed with relief and held him close, caressing him gently.

Henry was surprised to find himself in a clinic chamber. His father removed some of the apparatus attached to him.

"Please, don't scare your mother and me like this again. We've been out of our minds. You nearly ended your life."

"I'm sorry," Henry stammered, feeling remorseful for the first time in his life.

The following morning, his father woke him long before dawn. Rodger checked him over thoroughly, asked him questions, made him read a short passage from a book, tested his reflexes, and a dozen other things.

"You're very lucky, Henry. You seem to have made a full recovery. I'll be repeating these tests over the next few time frames to be sure there are no lasting effects. You need to learn many things about our family, but I don't have time to spend with you. Please, forgive me for that. I want you to go with your grandfather and stay with him until you have finished this molt. I know how uncomfortable you are, but obey me this time. I've given him plenty of herbs for you. Listen to your grandfather and think about your life. You no longer have the excuse of nymphhood."

In spite of all the training he had missed, Henry knew he faced serious consequences for his actions. No amount of talking would help this time. If the colony's Justice Council had not already made a decision, they would while he was with his grandfather.

He humbly followed his father out of the mound. Antony stood near the entrance with a basket of supplies.

"Are you strong enough to carry this?" he asked Henry.

Henry nodded and crawled beneath the basket, lifting it as he did so.

"Have a little faith," Antony said to Henry's father, stroking him once. "I know he's good at heart."

The sky lightened as Antony and Henry set off across the meadows.

"Where are we going?" Henry asked.

"To one of your favorite hiding places, which also has special meaning for me."

An h-unit later, they arrived at a grove of wood plants next to a pond. Henry carried the basket, in which Antony had been riding for the last few d-units, into the shelter of the low-hanging branches. He set the basket down and helped his grandfather out.

"Thank you. I tire easily these days," Antony said. He walked over to two memorial markers and lifted his front pods in meditation.

Henry waited. He had often wondered about those markers when he had come here to get away from training and other responsibilities. Although he wasn't excited about the next several days, he had a feeling he finally be told a lot about the past. He hoped it would include an explanation of this place.

Antony finally lowered his pods and pointed to one of the markers. "Geree' was your life-giving grandmother. She handed Henrietta your father's egg, the most precious gift we ever received, and asked us to give him a chance. I'm getting ahead of myself. I should start at the beginning. You may ask me questions any time, no matter how personal. When we leave here, you'll be an adult. I hope what I have to say will help you make better choices in your life than you have up until now."

They unloaded the basket together. Over the next quarter time frame, Henry listened as Antony related the whole of his life: his joys, his sorrows, his mistakes and his triumphs. When Henry asked him things, Antony answered in great detail. Usually reserved and in control, Antony let go of his emotions. Several times, they cried together.

Henry finally thrashed his way out of his exoskeleton on the sixth day. Antony stroked him until he slept, then covered him, keeping vigil as his adult exoskeleton hardened completely. He had expanded one and a half f-units. Like his brothers and sister, he was larger than his mother but not nearly as long or wide as his father.

After breakfast the following morning, Antony handed Henry a piece of parchment and an ink pot.

"What's this?"

"It's your contract with me. After all I've told you, did you think you were going to leave here without one?"

"No, I suppose not."

Henry read his contract carefully:

"I, Henry Dairier, confess that I am guilty of insulting many members of New South Dairy Colony 50 on numerous occasions; neglecting my duties in training and colony life; lying countless times; showing disrespect for others, and for my own life. To make restitution for these offenses, I place myself under the control of Antony Dairier or his designee, until I have fulfilled all the requirements of this contract. I pledge to return to training

and not be absent unless my father personally verifies that I am ill; not to use words in Roach which do not have polite equivalents in Ant; to seek pardon of every creature I have offended; and never to enter the clinic or dispensary unless supervised. I agree to spend the first season cycle of my job exploration in New South Dairy 50, closely supervised. If all goes well, I will spend the second season cycle in South Harvester 45. I may then spend one season cycle in Roacheria at the training center of my choice at colony expense. If I wish to remain there longer, I will make my own way. I understand that if I do not follow all laws there, no one from my colony will be able to defend me. If I break this contract, I agree that I should be banished to permanent underground work in North Carpenter Colony 5. Signed _____,
this 26th day of the Eighth Time Frame, 237th Season Cycle of The Combined Colonies of Insectia."

Knowing he had no choice, Henry signed it. He thought long over whom his grandfather should designate to hold the contract if something happened to him. "My brother, David," he said finally.

3.

A subdued Henry entered the training facility not just on time, but a little early the next morning. He faced his trainer humbly, antennae drooping. "I've caused a lot of trouble. I'm sorry, really ... I'm really sorry this time. I'm going to do better from now on."

Henry thought of the alternative. Some might consider it paradise, but the thought of being permanently confined underground in North Carpenter 5 was more than Henry could bear. Anyone who had ever visited, or came from there, talked on an on about how beautiful it was in that part of The Colonies. Vast forests filled with unusual wild insects covered much of the surface, while crystal clear bodies of standing and moving water abounded with a wide variety of creatures. Beneath the surface, the ants mined an abundance of plastic and mineral wealth. Food from the southern colonies flowed there, as a steady supply of underground resources moved south.

Roaches had never tried to settle that far north. They couldn't take the cold. Frozen sky water covered the surface at least four time frames of every season cycle. Ants spent that time deep inside the colony in winter inactivity. In midsummer, colony members often put in sixteen h-unit days to catch up.

"Welcome back, Henry," said his trainer, putting a pod on the back of his thorax. "We all want to help you. A little cooperation is all I ask."

"If you really want to help, say, 'North 5' whenever you think I'm daydreaming. If I prove myself to you for a time frame, will you allow me to study out in the meadows occasionally?"

"Perhaps. If I do, I'll give you a set time limit and quiz you thoroughly. Prove you've studied that way, and I will allow it again."

Henry was grateful for the courtesy others showed him, welcoming him back and never asking what had happened. His trainer never had to say, "North 5." Henry said it to himself often enough.

Each seventhday, Henry sought out one or two of the colony members he had insulted. Apologizing wasn't as difficult as he feared. He found in others and in himself a warm feeling he had not known existed.

One secondday evening after the fall harvest was complete, Antony knocked on the portal of Henry's sleep chamber.

"Come in, Grandfather."

Antony caressed him tenderly. "I'm proud of you. Your trainer says you've almost made up all last season cycle's work. I've always known you had it in you."

Henry smiled. "I still have a lot of colony members to talk to."

"It takes time. I expect that."

Henry looked down.

"What's troubling you?" Antony asked. "You may tell or ask me anything."

Henry leaned against his grandfather and cried. "How do I ask Uncle Gerry's forgiveness? It was my fault. I yelled at him not to eat the berries. It startled him and he fell and broke his back legs. He yelled, said I had ruined everything. I got angry. I went off and left him there. When I saw the mantis, and part of him ..." Henry began sobbing.

Antony wrapped himself around Henry. "What berries?"

"The red, poison ones," Henry moaned.

"Poison," Antony paused and sighed. "Release yourself from any guilt you feel over his death. You could not have prevented it. Your uncle knew he was in the early stages of chritinomalacia. He talked with me a long time and told me in confidence that he had seen too many suffer and die that way when he was growing up. He'd made a vow to himself that he would never let it happen to him. He planned to take his own life. I thought I had talked him out of it. After watching Renée suffer, I can't say

I blame him; although I did not approve of his actions, especially now that I know it involved you. I'm so sorry you happened to be there. I should have realized it when you were so hysterical that day. I wish you had told me this before."

He stroked Henry's antennae. "I was relieved when everyone viewed it as a tragedy. I think the truth would devastate your aunt. For her sake, let's keep this between us."

Henry nodded. "What about all the things I said to him?"

"Meditate on it. One day, you may find yourself in a situation where you can forgive another for similar offenses toward you. Then you will feel cleansed of it."

Antony remained with Henry that evening stroking him until he fell asleep.

*   *   *   *

Henry applied himself so well that he finished his basic training the first season cycle of his contract. As he entered job exploration, he thought less about North Carpenter 5 and more about his own future. He spent two time frames trying out archaeology, still with the thought that he was supposed to take up that work.

"How did my grandmother ever learn to read these symbols with no one to teach her?" he asked Master Donna, the archaeologist in charge of the Duo Pod manuscripts his grandmother had found. "I worked hard to learn to read in Ant, struggled even more with Roach, but this is impossible."

"Your grandmother was very gifted. I've been told she taught herself to read Ant in two time frames, skipping almost the whole first season cycle of basic training. Yet, she was a patient teacher. I remember how I struggled in the beginning, but I was determined to learn."

"I think it would be easier if you told me what it sounded like," Henry said, shifting on the stool and looking at the image rather than the text.

"That's something we may never know. The one thing in the chamber your grandparents found that might have told us was destroyed."

"What was it? How was it destroyed?"

Master Donna showed him an image of a machine that had a screen something like a video wall and a flat rectangular thing with all the Duo Pod numerical and writing symbols on it. "When the renegades stripped the chamber of artifacts, they took this one as well. On the way back to their camp, someone dropped it in the border stream and this part shattered," she pointed to the screen. "The renegades had no idea what they'd taken. They simply left it. By the time it was found again, the flat panel was ruined as well. Your grandparents had the manuscript that went with it."

Henry thought about what his grandfather had told him in the glen. Master Donna's statements made perfect sense when she continued.

"Since then, we've found out that it was powered by a flow of electrons and could do marvelous things. It could compute more complex problems than the fastest creature on a sliding bead calculator; record everything that was written into it with the symbols; and print out images and words. It had a voice imager as well. The manuscript with it stated that the flat, plate-shaped things with it contained as much as a hundred times the amount of information in all of the manuscripts we have here. Had it been saved, and had we been able to figure out how to produce a flow of electrons in a better way than the Duo Pods did, or convert it to lightning bug power, we could have heard the language and much more."

"Maybe someone will find another one someday."

"It's possible. Excuse me for a moment. I've got to finish this communication to Central Harvester 12."

Henry decided that although it was interesting, he had no talent for translating the writings, and would hate spending all his time underground. Perhaps the surface part of archaeology would be better. Master Donna arranged for him to spend some time in the Duo Pod ruins nearest them. He found the digging tedious. He understood the importance of learning about the past, but deep inside, he knew this was not what he wanted to do with his life.

Not long after that, he traveled to South Harvester 45 and began his second season cycle of job exploration. There, he stayed with his great-uncle, Andrew. He appreciated getting to know distant relatives on his grandmother's side of the family, and learned to do many things a little. But he did not find any work that truly excited him. He began to count off the days until he was free to make his own choices.

When that day finally came, Henry decided not to travel the intercolonial tunnel between South Harvester 45 and New South Dairy 50, even though he was now aware that his great-grandfather, also named Henry, had engineered the tunnel. He thought about all the things his grandfather had told him and about his antcestors, roach as well as ant, as he traveled the surface trail. By the time he got home, he knew what he wanted to say to his grandfather.

Antony was resting on a floor cushion talking to Genny when Henry entered. He greeted his mother fondly, then his grandfather. "I've missed you. I've missed everybody. You look tired. Can I get you something?"

Antony reached out and embraced him. "I'm fine. Feeling my age these days. You look wonderful. I've missed you, too." He rose from the cushion, breathing heavily. "I wanted to go back to the glen with you, but I don't think I can walk that far. Let's go down by the stream instead."

"I'll carry you," Henry offered.

"No, thank you."

Antony rose slowly, left the parlor and returned with a parchment in his pod. The two of them walked through the main tunnel, out of the mound, and down to the edge of the stream.

Antony looked into Henry's eyes. "You seem longer and taller, though I know you aren't. I know there is goodness deep within you. You have done everything I asked of you. I set you free now." He took Henry's contract and tore it in half.

Henry took his portion. In accordance with ant tradition, they ate the parchment.

"It is over now, consumed. Forever a part of both of us and behind us," Antony said.

"May I ask you something personal?"

"Of course."

"I know your name means 'all ants' and that it's the most frequently given name. I think it meant more for you, because you told me about how the old colony died the day you hatched. Did you do everything to build this colony to honor all those who perished?"

Antony looked at him steadily. "Yes, and to give life to my family, but not because I felt I was expected to. From the very depths of my being,

I wanted to. I also never realized in the beginning what I would go through to achieve it."

Henry spoke slowly. "I've learned a lot and tried many things. I'm still not sure what I will choose for my life's work, but I know I don't want to be an archaeologist or a tunnel engineer. I hope you're not disappointed."

Antony embraced Henry. "Have you thought all this time that you must have their life's work?"

"Yes ... Well, David and Dorothy both ... David told me once that I should honor her."

"He meant well, but you misunderstood. I'm sorry if you've felt pressured all this time. If you happen to like the same life's work as your namesake, that certainly is one way to honor that creature. But what is more important is to think about all that one's namesake was and did, and try to emulate those characteristics. Your grandmother cherished everyone unconditionally. She opened her mind and heart to new ideas. She accepted pain with grace and gave willingly of herself. You know how I hurt and betrayed her, yet she forgave me. When you find yourself faced with a difficult choice, remember her. Think what she might have done. Let that guide you and you will honor her."

Henry smiled. "I still don't know what I want to do."

"Perhaps you will find the answer in Roacheria," Antony suggested.

*　　　*　　　*　　　*

Henry stood at the mound entrance with Arthur and his mate and the carriers as they got ready to leave for Roacheria the next morning. Arthur checked each basket of trade goods. When each item ordered by Roacheria had been checked off his list he turned to Henry. "Ready?"

Henry nodded. A strange mix of excitement and fear rose within him. He looped one satchel around each front leg and slung them over his back.

"Rick will meet us at the Trade Center," Arthur said to Henry, then turned to embrace his mate tenderly. "It'll be dark when I get back, but don't worry about me."

Carriers picked up the baskets. Arthur gathered all the parchments into his own satchel and they set off down the trail from New South Dairy 50 to Roacheria.

Henry thought about Rick, so generous in giving each of his brothers, and now him, a home when they went to study in Roacheria. Rick was the youngest son of Master Roland, one of the first roach archaeologists his grandmother had trained to read the Duo Pod symbols. Henry's father had lived with Master Roland during the three season cycles he studied Roacherian medicine.

Arthur broke into his thoughts. "Henry, during your stay in Roacheria, don't take offense when someone insults you because you have been raised with Ant beliefs. You still get too defensive. Keep to yourself. Try not to stand out. It's the easiest way to get along."

Henry interrupted. "Please, no more. I've heard it all, over and over from everybody. I'll hate it. The conditions of those in the shanties without credit will sicken me. The economic system is unfair. Those with power will try to antagonize me. I know you mean well, but couldn't we talk about something else?"

Arthur smiled. "I guess we have overdone it. I'm sorry. We just worry, that's all."

"I must be the best prepared of any of us." Henry offered a change of subject. "Any news on getting a better bridge built on this trail?"

"No. Our council, The Intercolonial Council, and The South East Roach Control Board all feel that since most of the trade and travel still runs from South Harvester 45 on the wider, re-built Peace Bridge, ours will have to stay as it is," Arthur replied.

Henry made a comment about the pleasant day, and then lapsed into his thoughts once more. Arthur remained quiet the rest of the journey as well. As they lumbered across the narrow, wooden bridge over the steep-banked stream forming the border between The Combined Colonies of Insectia and Organized Roacheria, Henry thought of what it must have been like in his grandfather's youth. Then, the only bridge was the one on South Harvester 45's trail, often lined with fire ants and roach warriors on their respective sides. The stream (though only six to eight f-units across at the bottom of approximately thirty f-unit deep banks) represented a canyon of hatred, misunderstanding, and fear between two groups whose ways were far apart. Although his grandfather had helped bring an end to violent conflict, what would it take to build a bridge between their minds and essences?

*　　　　　*　　　　　*　　　　　*

Colony members had unloaded all of the trade goods and reloaded their baskets with another time frame's supply of plastic when Rick arrived to greet Arthur and Henry.

"Sorry I'm late," he said, breathing heavily. "I had to finish an article for tomorrow morning's City Bulletin. We get fined if we're late. I got bogged down checking out some facts."

"Don't worry about it. We had to finish loading anyway." Arthur greeted Rick in the way of ants, both front pods extended.

Rick grasped Arthur's outstretched pods and pulled him close. He turned to Henry and offered the same greeting. "I've waited a long time for the privilege of being your temporary family while you train here. Welcome."

Henry responded. "I've waited a long time, too. Thank you. It's good to be here." He turned and embraced his brother. "Don't worry about me. I'll be fine, and tell David I promise not to get into any trouble."

Arthur held him close, sighed, and then left with the carriers.

The Trade Center, a huge pavilion with no walls, sat in the center of the city of Roacheria. Stone and wood pillars every twenty f-units supported a wood and metal roof. Everything (plastic, produce, bulk quantities of every imaginable domicile need) came through it from The Colonies or other communities in Organized Roacheria. Things were redistributed to smaller markets where individual roaches could purchase them. Goods made in the city and plastic from its mines arrived here before shipment out. The South East Roach Control Board regulated it tightly to the advantage of Board Members.

Rick led Henry through the din and confusion. Henry looked about, taking it all in, a surge of excitement flowing through him. Larger roaches labored to load huge rolling carts. Some with authority checked lists on parchment and wrote out destination orders.

"This way," said Rick, leading him toward a raised platform at one end of the pavilion. Henry saw a large roach standing there. A round medallion signifying Board Membership hung around his head and dangled below his mandibles. He watched all the activity below and gave instructions to other authority figures.

Rick walked up the ramp, lowered his head and swept his front pods out to both sides. "Good afternoon, Sir. I work for the City Bulletin. Do you have any public information today?"

"Have I seen you before?"

"Yes, Sir, frequently."

"I thought you looked familiar. No, not today. Stop by fifthday. I'll have this time frame's totals and the regular report for you," he said, turning to another roach, never acknowledging Henry's presence.

The two went down the ramp and left the Trade Center.

"I'm going to take you directly home. I'm tired and I know you must be. I'll take you on a tour of the city tomorrow. The next day we'll get you checked in at the Training Center for Business and Professional Work. That was your choice, wasn't it?"

"Yes, I decided to do at least one thing the same as my brothers," Henry said following Rick down a wide thoroughfare, crowded with roaches. It reminded Henry of the main tunnel into South Harvester 45, except it wasn't underground. The buildings around him were not tall, none more than two or three levels. Many were built on the foundations of Duo Pod ruins, which Henry found interesting. Gradually they left the marketing and work areas behind. The lanes narrowed, curving and meeting at odd angles.

Rick led him up a short ramp and into a fairly large domicile. "This is home, the same one I grew up in. This way." He directed Henry to the second level to a chamber with a wall opening facing the lane. He showed Henry how to use the shutters, if he wanted the chamber closed. "This is the same chamber your brothers used, your father, too, when he stayed with my father many season cycles ago. I hope you'll feel at home. I know how important it is to be close to someone. Don't hesitate to ask me or my mate, Genelle, for comfort when you need it."

Henry set his satchels on the sleep cushion. "Thank you. I like the wall opening. I'm not like my brothers. I never liked it underground. May I ask you something?"

"Of course," Rick said lowering his abdomen onto the padded bench under the wall opening.

"I know you're about the same age as my father, but he never mentioned knowing you when he was here. May I ask why?"

"I wasn't living at home at that time. I had finished my formal training and was seeking a job with the City Bulletin. My father, praise The Essence for his wisdom, decided my education wasn't complete. You know he adopted Ant beliefs and taught them to me as well. He sent me on his own version of 'job exploration.' I worked half a season cycle digging in a plastic mine, then collected refuse several time frames.

"That was followed by stints cleaning chambers in the S.E.R.C.B. Building, serving food to Board Members, and other similar 'low ranking' jobs. I did all that for two season cycles, living in the shanties the whole time. With an entirely different outlook on life, I began to work my present, fairly good job, grateful for all I had, and determined to use my talents in a way that would support others besides any mate and nymphs I might have. My son, Ray, is now learning the same lesson.

"I met Genelle and we mated. We lived in a little bungalow not far from here. My father and I grew ever closer. When he left this world, he gave me this house because he knew I would carry on as he had. It made my older brothers furious. They never understood. When Genelle gets home from the market, you'll meet our 'household help,' a young, homeless female we've taken in, like so many my father did."

"Like my mother?" Henry Asked. "You and your father couldn't change the system, so you decided to save a few from it."

Rick rose and looked out the opening. Henry flopped back onto the sleep cushion.

"You understand a lot," Rick said.

"My grandfather told me more than he ever told anyone else. Do you think things will ever change? I mean really change?"

"Maybe. I don't foresee those on The Board ever giving up their wealth and status, but there are many more than there used to be who, like my father, provide opportunities for others. My generation is much more open than my father's. Our young are even more accepting, but they need someone to teach them. Change in the way our political and economic systems work will happen gradually when enough young adults have the courage to begin something radically different. But I don't know what that might be."

"The colony trainer told me once that we can't change rules by breaking them. We have to follow them completely, and know them so well that we can propose better ones."

Rick walked toward the portal. "I think your trainer is absolutely right. Let's go down and start supper."

Later that evening, Henry sat on the bench, looking into the night sky. He decided he would take training units in Roacherian politics and law.

4.

*H*enry looked at the title of the manuscript in front of him, Roachstory: From the Beginning of Organized Roacheria to the 100th Season Cycle. Trainer Renard called the names of those enrolled in this required unit.

"Henry Roach-Dairier," he heard.

"Yes, Trainer Renard." Henry rose, then stooped and swept his front pods out to the side.

"What kind of a moronic, plastic-depraved name is Henry Roach-Dairier?" Trainer Renard asked, rising to his full height. One of the larger variety of roaches, he towered over Henry.

"With all due respect, I've chosen to acknowledge both sides of my heritage," Henry replied, keeping his voice as steady as he could.

A roar of laughter swept through the chamber. Renard raised a pod. Instant silence.

"And what might that be?"

"I'm a member of New South Dairy Colony 50 and the son of one who was adopted by ants. I'm proud of that, so 1 chose to declare it with my name." Henry's brothers had hidden themselves behind common Roach names while in Roacheria and had advised him to do the same. Henry had decided to do the opposite.

Trainer Renard looked at him skeptically and moved on down the list.

Mid-day came. Henry took the bowl of food and the mug handed him by a scrawny male. "Thank you," he said.

He heard the stunned worker mutter, "You're welcome."

He turned and headed for a bench at one of the many eating surfaces in the large chamber. "May I join you?" he asked the group already seated.

"Well, well," said Reese, a male of the large type always found in positions of power. "If it isn't Henry Hyphenated. So what do you really consider yourself? A roach? Or a three-blobbed, only-fit-for-slavery-ant?"

"Maybe he's a Rant," taunted another sitting next to him.

Henry sat down and let silence settle before saying, "I've been trying to think of a good word for myself for a long time. Rant. Interesting. Thank you."

All of them, obviously expecting an angry response to their insults, stared in silence. Henry picked up his mug, raised it toward them in a silent gesture of approval and ate his lunch without another word, shaking inside like a leaf in a summer storm. He lifted up silent thoughts in meditation that his decision to meet their bigotry and insults head on would not prove to be foolish.

That first evening, Henry returned to Rick's home exhausted from the anxiety of the day. "Please, meditate with me," he asked Rick. The two sat on the bench in his chamber, looking up at the night sky. Henry took Rick's front pods in his and lifted his thoughts out loud.

"Guiding Essence, Wisdom far greater than my own, I am afraid. In one day, I have learned why my brothers hated it here. Give me strength beyond my own to return insults with compliments, and live what I believe with dignity. Let me know, somehow, that my choice to live my beliefs openly will help others to become more tolerant."

"Source of All Life," Rick began. "Let strength flow through me to help Henry. I've always kept my feelings hidden from others. Grant me courage to speak out, as he has. May the Essence flow from both of us to touch others."

The two remained in silence, pods joined and held high. Henry felt the light touch of another pod, Genelle's.

*   *   *   *

For the first two time frames, Henry endured the daily onslaught of insults from his fellow trainees and nearly as often, Trainer Renard. He gave the trainer due respect and faced his colleagues with courage, standing as their equal and never letting the hurt show.

"Henry, in what season cycle did Roacheria begin management of South Dairy 1?"

"South Dairy 1 was enslaved twelve season cycles B.C.C. and liberated in season cycle one."

"What!"

Henry's antennae shook. "Excuse me, I meant to say twenty one, Trainer Renard. Management began in the twenty-first season cycle."

"Get up here!" ordered Renard.

Not realizing at first that he was about to endure the degrading practice of being stepped on, Henry moved to the front of the chamber.

"Humble yourself."

Henry stooped low, felt himself pushed even lower. Renard's back pod came down hard behind his head. Pain shot through him. "Now say that again!" he heard.

Very softly, Henry said, "Management of South Dairy 1 began in the twenty-first season cycle of Organized Roacheria."

"Return to your place. Keep your facts straight from now on."

Henry noticed silent sympathy in the eyes of those who usually mocked him as he walked slowly to his bench. He wanted desperately to rub the back of his head with one front pod, but he didn't. Instead he lifted up a silent thought. "That was for you, Uncle Gerry. I forgive him. Will you forgive me?"

*   *   *   *

"May I join you?" The voice came from behind Henry as he sat alone with his lunch.

He began to nod, winced instead, and reached to rub the plate of his exoskeleton that covered the joint between his head and thorax. He looked up to see Gatlin, a small, thin male in his Roachstory group who never spoke unless the trainer addressed him directly.

Gatlin whispered in poorly pronounced Ant, "Will you be all right, Henry? Others say how cruel is Trainer Renard. He had no cause for that to you. The others, the ones who hate you, say so yes?"

Henry appreciated his words, especially since they came in Ant. "I'll be fine, thank you. Where did you learn to speak Ant?"

Gatlin switched to Roach. "My father is an interpreter in the communications center. He started teaching me last season cycle, but he doesn't get much time. I'm not very good at it."

Henry knew that interpreters had once made a great deal of credit. But now that there were more of them, there was less work. He wondered how Gatlin's family afforded his training fees.

Gatlin must have guessed what he was thinking for his next statement was, "I study here on a sponsorship."

"If you sit with me every day at lunch, I'll help you learn Ant," Henry offered.

"You would do that?"

Henry nodded.

Another roach approached them. "Henry," Gatlin said, "this is my friend, Rusty."

Rusty gave Henry a friendly nod. "I heard about you. Renard had no right to do that, just for a wrong answer."

Henry finished his mug of water. "I could have avoided the whole thing. I wasn't concentrating and answered out of habit, as I would have at home. From now on, I won't forget my point of view, or to add thirty-three to the season cycles I memorized long ago."

"What do you mean? Point of view?" Gatlin's voice revealed genuine confusion.

Henry explained. "Whether one sees the incident with South Dairy 1 as 'enslavement,' or 'management' depends on whether it is read in an Antstory manuscript or a Roachstory training unit. The same goes for the season cycle. Here it's counted from the beginning of Organized Roacheria, thus the twenty-first season cycle. In The Colonies, it began in the twelfth season cycle Before the Combined Colonies. I wasn't thinking quickly enough. From Trainer Renard's point of view, my answer was not only wrong, but a great insult. In his chamber, I must live by his rules. It's that simple."

"But he still had no right ..."

"Yes, he did," Henry interrupted. "Every trainer has the right to determine discipline and punishment within his own chamber. It's written in the Training Code I was given when I enrolled, and required to sign. I read the document carefully."

Rusty looked at Henry intently. "I remember someone saying, 'Here, sign this,' but I didn't read it."

Gatlin lowered his eyes then asked, "If you don't mind, I'd like to talk to you more sometime, about your point of view."

Whether it was Henry's display of courage while being punished, or the fact that the others hated Trainer Renard more than they hated Henry, he never found out, but no one insulted him after that day.

*   *   *   *

Henry gently corrected Gatlin's pronunciation of an Ant word and gave him a new vocabulary list. The two spent every lunch together. Rusty often joined them. Although Henry still disliked studying, he enjoyed helping Gatlin. Giving out information was much better than having to take it in.

"Henry, may I ask you something?" Gatlin asked.

"Ants have a tradition that it's impolite to ask anyone something about their personal life. But I know you want to learn, so I'll never take anything you ask as an insult," Henry replied.

"Is it true that ants never suffer from Plastic Deprivation?"

Henry brushed the seed crumbs from the table and said, "No, some ants do end up plastic deprived, but never intentionally. All larvae are properly fed, but sometimes, during the pupa stage of life, mechanical failure occurs. The apparatus that feeds plastic to the pupating young can break down. Sometimes, near the end of pupation, the sleeping young may kick it with a newly forming appendage. It doesn't happen as often these days because they've invented better equipment."

"What do the parents do when that happens?"

Henry thought of some of the plastic depraved roaches he had seen wander aimlessly around the city and the shanties, scrounging for food, eventually dying alone, abandoned by Roacherian society.

"They grieve. Then they take care of their young one. Sometimes the deprivation is only slight. The adult may be able to learn simple things, even work at some jobs with extra guidance. Others are cared for in the larva nurseries, cherished and protected, treated with dignity for as long as they live. After all, it isn't their fault. They get sick easily, even with the best medical care, and usually die ten season cycles or so after emerging as adults."

Gatlin looked thoughtful. "Why can't we do that?"

Henry had no answer.

As the term progressed, Henry found that more and more trainees sought him out, asking curious but respectful questions. Even if they seemed foolish, Henry never said so. He tried to answer in a way that did not belittle their ignorance.

Toward the middle of the thirteenth time frame, Gatlin asked, "Henry, if you don't have plans for Last Night's festival, would you consider coming to my home? I've been telling my parents about you and they want to meet you."

Winter Solstice, the end of the season cycle, was celebrated quite differently by ants and roaches. For ants, it was a solemn occasion. Ants began early in the morning with meditation services. They rededicated themselves to their beliefs, then shared a feast with extended family.

Roaches, on the other hand, celebrated at night, singing, dancing, and drinking ale. For those with wealth or political power, it was a celebration of success and the hope that the coming season cycle would be even more profitable. The first day of the new season cycle was a day off for everyone. No one worked and no markets opened. "That's so everyone can get over consuming too much ale the night before," Rick had joked to Henry one day.

"What time?" Henry asked Gatlin.

"About eight h-units."

"Oh, good. I was afraid it would be earlier. Rick will be home from his job around four that day and we will perform our ritual and share our feast. But we'll be finished by eight. How about joining us first? Then you can take me to your home. I still don't know my way around very well."

"I would like that very much," Gatlin said.

Rusty had been sitting quietly with them. "Could," he hesitated, "I come too?"

"Sure," Henry replied. He knew Rick wouldn't mind.

*   *   *   *

Henry opened the portal. "Gatlin, Rusty, come in."

He led them down a short passage and into the dimly lit parlor. "Sorry it's so dark. It's part of the ceremony, symbolizing the lack of daylight at the end of the season cycle. Here," he handed them some parchments. "I translated the words we'll be chanting into Roach so you'll know what's going on. Let me introduce you to everyone."

"This is Rick, and his mate, Genelle." Rusty and Gatlin both stooped low to show respect for Rick's relatively high status compared to the two trainees on sponsorships. The pair, both of the larger variety, seemed to tower over them in the dimness, their solid brown exteriors glossy from oil rubbed over them for the occasion.

"No need for that here," Rick said, extending his front pods. "On this day and in this home, no one is high or low. This is my son, Ray, and Rina, who lives here with us."

Rina, small and thin like most shanty females, extended her front pods and grasped Gatlin's. "It's nice to have you here. Don't worry about not knowing what to do. Last season cycle was my first time."

"Yes," Rick said, "and this will be her last with us, I'm afraid. Rina has accepted a position as a tutor to the nymphs of one of the Board Members in Sea Edge. She'll be leaving secondday."

"Congratulations," Henry said to her.

Ray, image of his father, extended his pods to Rusty.

Rick led them to floor cushions, placed around one lightning bug lamp, its shade nearly closed. As they lowered themselves onto the cushions and joined pods, Henry explained. "We begin with a mournful chant for the end of this season cycle. Then we recite our creed. That will be followed by silent meditation, during which the lamp shade will be gradually opened, symbolizing the increase in daylight as the new season cycle advances. We will share seeds and end with a song of joy and hope."

"On this last day," they chanted, "as we link one solar season cycle to the next and unite it with the thirteen lunar time frames, we remember that all things are linked to each other.

"Creator of the Universe, and all its cycles, and infinite variety of living things, we offer up our thoughts and dedicate ourselves once again to all that we believe.

"To us has been given the gift of knowledge and the wisdom to discern right from wrong. May we reach out to help each other carry the responsibility of this gift.

"We pledge to respect all living things and the delicate balance of the chain of life; to take care of the planet and seek full understanding of its many cycles; to take no more than we need; to replenish what we take and reuse what we have; to cherish our mates and families and care for each member of every colony, placing the needs and good of others above our own.

"Help us to meditate upon how well we have lived this creed; to seek pardon of anyone we may have offended; to generously forgive all who may have offended us; and to resolve to live the new season cycle even more fully. So be it."

Henry felt a strange mix of emotions as he meditated silently. This was the first time he had not celebrated Last Day at home. Even when he had lived in South Harvester 45, he'd still gone home for Last Day. He missed his family, but felt at peace, secure in the care of Rick and Genelle and in his growing friendship with Gatlin and Rusty. Joy swirled through him, for he finally felt free of all his past guilt. A sense of purpose he had never felt before began to grow.

Rick opened the lamp shade. "As the daylight increases, so does our resolve to live our lives in simplicity and charity."

Ray and Rina passed seeds around, one for each two of them. Together they said, "May the All Powerful Force which makes the grassfronds grow from a large seed to a great height in a single season cycle, nourish us now with this seed. May we grow with it to care for each other more fully."

They ate the seeds and sang the concluding song of joy. Henry could see a new understanding in Rusty's expression and even more so, in Gatlin's.

"I've learned so much this evening," Gatlin said during dinner. "Rina and Ray, why don't you come with us tonight?"

Rina hesitated, looking at Rick.

"Don't look at me. You don't need permission."

The dances and songs of the festival at Gatlin's home were quite different from those Henry was accustomed to at ant mating ceremonies, but not difficult to learn. He involved himself fully, downing one mug of ale after another, embracing the good that Roacheria had to offer, just as he had the bad. He felt sorry that his brothers had been so closed to it. There was a place for both ways. One only had to find the balance.

Henry staggered home several h-units later, supported by Rina and Ray. When he awoke in the morning, he found Rick had not been joking about the need for a day off. He vowed to be more moderate in his consumption of ale in the future.

5.

Days turned into quarter time frames and time frames. One warm evening, late in spring, Henry sat on the bench near the wall opening in his sleep chamber, gazing into the night sky. He had to make a choice soon about remaining in Roacheria. Part of him said he should go home and begin to help support the colony. Another part wanted to continue studying Roacherian law. Becoming a certified counselor would take two more season cycles. It was not a skill he could practice in South Dairy 50, so he did not feel comfortable asking his colony to continue to support him.

After meditating for a long time, he fell into a fitful sleep, filled with visions.

Something tough but translucent surrounded him, binding him tightly. He squirmed, pushed against it, to no avail. He kicked outward with all his might, but it sprang back when each kick ended. Exhausted, he gave up for a while, but the urge to break out of this prison rose again. He kicked and thrashed, then in desperation bit at it. The membrane ruptured, flying back with a ripping noise. Henry squealed.

A round, black face looked into his. Long, thin pods picked him up and cradled him. "Finally. Here, you are, little one. You had quite a struggle to hatch. Rest now."

A delightful sensation poured over him. The gentle pods stroked him from the end of his back legs to the tips of his antennae. The voice continued. "Welcome to life, my grandson. If only your mother could see how finely formed you are, but she is so sick. Nor could your father take charge. So many are sick, and he is our only physician. But I'm here, and I won't leave. I will cherish and comfort you all my days, my precious tiny one."

The soothing touch and voice lulled Henry as the vision faded then grew strong again. He heard voices.

"Dad, has it hatched yet? It's over due. Don't open the portal. I'm afraid I'll contaminate the chamber. I can hear you."

"Yes, you have another fine son, Rodger. He's perfect in every way. I'm glad I could be with him. It reminded me of that day long ago when you came into our lives."

"Praise The Essence. The news will help Genny, I know. She said last night she'd decided on a name: Henrietta or Henry. Now we know which."

"How is Genny?"

"Very weak, but she's responding to treatment. It will be quite a while before she is able to care for Henry. I'm leaving fresh food and honey dew here by the portal. Wait 'till I've gone. I don't want to risk exposing Henry."

"I was with your mother all through it. Why not me?"

"I don't know." The voice shook. "I'm simply grateful I still have you and that neither of us has shown symptoms," the voice ended, replaced by mournful wailing.

The pods surrounding Henry began to shake as they stroked him. The voice seemed to struggle for control. "Hold on, Rodger. Go back to Genny and let yourself grieve for your mother with her. It will give both of you strength. You must rest."

"What about you? Will you be all right?"

"I'll manage. This little one will give me strength with his energy. I'll stay with him as long as I'm needed."

It was quiet for a time after that. The gentle pods fed him a cool sweet liquid. Then came something shredded and crunchy. Henry's mandibles chomped it with delight and he squeaked, hoping more would come.

"No, not now. Shouldn't have too much of a good thing, little Henry." The voice broke into soft wails, unable to continue after saying his name. Henry felt moist drops on the back of his thorax, but the pods continued to stroke him. "I'm sorry, precious one. If only I could give my cherished mate ... Oh, how I miss her, your grandmother and your namesake. She was everything to me, life itself. Why? Why didn't she respond to the treatment? Why was she taken from me? Why couldn't I have gotten it too, and joined her?"

The wailing finally stopped, but the gentle caressing continued. "Forgive me for filling your first day of life with my grief. Let me give to you all the affection I would give her, if I could. You have a life to live, and I must move on and help you with it. She said there must be something more for me to do in this world. Perhaps it is you," the voice sang to him. Within the vision, Henry seemed to sleep and awaken.

"Good morning, little Henry. You must eat: meat and seeds for a strong body, plastic for a strong mind, and honey dew for its sweetness and joy. I remember when I helped care for my little brother when he was a larva—so different are we ants. My mother showed me how to grind the plastic finely and mix it with honey dew for him to lap from my pods. My mother said I needed to know how to care for my future young. How could she foresee that I would raise your father, a roach, instead? Well, your father turned out wonderfully, so your grandmother and I must have done something right. Now I have you, and not her." The voice deteriorated into mourning again.

"Oh, Henry, your grandmother and I worked so hard to bring understanding between ants and roaches. This truly is a new colony, where we live together in harmony. But this place isn't enough. Somehow, all roaches must learn that life can be better. Why won't colony life work for them? I have many friends in Roacheria. They understand, but they can't seem to convince others. Who will teach all roaches how to care for each other as we do? Who will go to them? Who will continue what I started here?"

The vision faded and Henry awoke with a start, stiff from his awkward position on the bench. He looked at the sky, where the stars told him dawn was still far off. Joy swept through him. At long last, he remembered hatching. Then other memories came to him. "... Try to be a little less like me and a little more like your namesake ... Perhaps you will find the answer in Roacheria."

Henry left the bench and crawled onto his sleep cushion. He knew what he wanted to do. A peaceful sleep came over him.

*　　　*　　　*　　　*

Master Riedel, Director of the Training Center for Business and Professional work, motioned for Henry to enter his private work chamber. Henry bowed politely and sat opposite him. "You are an interesting creature, Henry Roach-Dairier, so different from your brothers when they came here. They hid. You shouted who you were from the first day. They remained on the edges, while you gather groups around you at lunch. They always looked miserable. You seem content, even happy. Why?"

"Is my contentment a problem, Master Riedel?"

"No, I'm just curious. Would you like something to drink?"

"No, thank you. Your question is very personal, but I will answer it. David and Arthur came here after they had finished all their training and knew what they wanted for their life's work. They only wanted to find mates."

"What? No young female roaches in New South 50?"

"The few at the time were related."

"I see." Master Riedel shifted on his cushioned stool and tapped one front pod.

"So, what are David and Arthur doing now, if I may ask?"

"David works with the grasshopper herds. He has two nymphs. Arthur directs the colony's trade. He has one nymph, so far."

"And the rest of your family?"

"My sister, Dorothy, works in South Harvester 45's main chemistry lab. Drew spent one season cycle at the Advanced Training Center for the Sciences, found a mate and went home. He's nearly finished his mentorship with my father."

Master Riedel took a gulp of ale from his mug. "No mate for Dorothy?"

"A female need not have a mate to have a full life."

"So, what makes you so different? Why did you come? Not for a mate, because I know you're not looking."

"I came to find myself and my purpose in life. I believe I'll have that drink now, if I may." Henry pushed his nervousness deep inside. He knew how carefully he needed to proceed in this interview.

"Of course." Master Riedel reached for another mug and filled it with ale. "And have you found it? Your purpose, I mean."

"I believe I have. That's why I asked to see you. I have a request." Henry drank from the mug and took a deep breath to steady himself.

"I'm listening."

"I would like to stay here and study to be a certified counselor of law, but I need funding. My agreement with my colony lasted only the first season cycle. I'm not a citizen, so I can't apply for a sponsorship. What I would like to do is work for you in the mornings and be in training all afternoon. You've seen how many trainees are anxious to learn from me. I could teach Ant."

"There is some roach in you after all. You've tired of giving away knowledge for free, have you?" Master Riedel said with a laugh.

"You could look at it that way, but it is a skill that I have which you could use. Here's my offer. I'll teach all morning in exchange for my training fees, room and board here at the center, and a small allowance. Quite a bargain for you, compared to straight trainer salary."

Master Riedel looked at him seriously. "You certainly did your research, but you're too young to teach. How would you control trainees who are older than you are? Have you got any idea the controversy this could cause?"

"My grandmother was only seventeen when she began her mentorship. At nineteen, she trained roach archaeologists much older than she. Age has little to do with ability. The agreement every trainee signs concerning proper behavior will establish my authority, as it does for everyone else on your staff. I'm very aware that many still have negative attitudes toward me. You could use that to your advantage."

Henry looked intently at Master Riedel in silence. He could see that Master Riedel understood his unspoken words. If his teaching didn't work out, Master Riedel could send him home in disgrace, saying it had been an experiment that proved Roacherian ways were superior. If Henry succeeded, Master Riedel could declare that it was his forward-looking ideas that made Henry successful. Master Riedel might be able to advance his career. He won either way.

Master Riedel put one pod across his mandibles and looked thoughtfully at Henry. "You could become quite a counselor. You're persuasive, and you know how to think like we do. I'll agree to one term. If it goes smoothly, we'll renegotiate."

"You won't be disappointed. Perhaps you should have a written contract to protect yourself in this experiment."

"Or to protect you from someone like Trainer Renard? I may not say anything, but I know everything that goes on around here."

Master Riedel took out fresh parchment and ink and together they wrote out the terms of Henry's employment as guest trainer of Ant language and culture for one term. Both signed it.

Henry sent a brief message home: "I have suitable work and will be staying here for at least another half a season cycle. I will be living on my own, but will join Rick and his family every seventhday for meditation and dinner. You can still send letters to me there." He wanted desperately to tell his grandfather that he remembered his hatching and would be teaching, but decided to wait until he knew he had succeeded.

*   *   *   *

Henry looked over the quiet group before him. It wasn't as large as he'd hoped, but enough to start. Some he recognized as friends, at least one as an adversary, some completely new faces.

"The title of this training unit is 'Beginning Ant Language and Culture,' in case anyone is in the wrong chamber. During our sessions, and in this chamber you will address me as Trainer Henry, with all proper respect for that title. Outside this chamber, I am another trainee and you may call me anything you like."

He walked across the front of the chamber and stood next to a large piece of parchment he'd attached to the wall. "These are the regulations you will follow when you are in this chamber. You will address one another by name only. No insults will be tolerated. I am not here to try to induce you to adopt Ant culture or Spiritual Philosophy, but to help you understand it. If I perform any ritual here, it is for instruction. You will participate to learn, not because you must believe it. No one is considered 'high' or 'low' here, and you are to listen to each other's opinions with open minds. All are free to express their opinions. Anyone who cannot follow these guidelines should leave now."

Henry let his eyes sweep those in his audience, especially one he felt might be there to discredit him. No one left.

"The first time a rule is broken, I will ask the offender to leave for the rest of the session. The offender may return the next day after a proper apology. The second time, the offender may not return until an agreement has been reached with me regarding the terms of remaining in the group. If there is a third infraction, standard Training Center Procedures will be followed."

Several trainees shifted on their benches, but no one said anything. Henry returned to the center. "If you are uncomfortable, you may move about, stand, or sit. Bring a cushion tomorrow if you like. I know how these benches feel. We have no manuscripts, so I'd like you to bring plenty of parchment and ink. You'll have your text when we finish. Let's begin."

He took out a cushion and sat in their midst. He explained the Ant custom of not asking personal questions, and gave several examples, then rose and stood near another large, blank piece of parchment tacked to the wall, ink pot in one pod.

"I'd like each of you to introduce yourselves, telling as much as you want to about your family. Tell us your goals for training and work, and why you chose to take this unit. I'll begin with myself.

"I am Henry Roach-Dairier. I hatched and was raised in New South Dairy Colony 50. I have three brothers and one sister, all older than I am. My parents are Rodger and Genny. Genny grew up here in Roacheria in the shanties. My father met her while studying to be a physician. My grandparents, Master Antony, author of the peace agreement of 221 O.R., and Master Henrietta, may her essence rest, adopted my father. They found a mortally wounded female named Geree' shortly after New South 50 was established. She asked them to take her egg as she died. Her mate, George, was one of the warriors killed during the last violent conflict, 219th season cycle, O.R. I do know who Geree's family was, but they have a right to their privacy." Henry wrote the names on the parchment and drew lines indicating the relationships as he proceeded.

"Master Antony's parents, David and Dorothy, along with his brothers and sisters were also killed in the conflict of 219. Master Henrietta's parents were Adeline and Henry, of South Harvester 45. He was a famous tunnel engineer, by the way. I don't expect this kind of detail from you. I share it because it demonstrates my family's unique position in both The Combined Colonies of Insectia and Organized Roacheria."

He moved back to the cushion and sat down. "That unique position is why I asked to begin this training unit. Although we have peace, we do not have understanding. I've chosen to follow the mission begun by my grandfather when he established New South Dairy 50. My goal here, besides teaching you, is to continue to study Roacherian Law in order to increase my own understanding of my Roach heritage."

Henry pointed out one of the trainees. "Now that you know about me, please, introduce yourself."

The large male looked surprised. Silence hung heavily. Henry had deliberately chosen his enemy. "I am Reese, and my father is Sir Reese, Chief Executor of the South East Roach Control Board. This is my last term of training. Then I will join my father on The Board. Trainer Henry, you know I don't like you personally, but I will follow your regulations in this chamber. I took this unit because my father says it's important to know your adversaries well."

Henry nodded. "Good advice. Next."

"My name is Gatlin. My father is an interpreter. I study here on a sponsorship. I'd like to work for the City Bulletin. Trainer Henry has been teaching me at lunch for a long time and I wanted to learn more," Gatlin stated. He smiled at Henry, which seemed to relax the others.

Henry gestured to Rusty, sitting next to Gatlin. "My name is Rusty. I'm a friend of Gatlin's. My parents work in a Basic Training Center, teaching nymphs to read. I'm also on a sponsorship. I'd like to work in the Trade Center, and I took this unit because Gatlin did."

Henry looked at the next trainee, slightly smaller than Henry, he was obviously a mix of the larger roach variety like Henry's own father (common among government officials, warriors, and those with power and wealth) and the small, slender roaches like Henry's mother. Many of this mix existed in Roacheria, because wealthy males fathered nymphs with shanty females unofficially. Such relationships, and the resulting nymphs, were frowned upon by Roacherian Society. Hatred for Henry grew from his mixed parentage as well as his Ant origins, something else he hoped to change.

"I am Rundell. I'd rather not discuss my family. I hope to manage and maybe own a market stall. I'm here because I'm curious."

Before Henry could acknowledge Rundell, the portal flew open and Trainer Renard stormed in.

"What right have you to be in this place poisoning the minds of these trainees, you miserable piece of fly bait?" Renard demanded, standing over Henry.

Henry rose from his cushion and faced Renard. "I have a contract with Master Riedel as a guest instructor, Trainer Renard. You may check with him if you like. You are entitled to your opinion about poisoning minds, but I will not tolerate your personal insult. You will address me as Trainer Henry inside this chamber. Please, leave. If you wish to return and observe a session, I expect a formal apology."

"Contract! We'll see about that, pond scum! You're all pond scum." His eye caught Reese. "What are you doing here?"

Reese rose, quickly swept his pods to the sides and said, "My father's orders."

Fury replaced Renard's anger. "I'll see all of you expelled!" He raised one front pod ready to strike Henry.

Henry stood firm and said quietly, "You have no legal right and you know it. When I was a trainee in your unit, I accepted your physical and verbal abuse, because it was your right within your chamber. Now, I am the trainer and this is my chamber. You are obliged to follow my regulations." He pointed to the parchment on the wall. "You have now insulted me twice, and the group once. Leave. You may not return without a formal apology and the group's permission."

Trainer Renard looked at the parchment and raised his pod higher.

Henry remained still, his head positioned at prime distance from the threatening pod. He forced himself to retain a calm exterior. Indescribable anxiety filled him. "I don't think you want to add assault to this, not in front of all these witnesses."

No one moved.

The trainees' eyes shifted. First to Renard. Back to Henry. The sound of breathing became noticeable. Henry fixed his eyes on Renard. Time suspended itself.

Trainer Renard slowly lowered his pod, then turned and stalked out of the chamber, slamming the portal behind him. Henry slumped down onto the cushion. Murmurs of relief spread through the chamber.

"Trainer Henry, you will charge him, won't you?" Gatlin asked.

Henry took several deep breaths before responding. "No. He did not touch me. I made my point and he acknowledged it. I will never lower myself to his standards. If he apologizes to all of us, with sincerity, he may observe any session. I don't expect that to happen, though. Now, where were we with our introductions?"

*   *   *   *

The following morning, Master Riedel observed the session, which involved learning common greetings. Henry chose to greet Rundell first, taking both his front pods in friendship. "The fact that I take both your pods and stand face to face with you demonstrates friendship and mutual respect. Common courtesy and caring for all replace the belief that one should be higher than another." He greeted each of them in the same way and had all of them greet one another, including Master Riedel.

Master Riedel remained when the session ended. "I no longer have any doubts about your abilities, Trainer Henry, future counselor."

Henry smiled. "Thank you."

6.

*T*he term proceeded smoothly. Henry based his culture lessons on comments and questions from the group. He presented the language in an orderly way beginning with greetings and the words used most frequently in conversation. Between preparation for his unit and his own studies, he had very little free time. Letters home were infrequent, but he always went to Rick's home on seventhdays. There, he reaffirmed his goals through meditation with those he cared deeply about. Rick's son, Ray, often joined them.

"Henry, I want to show you something," Ray said one day. He took a cord made of braided plastic strands about eight f-units long from his satchel. "I'm going to see Ramona's father tomorrow. I wondered if you would help me with the wording of the contract."

"Congratulations! I knew you cared about Ramona, but I didn't think you were that serious. I finished that section of study last time frame, so I know how to do it. We'd better work on it now. I never have extra time on training days."

The two moved into the parlor and Ray took parchment and ink from his father's writing surface. "We made an Ant mating promise last night and my father says we can have a small ceremony here, very private, since Ramona's father doesn't approve of Ant ways. He doesn't know we both believe in it. That's why I need a good contract."

As Henry helped Ray with the legal wording of a Roach mating contract, he thought about the symbolism of the plastic cord. If Ramona's father accepted Ray's contract, he would use the cord to bind the two together. It would be tied from Ramona's front pod to Ray's back one, for females were subservient to males in Roacheria. Later, it would be fed to their first nymph. In the document, Ray would pledge to accept legal responsibility for any nymphs Ramona hatched and vow publicly to insure that they would be provided with sufficient plastic.

Subservience was something Henry could do without, but a male committing himself to the nourishment of young was another of the good things about Roacherian law. Henry regretted that so many females gave themselves in mating without the protection of this legal bond and later found themselves with nothing but nymphs to raise alone. Since all nymphs belonged to the first male who mated a female, those who were deserted seldom found another willing to assume the responsibility.

"I'd also like to state that I will be faithful to her," Ray said when they had drafted the main part.

"That's not necessary, Ray."

"I know, but I want to assure him that I'm more serious than other males who may approach him. I know I would never leave her. But if I state that I also promise her monetary support in the event that things don't work out, he's more likely to accept my contract over another's."

Henry dipped his pod in the ink again. "Do you have competition?"

"Not directly, but Ramona's father has been talking about her to his boss, who has a son. He might be better off financially than I am, but he would never care for her as I will."

Henry nodded and stated it in appropriate legal terms. "All right, here it is. You should copy it in your own script."

"Thanks, you just saved me a counselor's fee. Will you stand as my first friend when we celebrate here?"

"I'd be honored. Ask me any time you need something legal done. If I know enough about it, I'll do it for you."

*   *   *   *

Henry looked at Rundell. His mood had changed during the last time frame. At the start of the term, he'd been open and talkative. Now he rarely spoke and moved with an awkward stiffness uncharacteristic of adult roaches. He seemed more like a nymph, but if that were so, he would not have been admitted to this training center.

He approached Rundell, looking steadily at the wild-eyed young male. "Rundell, what's wrong lately? You aren't yourself."

"Nothing! Leave me alone," Rundell shouted, sending a hush through the other trainees.

Henry reached out to touch Rundell, but at that moment Rundell screamed, and flung all his appendages outward. One back pod caught Henry and sent him sprawling. The group gasped. Henry picked himself up, realizing that Rundell had been hiding his youth, silently suffering through his final molt.

"I'm not hurt," he reassured the others. "Stay back. It seems Rundell is a bit younger than we thought."

A sigh of relief went through the trainees as they moved away from the struggling Rundell. "The rest of you are dismissed for today," Henry stated. "I'd appreciate it if none of you mentioned what happened here to anyone."

Everyone nodded agreement and filed out quietly. However, Rundell's cry had not gone unheard in the center's passageways. Even though the others, including Reese, refused to say what had happened, Master Riedel arrived an h-unit later with an Enforcer. Rundell had trashed his way free of his last youthful exoskeleton and lay limp on the floor, helpless. Henry had nothing with which to cover him.

"Trainer Henry, what in ..." Master Riedel began, and then stopped when he saw Rundell.

"It's not what you think," Henry tried to explain.

"It's out of my pods. Someone passing by heard it. I cannot deny that an assault took place."

"I was not assaulted. There was no intent to injure. Had I realized a moment sooner, I'd have gotten out of the way," Henry persisted. "He only did what all of us do. If he's guilty of anything, it's concealing the fact that he was not yet an adult. Please, Master Riedel, tell the Enforcer to leave. This young male does not deserve to be condemned to the mantis compound."

"I can't ignore center policies. You know that," Master Riedel said motioning to the Enforcer.

"No! Wait!" Henry shouted. "At least let him harden. Have you no compassion at all?"

"All right. We'll return tomorrow morning. But I'm posting two outside the portal. No one enters. No one leaves. I have a reputation to uphold, Trainer Henry."

"Thank you. Could you have someone send in a bit of food and drink?"

Master Riedel grunted. "I suppose. I'll include something to cover that pathetic creature."

When the items were delivered, Henry covered the terrified Rundell and stroked his antennae until he slept. He ate a little and then began to meditate.

Rundell woke during the night, adult exoskeleton having hardened, and accepted the food Henry offered. "Why did you do that? You've only postponed things. Nothing can save me."

"I needed time to think. I happen to believe that you are worth trying to save. There may be a way, if you are willing to trust me and answer everything I'm about to ask you with absolute honesty. I know you did not intend to hurt me."

"Trainer Henry, you are among the few creatures who have been kind to me. I wish I could undo what I did. I'd do anything for you. I'll never forget you, even if I end up being breakfast for a mantis."

"Tell me how you managed to be admitted to this center though still a nymph, why you did it, and about your family," Henry said, gesturing toward two cushions.

The two settled themselves and Rundell began. "I have no family. My father deserted my mother when I was about two. I watched my mother slowly starve herself to make sure I had enough food and plastic. I don't know for sure, but I think she laid other eggs and crushed them."

Henry cringed at the thought of anyone intentionally ending the life of an unhatched egg, but he knew it was a common practice among the poor, who felt that was better than growing up in poverty or suffering from Plastic Deprivation.

Rundell continued, his voice shaking. "I watched many abuse her and then offer her a pittance of credit to give them pleasure. She killed herself two season cycles ago."

Rundell broke down and Henry wrapped himself around the youth, giving him comfort, as he had often received it.

"I lived by scrounging. One day, I happened to wander to the farthest edge of the refuse piles, in search of something not yet too rotten to eat. I saw several flies hovering and realized they were about to lay eggs. I knew it was a lucky find and gathered the whole lot. I went back on a regular basis. I also learned how to collect good bait from refuse bins to attract even more flies. I always made sure no one saw me, so my gathering place in the refuse piles remained a secret. At first, I sold them to market managers, but they often cheated me. I couldn't get my own market stall, so I started selling them directly to the rich. Many liked it that I delivered them fresh on a regular basis."

"You know," Henry interrupted. "I never thought about how fly eggs got to the markets."

"It's not a bad living. One of the Board Members I delivered eggs to let me live in a storage chamber in the lower level of his domicile. The tutor he had for his nymphs taught me to read. I still live there. I tried to get a sponsorship but they'd given them all out. I did get a deal to pay my fees by the time frame. I spend every sixth and seventh day spreading bait and gathering eggs. I make enough to pay my fees."

"Why didn't you wait until you'd molted?"

Rundell rose and paced the chamber. "I'm past thirteen. I got tired of waiting. I had proof of age, the one thing my mother did give me, so nobody asked when I enrolled. Just so the fees got paid. Lot of good that does now."

They sat in silence for several minutes. Then Henry asked, "Are you willing to place yourself in my custody for at least one season cycle? I would take legal responsibility for you, but you would be completely under my control. I'd have the right to condemn you for any infraction, anywhere."

"What for? Day after tomorrow I'll be dead."

"What if I could convince Master Riedel to try something else? Would you be willing to do it? Even declare it publicly?" Henry asked, looking into Rundell's eyes.

Rundell returned his gaze. "Yes, if I were offered that chance."

"When Master Riedel comes in, stand in back of me. Don't say one single word. If you can keep still, no matter what I say, I'll know I can risk anything and you'll make it. Let me argue this out. If I succeed, you'll be the first in Roacheria to live under an Ant Probationary Behavior Contract."

Rundell managed to sleep again, but Henry spent the rest of the night meditating. Master Riedel actually knocked on the portal before entering. The two Enforcers who had stood guard entered with him.

Rundell moved behind Henry.

"I'm sorry, Trainer Henry, but you know what I have to do."

"Master Riedel, do I not have the right to determine punishment within my own unit?"

"Yes, but..."

"Do I have the right or not?"

"Yes."

"Then hear me out. You know the truth. This was not assault. If you'd checked better, he would not have been admitted. But I know the reality here. Neither of us can let this go. This unit was to be a cultural experiment, correct?"

Master Riedel looked skeptically at Henry and answered cautiously, "Yes."

"Then give me my right to determine punishment by that cultural experiment."

"The fact that I'm listening to you should not imply approval at this moment," Master Riedel said, signaling the two Enforcers to stand outside the portal again.

"I understand. In an ant colony, when a young adult makes a mistake, he or she is given a second chance. The offender is placed under a probationary contract held by a party familiar with the offender, the nature of the offense, and the contract process. The holder of the contract takes full legal authority for the offender. The offender no longer belongs to himself or herself, but to the holder of the contract. The document stipulates what the offender must do to make restitution, and the consequences for breaking the contract."

"And the consequences are?"

"It depends on the individual, but it is generally something the offender considers worse than death. For example, an offender who likes being on the surface might be confined underground. For someone most comfortable underground, surface work would be a better punishment.

Under the circumstances we have here, the consequence of breaking the contract would be immediate condemnation."

"And what would you consider breaking the contract?" Master Riedel asked, beginning to walk slowly around the chamber.

"Any offense to anyone during training hours, any breach of civil law outside training." Henry felt Rundell put a pod on his back. It was shaking, but he remained silent.

"And I thought ants were soft on punishment. What if Rundell doesn't want to do this? Or doesn't think he can be that perfect? How long a period of time are you talking about here?"

"One season cycle. It isn't meant to be easy. Rundell's already agreed, and I believe he will meet the terms of the contract."

Master Riedel sat down on one of the cushions. Henry remained standing. "You'd be the one to hold this contract, I suppose?"

"Yes."

"The whole center already knows something's happened. Are you willing to make this public?"

"Rundell and I will stand before an assembly of the entire training center, staff and trainees, and tell them exactly what happened and my course of action. Let it be a continuation of our experiment. If we succeed, we consume the contract in one season cycle, in accordance with Ant tradition. Rundell will be completely free of it." Henry paused. The words he spoke next did not seem to come from himself. "If he fails, you may condemn me along with him to protect yourself."

Rundell slumped to the floor. Master Riedel stared at Henry, his mandibles opened in astonishment. Henry felt a strange confidence. He had read about ants who felt prompted by The Essence to speak and act in certain ways, but he'd never thought it would happen to him.

"Why put yourself up with him?" Master Riedel asked. "You're insane!"

"Maybe," Henry said, his voice calm, "but I believe I will show you it can be done, just as I have with my training unit. You have nothing to lose and everything to gain. Do you accept my offer?" Henry reached back and put a reassuring pod on Rundell's head.

"All right," Master Riedel said.

Henry took out fresh parchment and ink and wrote out Rundell's contract. All three of them signed it. Later that day, he and Rundell stood before everyone at the training center and read it aloud. No one drummed their pods on the floor in approval; neither did they call out in protest. The members of Henry's unit stood in silent respect.

*   *   *   *

The last day of his first term came on sixthday, the 27th of the thirteenth time frame. Henry decided he would demonstrate the Last Day ritual, which he would celebrate formally with Rick and his family on its proper day. He had given his trainees copies of the words in Roach and instructed them to bring cushions.

As he closed the shutters in the chamber and turned the lamps as low as he could, he heard a commotion in the passageway. "The Supreme Executor is coming," he heard several passing trainees say as they hurried to move to the sides of the passage.

Sir Reese, the elder, strode toward him. Young Reese walked behind his father. Everyone stooped low and swept pods to the side as he passed. Henry did the same as they reached him.

"To what do I owe this honor, Sir?"

"My son says you told them early in the term that any ritual you performed was only for instruction. I came today to make sure of that."

"Welcome," Henry said, noticing that Reese carried two cushions.

The relaxed atmosphere Henry had worked so hard to achieve with his group evaporated as each trainee entered and saw The Supreme Executor. Henry couldn't help feeling that Sir Reese's presence would spoil the effect he hoped to make on his trainees. He closed the portal and decided he would not change who he was or what he believed, even for the Supreme Executor. He moved to the center of the group and took his place.

He explained briefly what they would see then said, "I've tried for the last several days to chant the words in Roach, but the tones don't fit. Reese, I don't have an extra copy of the translation, so I would appreciate it if you would share yours with your father. I invite you to hum along. During the time of silent meditation, I would like you to reflect on all that you have learned this term."

Henry found his nervousness subsided as he began the chant. He closed his eyes and lost himself in words and tones he had known since early nymphood. Peace filled him. He chanted with a clarity he had never experienced before, as if it were some other voice and not his own. He heard Rusty and Gatlin chanting the words in Ant, as well as Rundell's off-tone attempts.

During the silent time he reached out and took hold of the front pods of those closest to him. The gesture spread. Henry centered his thoughts on his family, growing friendships, and the tiny seed of understanding that had sprouted as a result of his work. He hoped The Essence would continue to guide his choices and help him continue what he had begun.

When the ceremony ended and his trainees filed out quietly, Sir Reese lingered. "Your demonstration for instruction could lead to lasting impressions on some, but not on me. I'm not like the former Sir Reginald. Nor am I like another. I will never agree with or adopt your philosophy. Neither will my son. But he's learned what I sent him here to learn. You have my respect for that."

Henry nodded.

Sir Reese turned to leave. Half way out of the portal, he looked back and said, "Somehow, I don't think we have heard the last from Henry Roach-Dairier."

7.

*W*ith the exception of Reese, who had completed his training, all of Henry's group returned for a second term. Henry began another group for new trainees. His own studies demanded more of his time as well. Rundell continued in his training group and ate all his meals with Henry. The two went to Rick's home each seventhday morning.

"Rundell, I think I'll join you on your trip to the refuse piles today," Henry said as they left after dinner one day in the spring.

"I don't think you'll like it."

"Let me judge that. Don't worry, I won't tell anyone where your gathering place is."

"All right, but don't say I didn't warn you," Rundell replied.

Rundell led Henry to some of the better areas of the city first. They went up and down the lanes behind domiciles and Rundell picked up his bait, the rank remains set out for the refuse collectors.

"I know every collection route," Rundell explained. "This is the best one. The rich put out good leavings and the collectors come here firstday mornings."

He handed Henry a cloth when they reached the refuse area. "Here, put this over your antennae and face. It won't cut out all the smell, but it will make breathing a little easier."

Rundell was about half way through collecting his eggs when Henry gave in to his nausea.

"Don't feel bad about it," Rundell said. "I got sick plenty in the beginning."

"I don't think I'll ever eat another fly egg," Henry said weakly after they left the refuse piles behind.

Rundell laughed and asked, "What do ants do with their refuse? Surely, you do have refuse."

"Everyone sorts it by type before it's collected. We have containers for each type, which are used over and over until they break. Then the materials are melted down and made new like everything else. Any wood or parchment is shredded to make new parchment. Things made form woven thistledown are also shredded. The fibers can be spun and woven again. Organic waste has its own container. It's taken to the fungus growing areas deep within each colony, mixed with soil and used as fertilizer for fungus and grassfronds," Henry explained.

"Sounds like an awful lot of work."

"Yes, many workers are involved in reuse centers, but in the long run it saves time and resources. It's much better than the mess we just left. Healthier, too."

Rundell said nothing more. He led Henry through his delivery route, bowed politely to his regular customers and collected his credit. When they returned to Henry's quarters at the training center—which Henry now shared with Rundell—Rundell said quietly, "It may not be pleasant, but it pays my fees."

*   *   *   *

Henry looked at the bewildered faces in his beginning group and tried again to explain the difference between things one needed and those one wanted. "As an adult, I want plastic, but I no longer need it. So if I don't have enough credit, I skip it. Nymphs should have enough first. In an ant colony, everyone's basic needs are met. Then any extra is shared by all."

"But we have to save some for difficult times. Nobody meets our basic needs," one trainee said.

"Yes, that's the difference between us," Henry said. "But what if I accumulate more plastic than I could possibly eat in a life time? What good does it do me when I leave this world?"

"You feel secure," the trainee said.

"Why not try different ways? Then all would feel secure without some having more than they need while others suffer without."

A knock at the portal stopped the discussion.

"Excuse me, Trainer Henry," the clerk apologized, "your brother, David, is in the central work chamber. He says he must see you immediately."

Henry turned to his trainees. "I'll be right back. Practice the writing symbols."

Henry followed the clerk, wondering why David would come to a place he had sworn he would never lay eyes on again.

"Henry, you've got to come home. Grandfather is dying and he's asking for you," David said before Henry could even embrace him.

Henry stopped and stared. "Grandfather? But ..." It couldn't be, he thought. Antony would always be there for him. His mind swirled around him.

"Henry," Master Riedel's voice broke into Henry's thoughts. Henry hadn't even noticed him standing there. "Go on. Take all the time you need. Someone will dismiss your group. I'll let your afternoon trainers know you'll catch up when you return."

"What about Rundell?"

"Don't worry about him. He's too busy being perfect for your sake. I'll keep an eye on him."

"Thank you, Master Riedel. I'll send word."

Henry had never seen David move so fast. He ran to keep up. David didn't slow down until they'd crossed the bridge to New South 50's surface area.

"What's wrong with him?" Henry finally asked.

David informed him that Antony had been fighting degenerating breathing organs for six season cycles. "Not that you'd have noticed," he added sarcastically.

They argued about Henry's lack of consideration and letters home. Henry lapsed into silence. He knew David was right. Henry had never paid any attention to the signs, but it all came back to him now. His grandfather's wheezing and fatigue. The herbs he had taken during the days before Henry's molt. They had gone to the stream, not the glen, before he left home. He had taken his grandfather for granted.

His antennae drooped in shame and humility when he and David entered their nymphood home. Several family and colony members sat in the parlor, talking quietly. Henry entered his grandfather's sleep chamber.

"Dad," he heard his father say, "let me move you into the clinic. You need breathing apparatus."

"No," was the quiet reply.

Antony caught sight of him. "Henry, I knew you would come."

Henry choked back tears at the sight of his grandfather, a frail shadow of the strength Henry remembered. He knew he should comfort his grandfather, but instead he wanted that feeling of peace Antony had always given him. Rodger moved aside for Henry.

With what Henry later realized was his grandfather's last bit of strength, Antony embraced Henry and stroked him. Henry told Antony about his teaching and about Rundell.

A spark of joy came into Antony's eyes. "Your father keeps asking me what I want on my marker. I told him you knew. How's your memory?"

"Excellent."

Antony spoke about Henrietta's death and her peace at knowing others would carry on her work. Now Antony could be at peace as well, his work was finished. Henry saw that, even though he hadn't said it directly, his grandfather understood that Henry had remembered his hatching and found his purpose in life. He would continue Antony's work.

The quiet dignity and simplicity of ant tradition presided over the covering. Rodger laid his father in the hollow others had dug next to the place where Henrietta and Antony's family had been covered. Ants never wrapped their dead. It prevented the body from completing its purpose, feeding the earth. Rodger, his sons and daughter emptied baskets of dirt over him.

Each creature present spoke in turn, as if Antony were standing there, knowing The Essence heard.

"All that I am," Rodger said, "I am because you gave me the chance to live and cherished me."

Genny spoke through tears. "I will always remember how you accepted me and my sister as part of your family. You always made me feel important."

"You sent someone to search for me and convince me to come here," Renée's mate, Rita, said. "You forgave so completely and let Renée and I have a life here we never would have had. You filled me with peace when he left this world."

"You taught me to love dairying," David said. "As you and your father did."

Many colony members spoke of how Antony had inspired them to accept all creatures, not only ants.

Henry waited until last. "You taught me that change is a choice. I will live to honor my namesake and you. I will take your lessons far beyond New South Dairy 50, not because I feel expected to. Form the depths of my being, I want to."

After the covering ended, Henry shared a seed with his father. The words, "Change is a choice," were to be written on the memorial marker. Henry explained that he needed time and privacy to write the rest of his grandfather's marker, everything he had told Henry about his life.

Henry went to South Dairy 50's communication center and sent a brief message to Master Riedel and Rundell. He wasn't sure how long he would be. Then he went to the training center and asked for a large supply of parchment and ink. As he sat at the work surface in his old sleep chamber, the words poured forth. He remembered everything his grandfather had told him with absolute clarity. The stack of completed parchments grew.

"You need some rest," his father said, stroking him gently.

"I'm not tired."

"At least eat something," Rodger said, setting a bowl of roasted seeds and a mug of honey dew where Henry could reach it.

Sometimes he dozed over the parchment and woke to find a coverlet over him. Off and on, he was aware of his mother's or father's presence as they set more food and drink down next to him. Several days passed.

"Henry, I must talk to you."

Henry looked up to see his father standing there.

"I've been reading some of what you've finished. I'm proud of it. Do you plan to include what he told you about my season cycles in Roacheria?" Rodger asked.

"Only with your permission."

"You have it. Here is the letter Sir Ronald wrote me when I left, and the one Ronda wrote after her grandfather died. I haven't heard from Ronda since, but I didn't expect to. The letters might help you when you go back there, since they acknowledge my relationship, and therefore yours, to that family. I don't know how I feel about your choice to live there. I'd rather you came home to stay, but your life can't be what I wish."

"Thank you for understanding," Henry said. "I'll be finished by tomorrow. Will you have someone check it for syntax errors? I've got to get back."

Rodger nodded and embraced his son.

8.

*F*ourteen days from the day he had left, Henry returned to Roacheria. The training day had ended, but Master Riedel was still there. Henry reported to him.

"I was beginning to think you'd decided not to come back," Master Riedel said.

"Didn't you get my message?" Henry asked.

"Yes, but it's been much longer than I thought you intended."

"My grandfather and I were very close. Five season cycles ago, during my final molt, my grandfather told me his life's story. He said I could write it down after he'd left this world. I knew if I didn't do it right away, it wouldn't get done."

"You wrote a whole book since you left?" Master Riedel asked.

"I've had five season cycles to think about it. I did nothing else. I didn't sleep much. It's not edited, either. Was everything all right with Rundell?"

Master Riedel glared at him. "Everything was fine until last fifthday. I haven't seen him since. I was about to let the Enforcers find him."

"Rundell gathers and delivers fly eggs on seventhdays. Something must have gone wrong," Henry said, distress rising inside. "I'll find him."

"Two days of unexcused absence is, to me, a violation of his contract. I'm warning you, Henry, if you're not back here with him by morning, I'll send the Enforcers after both of you."

Henry hurried out of Master Riedel's work chamber. He threw his satchels in his quarters, shuffled through the parchments on Rundell's work surface, grabbed one, and ran from the center. Breathless, he arrived at Rick's home a short while later.

"Rick, did Rundell come here on seventhday?" he asked before Rick could even greet him.

"Of course. What's wrong?"

"He didn't go back to the training center firstday."

Rick put a pod on Henry's thorax, sensing his anxiety. "We meditated as usual. Then he left to go collecting. I told him I'd buy any extra eggs he had. When he didn't return, I thought perhaps he'd sold them all. Do you know his route? We'll search together."

"I found his list," Henry replied, holding up a crumpled parchment.

"Let's get going then. It will be dark soon."

The two of them headed out to the refuse area. When they reached Rundell's collection spot, Henry said, "There are no eggs. He must have gotten this far. Nobody else knows about this place. Come on. We'll go to all the domiciles where he delivers and ask who has seen him. I've got to find him before morning or we're both dead."

"What do you mean?" Rick asked.

Henry explained Rundell's contract.

Rick let out a long whistle between his outer mandibles. "Let's run," he said.

A female servant came to the back portal of the first domicile on the list.

"Please pardon the lateness of the h-unit," Henry began. "Did Rundell come on seventhday with your egg supply?"

"Yes, on time as usual. Why? Is he in trouble?"

"No, but he's missing."

"I hope nobody got him. My master wouldn't want to lose his supplier."

Henry thanked her and hurried on. As they went down the list, and heard similar replies, both grew more anxious.

"You don't suppose someone attacked him?" Rick said.

"That's what I'm afraid of. Each place we find he's been narrows it down, but there's only one left: Sir Rubin."

Sir Rubin was a young Board Member, the one who had allowed Rundell to live in the storage room of his domicile. Terror struck Henry as they approached it. The domicile lay in rubble, smoke still rising from it. Two Enforcers stood guard.

"Let me ask," Rick said. "I know many of The Enforcers from gathering reports for the City Bulletin. Stay back. No offense, but they don't like your type."

Henry nodded, slunk into the shadows and watched. Rick talked to one Enforcer, was directed to the other, who pointed around and nodded. Rick poked about the charred remains of the domicile and the garden area. Henry watched him pick up something and return to the Enforcer. They talked again. Rick waved good-bye and started toward Henry. With dismay, Henry saw that the object he had was Rundell's basket.

"Come, quickly," Rick said. "We've got to go to the medical center. Rundell was here, as you can see by his basket. When the Enforcers arrived, they found Sir Rubin and his family sprawled out on the ground, unconscious. Two other roaches, both injured, were with them: a large warrior, and one matching Rundell's description. All were transported to the medical center. The Enforcers say that one of the two attempted to kill Sir Rubin and lit the fire. The other heroically hauled all of them out. They suspect Rundell committed the crime and say the larger one is the hero."

Henry knew from previous training that Enforcers almost always accused those of mixed variety when given the chance, but he had never realized how easily it could happen.

"Will you handle it again when we get there? They won't listen to me, will they?"

"Probably not. I won't say anything about your contract with Rundell. Don't you either," Rick cautioned.

✝   ✳   ✳   ✞

Henry walked behind Rick when they entered the Medical Center. He tried to look humble, as though he were Rick's servant. Rick approached the receiving clerk.

"Excuse me," he said. "Could you tell me where Sir Rubin and his family were taken?"

"Are you related?" the clerk asked.

"No, but I have important information for him. If an Enforcer is here, I would like to talk to him, too."

"Who's he?" the clerk asked, pointing at Henry.

"He's with my household."

"One moment."

The clerk entered a chamber behind him and came back with an Enforcer. The large roach stared at Rick and Henry then said, "You have information regarding the crime committed against Sir Rubin?"

"Yes," Rick said. "I've met you before. I work for the City Bulletin. I know one of the two roaches brought here. I can tell you who committed the crime. Could we speak privately?"

The Enforcer nodded. "I remember you. You're the son of some famous archaeologist aren't you?"

"Yes," said Rick. "Master Roland was my father."

They were led to a small chamber. "This is Henry Roach-Dairier," Rick said when the portal closed. "He teaches Ant language and culture at The Training Center for Business and the Professions. The smaller roach found at the scene is Rundell, one of Henry's trainees. He earns his training fees selling fly eggs. Sir Rubin is one of his customers. Rundell was there on seventhday to deliver eggs. This is his basket," Rick held it out. "I found it there. I know Rundell well through Henry. There is no doubt in my mind that he is the one who saved the family."

The Enforcer said, "Since you come from a notable family, Rick, I am tempted to believe you." He looked skeptically at Henry. "Do you have some identification?"

Henry swept his front pods out to the sides and then reached into his satchel. He took out the parchment he always carried stating his name and status as guest resident. It was signed by Master Riedel. He handed it to the Enforcer.

The Enforcer read it and asked, "Why didn't you come forward before now?"

"I returned to Roacheria this afternoon from New South Dairy 50. I've been away, due to my grandfather's death. When I learned that Rundell was missing, I was concerned. He's ... special to me because of his intense interest in Ant culture. I went to his room at the training center and found this." Henry held out Rundell's customer list. "These are all highly respected citizens. At each place, I enquired if he'd been there on seventhday to deliver their eggs. He had. Any of them will vouch for Rundell. We arrived at Sir Rubin's last since he is at the bottom of the list. That was when we learned what happened."

"Sir Rubin has not regained consciousness. His mate said, 'He saved us,' before she died. But she didn't say which one. That's the reason we brought both of them here. Sir Rubin's older nymph is away in Sea Edge. The nymph who was saved is too young to say. I will take you to the one you call Rundell and watch you carefully."

They followed the Enforcer down a passageway and into a large open chamber filled with several sleep mats. Henry looked about in dismay at the stark area. He could see no medical attendants anywhere. He looked at Rick.

"This is where those without credit end up," Rick whispered. "If some wealthy patron takes pity, they get treated."

It wasn't difficult to spot Rundell and the other roach. Several Enforcers stood around them. Rundell lay with his back to them, moaning. They saw that one of his back appendages was splinted, but he had received no further treatment.

Henry walked around to face Rundell and said. "Rundell, I'm here."

Rundell raised himself and smiled in spite of obvious pain. "Trainer Henry, praise The Essence you've come. They say I tried to murder Sir Rubin. Please, tell them who I am. They don't believe me. They wouldn't even send a message to Master Riedel. They don't believe I'm in training."

Henry took Rundell's front pods. He wanted to embrace him, but didn't dare in front of the Enforcers. "We'll get all this straightened out," he said. "What happened?"

"When I reached the back portal, I heard a yell. I know Sir Rubin's home well. Remember when I told you about the tutor he had for his nymphs teaching me to read, and how he let me live in that storage bin? Anyway, I went in. Sir Rubin's mate was screaming as he fought with that one," he pointed to the large roach also being guarded by Enforcers. "He managed to block Sir Rubin's breathing. Sir Rubin collapsed. I fought with him." He pointed again.

Rundell's voice shook as he continued. "He caught my leg in his mandibles and broke it. I cried out and fell backward. Then he started the fire and left us there to die in it. But Sir Rubin's mate threw something at him and he fell, knocking part of the burning wall down. He was pinned under it."

"How did you get out?" Henry asked.

"The fallen wall stopped the flames for a while but smoke was everywhere. I managed to drag Sir Rubin out. I went back for his mate, dragging my broken leg. When I got her out, I heard the nymph scream. I thought I'd pass out from the pain, but I kept going and got her, too. I felt like leaving that one behind," he pointed again, "but I thought about all I've learned from you. I couldn't leave him."

"Likely story," said the one Enforcer standing guard by the other roach, whose thorax was cracked and plastered. "He's too small to drag any of them. The sooner he's condemned, the better. One less of his kind around." He glared at Henry with destain.

"I take financial responsibility for Rundell," Rick said. "I want his injury properly treated immediately."

The Enforcer who had brought Henry and Rick in said, "Get someone in here and do as he says. But we will still wait for Sir Rubin to regain consciousness and verify what happened."

Henry said, "I will stay here and wait." It was a risk, but if he didn't let Master Riedel know what had happened, the risk was even greater. "If I write a message to Master Riedel, would someone please take it to him. I told him I'd send word as soon as I'd found Rundell."

"I suppose," grunted the Enforcer in charge.

Henry wrote the message quickly and one of the Enforcers left with it. Henry sat down next to Rundell. The Enforcers glared at him. An h-unit later, the one who had taken the message returned.

"You aren't to leave here," he said to Henry, "until this is settled. Either you'll both be free, or some mantis will get dessert as well as lunch, pond scum. If you do walk out of here free, Master Riedel expects you to be on time for your units."

Time dragged.

Near midnight another Enforcer entered. "Sir Rubin woke up. Haul that one out of here," he said, pointing to the larger roach on the mat next to Rundell. Then he pointed at Rundell. "Take this one to better quarters. Sir Rubin is paying the charges. Had nothing but praise for him."

It was three h-units past midnight before all the statements for the Formal Inquiry were completed, detailing Rundell's heroism and the other's guilt. Rick went home, but Henry stayed with Rundell, who now lay in a proper Medical Center chamber with his leg carefully plastered.

"You've saved me twice," Rundell said when they were finally alone. "I was so afraid I would never see you again. If I were you, I'd go back to New South Dairy 50 and stay there. I wish I had someone to be close to like you do."

Henry embraced him and stroked him affectionately. "You have my friendship always. You're beginning to feel like family. I won't abandon you, even when you've completed your contract. I'd probably better leave for now, though. Master Riedel is expecting me to teach in a few h-units. I'll be back after training. I'll take care of you when you are able leave here. Trainees in my group will carry you wherever you need to go and we'll take care of your customers until you've recovered."

*   *   *   *

Physically and emotionally exhausted, Henry stood before his trainees and explained the events of the previous half time frame and the situation with Rundell. They agreed to help.

"Why have you ended your grief for your grandfather so quickly?" asked one trainee.

"I still grieve," Henry explained. "We do not isolate ourselves as prominent citizens do here. I miss my grandfather very much, but he was old and sick. His time had come. How could I be sad over a long life so well lived? I am at peace about it. Besides, we believe that although the body joins the earth again, the essence goes on. Although I can't hear or see my grandfather anymore, I can feel his presence inside me when I meditate. That's very comforting."

Each explanation led to another question in both his groups. He had them write all their questions down. It made his planning easier. That gave him time to concentrate on all he'd missed in his Roacherian Law units. His trainers were not willing to give him much time.

*   *   *   *

A time frame later, Henry stood in front of an elaborate domicile in one of the best parts of the city. It had two levels with many wall openings. The wooden shutters were painted with a variety of bright colors, setting them off from the walls built of well-shaped pieces of synthetic stone. Roaches used such building materials from old Duo Pod ruins in government buildings and other public structures, but only the very rich could afford to buy stone chunks for private domiciles.

Henry tapped on the portal. A scrawny servant opened it. "Yes?"

"I am Henry Roach-Dairier. I have an appointment with Ronda."

"She's expecting you. Come with me."

Henry followed his guide through the entry chamber. The walls were covered with interesting designs in greens and blues. The soft cushion of woven thistledown covering the floor sank slightly beneath his pods. Though he had never seen it with his own eyes, he knew the place from the description given to his grandfather by his father. He was pleased that his own writing had been so accurate from their accounts.

He entered a spacious parlor at the back of the lower level. Opened shutters let in the afternoon sun and provided a view of well-kept gardens filled with fragrant blossoms and graceful wood plants. Soft floor cushions and padded benches covered with brightly printed fabrics lined the walls. Small surfaces stood between them, some with decorative lightning bug lamps, others had sculpted forms. It was quite a contrast to Henry's small chamber at the training center which contained two sleep cushions, two writing surfaces with stools, a shelf for manuscripts and no wall opening.

Ronda rose from a bench by one of the wall openings and greeted him. "So, you are Henry, the only one of your family to ask to see me. Why you and not them?"

Henry bowed graciously to his father's cousin. Even in middle-age, her beauty was striking. No wonder his father had been attracted to her. Although of the large roach variety, her features were delicate. The soft brown of her exoskeleton was marked with a distinct line down the center of the back of her thorax, the "lucky band," the mark that Sir Ronald had known proved Rodger was the nymph of his eldest daughter. Neither Henry nor his siblings had inherited the trait. His father had explained it to him: the rare mark was passed from mothers to their sons. If a mother had it, all male nymphs would. But both parents must have it for a female to inherit the mark. A father would only pass on the possibility.

Ronda pointed to the bench near her. Henry sat down.

She looked at him with the saddest eyes he had ever seen. "You favor your father."

"I've written my ant grandfather's life story, as he gave me permission to do. My father agreed that I could state the sections about his time here. It will be distributed throughout The Combined Colonies. I know it may reach Roacheria one day and I wanted your permission as well."

Ronda sighed. "My grandfather's acknowledgment of Rodger as his grandson is already public record, though I've appreciated the fact that it's not well known."

"My father rejected everything about Roacheria," Henry continued. "So did my brothers when they came here for training. Until now, I've thought you deserved your privacy. I wasn't sure how you felt about us."

"I had my reasons for not communicating, but they don't matter anymore. When I first met your father—oh, what a handsome creature he was—I practically threw myself at him. I begged my grandfather to find out about his parents and let them know I was available, and a good catch as a legal mate. I was deeply hurt and very bitter when my grandfather informed me that Rodger already had a legal mate. When my grandfather died, and I found out the truth, that he'd known all along that your father and I were cousins, I was furious. It took me a season cycle to be able to write the one communication I did send."

Henry thought of the words on the faded parchment his father had given him:

> "Dear Rodger,
> "Our grandfather is dead. Your assets have been turned over to a group consisting of the heads of four advanced training centers. As set down in his last wishes, they will pay the fees for worthy but needy young adults. I hope you're happy. Ronda."

"I can understand how you must have felt," Henry said.

"No, you can't. I adored your father. Oh, I know, he thought he was sparing my feelings, that I wouldn't want to live in an ant colony, couldn't give up my luxuries. Knowing that only added to the hurt at thinking Rodger already had a mate, and my anger at learning he didn't, at least not then. My grandfather was right to keep the truth hidden for a time. He couldn't very well encourage a mating between cousins, and your father had made it clear that he didn't want to find his Roacherian relatives. There really was no other way."

She got up and paced about the chamber. "The truth is, I'd have followed your father anywhere. I hated your mother for many season cycles because she got him, not me. Your mother was so lucky. She got a faithful and caring mate, much better than the sorry excuse I ended up with. I'll admit, my mate put up a good front. My grandfather knew he was well off financially and would honor the legal end of our mating contract. When I produced no eggs, and he found out my grandfather had made sure all assets remained in my name, he left me. A season cycle after my grandfather's death, I was presented with legal documents ending the mating. I moved back to this domicile."

She returned to the bench and stared out into the garden.

"I'm sorry. My father and my grandfather explained a lot to me, but I had no way of knowing this," Henry said.

"Don't worry. I'm over it now. You have my permission to publish as long as it doesn't include the conversation we just had."

"Thank you. I wrote only from my father's and grandparents' points of view. I won't reveal what you felt," Henry said, rising to leave.

"You're welcome. Come again if you'd like."

Henry let himself out. When he returned to his sparse chamber, he thought about his cousin. She lived lonely and miserable amid splendor. He could use a little more, but the bond he felt with his family and friends was far more valuable than her glittering domicile. He decided to visit her as often as he could.

*   *   *   *

At the end of that term, Henry headed for Master Riedel's work chamber. "I have an appointment with Master Riedel," Henry told the clerk.

"He's expecting you. Go on in."

Henry entered Master Riedel's work chamber. New images covered the walls. The woven reed mats on the floor had been replaced with softer ones of thistledown.

"Good afternoon," Henry said, bowing respectfully. "You sent for me."

"Yes, have a seat." Master Riedel pointed to a softly padded bench, also new, and held out a basket of crisp fried bees' wings. "Please, share some refreshments with me."

"Thank you."

"I'm pleased with the way our experiment has gone. I'd like to expand your teaching duties. Do you think you could handle three groups when the fall term begins?"

"Could we spread them through the day, so I can finish my law units? One of the units I need for certification is only taught in the morning."

"I think that's possible, if you will make an obligation to a full season cycle of teaching. Since I have given you more responsibilities, I will increase the amount you receive as allowance. You can continue to live in trainee housing until you complete your studies."

"Rundell will complete his contract with me soon. He's recovered from his injury, but I'd like for him to be able to continue sharing my quarters without charge, if he chooses. Any chance of a larger chamber? You're still getting quite a bargain." Henry felt comfortable pushing for more. There was a waiting list of trainees who wanted to take his unit, and Rundell's heroism had brought the kind of attention to the Center that Master Riedel liked.

Master Riedel rubbed his mandibles with one pod. "At the end of the passage on the lower level, there is a storage area next to one chamber. I'll have workers break down the wall and enlarge that space into a suite. It would be easy to install a private sanitation area. I'll have better furnishings brought in and a cooking box and small cold storage unit. Then you can have outside food, in case you get tired of the offerings in the trainee dining facility. The lower level might make it seem more like it's underground."

Henry smiled to himself at the reference to being underground. Since Master Riedel was trying to be accommodating, he didn't say that he preferred the surface, and would have liked a wall opening. "That will be satisfactory," he said.

"Why don't you draw up the contract yourself and I'll sign it tomorrow."

9.

*H*enry looked at the title of the manuscript for his next law unit: The Rights and Privileges of Classes of Roacherian Citizenship. His encounter with the Enforcers and the Formal Inquiry that cleared Rundell had shown him that his status as a non-citizen of mixed variety left him quite vulnerable to the whims of those in power. He knew he had a lot to learn. He felt very small and alone. Everyone else in the group was of the large roach variety.

The trainer spoke. "Most of you are partly aware of the regulations we will cover in this unit. One must be of pure, large variety for complete privileges. These include, but are not limited to, appointment to the South East Roach Control Board; full possibilities of working at any profession; ownership and control of surface area; and complete choice of domicile location. Knowing this, one wonders why Henry Roach-Dairier is so persistent in his course of study. Perhaps he'd enlighten us as to why he chose this career when he can't legally accept payment for his services?"

He looked down on Henry, waiting for an answer.

"Perhaps my purpose isn't to earn credit," Henry replied.

The trainer laughed loud and long. "And what do you plan to live on? Or are you going home where you belong after all?"

Henry took a deep breath. "I intend to keep teaching."

"Ever notice that most of the staff have other businesses and professions? We wouldn't make enough to support a mate and nymphs if we didn't. If you don't like celibacy, you'd better get used to the shanties," he laughed, "or maybe you and that little trainee you own with your contract ..."

When the rest of the group had finished laughing and Henry's mandibles ached from clenching them for control, the trainer continued his lecture. Henry heard none of it.

When his day ended, Henry stormed into his "suite of chambers" and threw the Rights and Privileges manuscript at the wall. "Every time I think I might make it here!" he shouted.

Rundell looked up, stunned. "What happened to you?"

"After all I've been through, I find out I can't take credit for any legal advice I give!"

"I thought you said you were always going to teach. You're too honest to be a legal counselor anyway. It's not in you."

Henry stomped about their tiny parlor and slammed his pods down on his writing surface, breaking it. Then he slumped to the floor and cried in frustration.

He felt Rundell's pods surround him awkwardly. "Please, Henry, calm down. This isn't like you. Shall I fix you some tea?"

Henry nodded.

Rundell tried to comfort Henry and he had often been comforted.

When his anger had passed, Henry said, "I'm sorry I lost control."

"It's all right," Rundell said, smiling at him. "In a way, I'm glad you did. Now I can see you're a normal creature."

"I do intend to keep teaching, but I'd hoped to earn some on the side counseling the underprivileged for whatever they could afford to give. Then I could support a mate and nymphs, if I ever meet a female I cherish who'll have me. Naturally, my trainer made a point of the fact that most staff here have other professions. But it was what he implied about you and me that made me the angriest. He as much as said we ..."

"No, don't," Rundell cut in. "I've heard many mumble it behind our thoraxes. I don't care what they think. Those who know us know the truth. The rest of them don't matter anyway. Besides, you can always go home if things don't work out here."

"I don't want to go home. I mean, I do want to, I cherish my family. But my work is here. I want to try to change the attitudes of those who are so full of hatred. My teaching is beginning to make a difference."

They sat silently for a while and Henry finished the mug of tea.

"Henry, I know what we can do. When you finish your training next spring, we'll move out of this hole. We'll find some shack in the shanties with natural wall openings. You keep teaching and I'll keep gathering fly eggs. You counsel for free. Tell your clients to buy lots of eggs at the market stall I'll have as a way to thank you. We'll share everything, a colony of two, both get mates and show the lot of them."

Henry sighed heavily and then the two of them chuckled at Rundell's idea.

The term progressed. Henry searched for some kink in the web of regulations used to keep the lowly where they were and reserve places of power for the descendents of a few. He thought of what his father had said when he gave him the letters Sir Ronald and Ronda had written. Perhaps there was a way to use them to gain the privilege of counseling for credit.

"I've got it! I think," he said to Rundell one evening. "Listen to this: 'Proving purity of line in the large roach variety: since some natural variation occurs, other means besides size may be argued. In a family where power and privilege have already been established, all nymphs hatched to descendents in legal matings may be assumed to be pure.'"

"So all you have to do is show them those letters you have, right?" Rundell asked.

"It's not quite that simple. I have to prove that everybody was legally mated."

"But if Sir Ronald was a Board Member, and he acknowledged your father."

"Think, Rundell. Geree mated one of Rex's renegades, against her father's wishes. He banished her in order not to be associated with Rex in any way. My parents did not mate in Roacheria. There was no written contract like one would have here," Henry explained.

Rundell sighed. "Give it up. It's not worth it. Things will never change here."

"I don't want to give it up! Don't you see? This isn't only about my being able to practice counseling. It's about all those of slender variety, and everyone like you and me who's a mix. If I can punch one small hole in this synthetic stone wall of restrictions, many can crawl through it. Maybe I can find some vague phrase in the definitions on legal mating that I can use, such as this one for establishing purity."

Henry kept thinking about Geree and George. He remembered something Renae' had said so long ago about them. George had stated that he would prove to Geree's father that he could be a good mate. Had he intended to assume legal responsibility? Henry poured every extra moment he had into research. By the time the term ended, Henry had prepared his argument.

*   *   *   *

The nine members of the Legal Counseling Services Committee stared at Henry. Their abdomens rested comfortably on padded benches on their side of a long, flat wooden surface covered with legal manuscripts. Derision filled their eyes, mixed with a look that said they would enjoy what they probably foresaw as Henry's humiliation.

Henry stood behind a small surface with his evidence—copies from selected manuscripts, publicly recorded documents, and the letters his father had given him. It had taken firm arguments to reach this committee. He had spent the previous evening deep in meditation, asking for strength and restraint with his words. A calm presence moved through him—meditation answered.

"Henry Roach-Dairier, you have requested the opportunity to try to prove your purity of variety. Your outline states you wish this so that you may practice legal counseling as a guest resident. You are not seeking citizenship in Roacheria at this time?"

Henry stooped low and spread both front pods out to the sides. "Thank you, Esteemed Committee Members, for agreeing to hear my case. At this time I do not seek full citizenship, only the privilege to use my training as I see fit."

The Head Committee Member spoke again. "Looking at you, knowing who your parents are, this ought to be quite entertaining." A snicker spread through the group.

Henry stooped again and began. "The first piece of evidence I wish to present is this quote from page 336 of the Procedures for Establishing Purity Manual." Henry read the quote regarding the use of physical size that he had read to Rundell. "This proves that my stature is not an issue. Let me trace my biological line for you. I am the son of Rodger Dairier. Rodger was, as you know, adopted by Master Antony and Master Henrietta of New South Dairy Colony 50. His biological parents were a female named Geree', and a male named George. Geree' was Sir Ronald's eldest daughter. Sir Ronald owned the Number 2 plastic mine and served on The South East Roach Control Board for many season cycles until his death in 246 O.R. This letter from Sir Ronald to my father, and this one from his granddaughter, Ronda, and this certified copy of the document Sir Ronald filed with the Agency for Document Registration, establish my membership in this clan with previously proven power, wealth, and authority."

He handed the parchments to the Head Committee Member and waited as he, and the other members read them. The easy part was over. The rest of his arguments dealt with legal opinions and attitudes rather than indisputable facts.

He searched their faces for some sign of favor. At the far end of the line, Henry's eyes met those of the youngest Committee Member, Master Robin. Henry gazed at him steadily. Master Robin's look softened and Henry caught an upward movement of his middle pod, a small gesture that meant, "I'm with you."

After each committee member had read the letters and the document, the Head Member looked at him and said, "Continue."

"I now wish to show precedents by which the matings of Geree' and George, and of my parents may be considered legal in Organized Roacheria. May I recall for you some basic Roachstory facts? In the 98th season cycle of Organized Roacheria, a huge area of surface, from the convergence of the two great rivers eastward to the sea, then known as East Roacheria, petitioned the South Roach Control Board to unite with them in a stronger, more centralized government. This resulted in our present South East Roach Control Board."

"We don't need a lesson in Roachstory, Trainer Henry," the Head Member interrupted. "Make your legal point."

"Among the many legal procedures worked out at that time were several provisions that established acceptance of customs in East Roacheria which were not practiced by South Roacheria. Though little used, they are still in effect. May I quote from Regulation 5 concerning legal matings?"

"If it doesn't waste all our time, yes."

Henry picked up a parchment and read:

> "A male who wishes to take responsibility for nymphs he fathers need not have the permission of the female's father in all cases. It is recognized that a female's father may not be available. Such a male may register the contract himself with the Agency for Document Registration. Such a union shall be considered legal."

Henry picked up another document. "I now give you a certified copy of the document George registered concerning his mating to Geree." It had taken him two time frames of searching in the basement of the Agency For Document Registration to find it. The looks on their faces made it worth it.

"This last parchment," Henry held up a small one, sent to him from South Dairy 50, "is a copy of the page in South Dairy Colony 50's Record of the Mated, showing the inscription by my parents. I might add that a mating among us is a life-long moral commitment of loyalty and fidelity between a male and female. Unlike a Roacherian mating contract, only the death of one of the pair can break the bond."

Henry walked up to the Head Member and handed it to him.

"I have one final point, Esteemed Members." Henry took a deep breath, since this was the shakiest point. "I call your attention again to the letter from Sir Ronald to my father. The letter was in a gift he presented to my father at the Completion Ceremony when my father finished his medical studies. Sir Ronald said to him, 'Please accept this parting gift for your mating and for the completion of your studies.' The gift was 50,000 credit units. Now I ask each of you personally, would you give your son or grandson a mating gift of that size if you didn't approve and consider the mating legal?"

The Committee Member next to the Head Member rose and shouted at Henry. "You come to us with these ancient, rarely-used points of law and expect us to honor your request in this far-fetched scheme?"

"The points of law are valid," Henry responded calmly.

"You twist the law to your own purpose!" shouted another.

Master Robin rose. "What's the matter? Does it bother you, Committee Members, that this young male can research the law, present his point well and use it to his advantage better than you can? Isn't that what we all do? Find the points we can use to advance our case and bring dishonor to another? You're jealous of his abilities! He's out argued you and you can't stand it. For my part, I'm honored that someone of his integrity wishes to become part of our esteemed profession."

The Head Committee Member cut off the discussion. "Enough! We will discuss this in private. Henry Roach-Dairier, you will return tomorrow morning at this same time and we will announce our decision."

Henry bowed and left the chamber.

The following morning, he stood before them again. Master Robin was the only one smiling. The wooden surface lay bare, except for a small stack of parchments in front of the Head Committee Member. Henry remained silent.

The Head Member pulled one front pod across his outer mandibles making a disgusting, clicking sound used to show contempt for a member of a lower class, picked up the parchments before him, then said, "Henry Roach-Dairier, we find that all your points of law are valid. We had considerable discussion concerning the opinion that your parents' mating should be considered legal in Roacheria. A simple majority vote ruled in your favor. We hereby grant you the privilege of practicing as a legal counselor, pending successful completion of your studies, of course. We return these documents to you."

Henry bowed respectfully, smiled toward Master Robin, picked up his documents and walked out. That evening he celebrated with Rundell, Gatlin, Rusty, Rick and his family.

*   *   *   *

The clerk entered with proper humility. "Excuse me, Trainer Henry, I was asked to bring you these messages immediately."

"Thank you," Henry said, taking them from her. He glanced at the opened one from Master Riedel. "Tell Master Riedel I'll be there."

The clerk bowed and left.

When the session ended, he broke the seal on the other message and read, "They wish to see you fail your final examination." There was no signature, but Henry could guess Master Robin had sent it. He pondered what he could do to protect himself as he finished his other training and study units.

At the appointed time, he entered Master Riedel's chamber. New woven coverings adorned the wall opening and an expensive looking sculpted piece sat on the writing surface.

"You wished to see me," Henry said politely.

"Yes, you've brought me good fortune," Master Riedel said, sweeping his pod around the chamber. "It seems someone at the Trade Center thinks it's a good idea to have all the overseers there who deal with The Colonies take at least one of your training units. Would you consider continuing here as part of my full time staff? Would you teach the unit for the Trade Center workers in the evenings? I would, of course, increase your salary," he paused, "far beyond the standard amount for my staff ..." his voice trailed off.

Henry thought about the warning note and looked around the chamber again. "I will continue to teach for you in the mornings and I will conduct the evening sessions. But I must have my afternoons free for other pursuits. I have enemies enough without other staff members resenting the fact that I would earn more than they do. I will not accept more than the standard staff amount. I will also find my own lodgings when this term has ended since I will no longer be a trainee. I do ask another favor though, one which will not compromise either of our ethics."

Master Riedel's antennae twitched. "And that is?"

"What can you do to protect me from this?" Henry asked, handing him the anonymous note.

Master Riedel looked at it and dropped it, his pod shaking. In that instant, Henry knew who was behind the new furnishings and the salary offer.

"I'm not sure there is anything I can do about this," Master Riedel's voice shook. "Your law trainers are the ones to say if you pass or not. It's very subjective."

"But I can request that you, as head of this facility, oversee the process. If I feel I've been wrongly failed, I can request a Formal Inquiry."

Master Riedel touched the sculpture with his pod. "You wouldn't do that, would you? It would be awfully difficult to prove conspiracy."

"I proved my purity, didn't I? If I pass the exam, I'll continue teaching for you as I stated earlier. If I fail, I'll go to another training facility. Do the right thing, Master Riedel, whatever that is for you."

*   *   *   *

The chamber filled slowly with counseling trainees, all twitching in anxiety. Henry took his usual place and removed a stack of clean parchment and an ink pot from his satchel. His anxiety level was high too, but not from fear that he wouldn't do well on the exam.

The "Rights and Privileges" trainer approached him. "We've received an anonymous note that some trainees may be trying to cheat. In order that you might not be accused, I request that you come with me and take this examination in my presence alone."

Henry picked up his supplies and followed, wondering if this ploy was really to protect him, or to make it more difficult for him to file a conspiracy charge. They entered a small, empty training chamber. Henry sat down at a writing surface and reached out to take the exam parchments.

The trainer stood behind him as he began to write. More than anything, Henry wanted to ask him to move away, but he knew he shouldn't. He closed his eyes briefly and lifted up silent thoughts in meditation. Then he blocked out everything around him and focused on the exam questions.

Three h-units later he finished, handed the stack of parchments to the trainer and said, "I am very confident that my answers are correct. You can testify to the fact that only you and I were here, and that I had no access to any help. I request that Master Riedel oversee the grading, as is my privilege."

He walked out quickly and headed for the dining area before it closed for the day. Rundell was waiting for him.

"How did it go?"

"I know I did an excellent job. You know how hard I've studied. Whether I passed or not depends on how much they offered Master

Riedel, and whether or not he has learned anything during my time here. Either way, we'd better start packing our things."

"You'd think he'd be grateful for all the good publicity you've brought this center," Rundell said.

Henry shook his head. "He's only doing what so many others of his rank do, grab each better opportunity as it comes along. We both helped him advance, but if he thinks he can do better, he has no use for us... unless I've managed to show him there is a better way."

"Well, I have some good news. I found a small market stall for rent. It's a bit run-down, but stable and affordable. There are two chambers. The one at the front is large enough for my egg shop, and a record keeping area. The smaller, more private one in the back will be for you, Counselor."

Henry smiled at him. "Thanks for your confidence. With that, and Rick's offer of a place to live as long as we need it, we'll get by, no matter which way this turns out."

A quiet tapping interrupted their packing later that evening. Henry set down a stack of law manuscripts and opened their portal. Master Riedel stood before him with a strained attempt at a smile. "Welcome to my permanent, full time staff, Counselor Henry. You will be free for other pursuits from noon to the fifth h-unit as you requested."

10.

"**R**onda is in her studio," the servant said. "Come with me, please."

Henry followed the thin female up the ramp to the second level. He had managed to visit his cousin about once a time frame since their first meeting, but they had always talked in the parlor.

"In here," the servant said, opening a portal at the end of the passage.

"Welcome to my studio," Ronda said.

"I didn't know you painted images."

"Maybe that's because I never mentioned it," she said with a smile. "I have to fill my days somehow, don't I? Actually, I've been painting since my nymphood. I did the walls in the entry way a time frame before my final molt."

Henry looked at the studio walls, all done in murals of meadows. "You're very good. What do you do with the things you paint, besides decorate this place?"

"Well, I certainly don't need to sell them for a living, thanks to my grandfather. I give them away," she replied. "I did a portrait of my grandfather to hang in the S.E.R.C.B. Meeting Chamber in his memory. This one is for you, Counselor, congratulations."

"Thank you," Henry said as he unrolled the fabric she handed him. About three by five f-units, the image showed Henry seated in the midst of several trainees. It looked exactly like his chamber in the training center. Henry looked at her in surprise. "How did you ..."

"I stopped by to see you several times. You were always so engrossed in your group I never had the courage to interrupt. I'm glad you plan to continue there. You're much too honest to make a living counseling."

Henry smiled. "Why does everyone keep saying that?"

"Because it's true. If you don't mind my asking, what made you choose counseling anyway?"

"If you want to get along in a place, it's best to know the rules. If you don't like the rules, you'd better know them thoroughly enough to propose changes. I plan to use my skills to help those who need it most, for what ever they can afford to give."

"You are your father's son, through and through. I admire you. I truly do, but be careful. There are a lot of powerful Board Members and others who like things just as they are," she said.

"I know. I've already met some of them."

"Do you plan to visit your family any time soon?"

"Yes, next quarter time frame."

"Good. Will you take this to your father?" she said, handing him another carefully rolled and bound painting. "I didn't really want to risk sending it with the traders. Tell him I finally buried my feelings."

"I'd be happy to."

They walked down to the parlor where Ronda's live-in help served them crisp fried bees wings and ale, and talked about Rundell's market stall. When Henry finally rose to leave she said, "Henry, if you ever need anything, please, don't be too proud to ask."

*   *   *   *

Henry found his father in his study, poring over medical research reports. He'd already spent two h-units with his mother.

No longer afraid to interrupt, he embraced his father fondly. "Whatever it is, Dad, let it go for a while."

Rodger returned his affection. "I've been thinking about you a lot lately. Have you been getting my letters?"

"Every one of them. I'm sorry I haven't replied more often. I have something for you from Ronda," Henry said. He had never told his father about his first conversation with Ronda, but he could see a hint of old pain in his father's eyes. "I've been to see her several times. She wanted me to tell you that she finally feels free of the past."

He handed his father the bound image and continued. "She is a talented artist, and she did this for you."

Rodger cut the binding strands and unrolled it. Tears came to his eyes as he looked at it. The image showed Rodger as Ronda had first known him, a young medical trainee tenderly performing therapy on her grandfather's painful leg joints, as he had been hired to do. The note with it read:

"Anyone who could tend a stranger (for that was how you knew him then) with the compassion you had, must be this world's best physician. With much affection, your cousin, Ronda."

"I have something for you, too," Rodger said after he recovered from the flood of emotion brought on by Ronda's gift. "Your rendition of your grandfather's life has been distributed throughout The Colonies. This came from The Intercolonial Council, and this is from Uncle Andrew." He handed Henry a letter and a parcel.

Henry opened the letter:

"From The Intercolonial Council, on behalf of all ants:
"Dearest Henry,
"It must have been most difficult for Master Antony to open himself to you in such depth, and equally difficult for you to prepare it to share with all of us. Thank you, for this precious memorial gift in his honor. May The Essence always be with you as it must have been when you wrote those words. We have decided it should be required reading for all basic trainees. Catrina Carpenter, Intercolonial Council Chief, fifthday, Sixth Time Frame, 243rd season cycle, C.C.I."

The parcel from Uncle Andrew, youngest brother of Henry's grandmother, contained the personal journals of Andrew's parents, Henry and Adeline Harvester, and a letter about how much Andrew appreciated Henry's writing. Henry spent most of the night reading treasured words his great-grandparents had meant only for each other.

*   *   *   *

Henry's late morning training group sat before him. The other groups had gone well. The first session, those who had been with him from the start, now concentrated more on language than on culture. They spoke only Ant during the session. The second group spoke half in Ant, half in Roach and still got a healthy dose of culture. This group would receive his usual opening: his regulations, his introduction and background, and their introduction of themselves. He would repeat the procedure this evening with the Trade Center group.

He was pleased to see three females sitting at the very back: one of the large variety, one slender, and one a mix. Their presence seemed to make some of the males nervous. Since Henry had won his case concerning his variety, several legal counselors had made good credit helping others prove the same thing. More roaches got better paying jobs and could send their young for training as a result. Master Robin had argued the case before The Board that females should not be denied entry to Advanced Training Centers.

When he asked for a volunteer to begin the introductions, the large female rose and said, "I am Racine. My father is Master Robin. He sends you his greetings, Trainer Henry. My father knows the time has come for females to be better educated. He says there are some things tutors cannot teach. That's why I'm here."

"Oooo," said a large male, "and eligible, too, I'll bet."

A snicker rippled through the group. Henry cut it off by raising one pod for silence. He looked directly at the instigator. "I've already made my regulations clear. I will not tolerate your rudeness to our female members. You will not oogle over how important you perceive Racine to be. Nor will you make any reference to whom, in your opinion, the others are not."

The male humbled himself immediately. "I," he stammered, "I'm sorry. Habit, you know." He fidgeted.

"Apology accepted. Start a new habit. Think before you speak. Introduce yourself properly, please."

"My name is Regi. I'm from Nauroach, where my father is on the local Control Board and owns a small plastic mine. He wants me to take over trade there, so he sent me to this facility and said I had to take this unit."

"Your father is wise. I'm sure you will take an improved attitude back to your community along the northern border," Henry replied. He was surprised that his reputation had spread that far.

When the session ended, the thin female, who had introduced herself as Ruth but said nothing else, asked if she could speak to him privately.

"What is it, Ruth?" he asked after the others filed out. "Do you mind if I leave the portal opened? It's an important habit."

She looked around, then said in a soft voice, "My family lives in a very old domicile. Recently, my brothers had a fight and knocked down part of a wall. We found this between the partitions. My father said I should take this unit and try to find out to whom it should be given. From what you said, you are one of them." She handed him a package, wrapped in old, yellowed parchment.

Henry could barely make out the words: "To the descendants of Henry, Herbert and Howard, three tunnel engineers from South Harvester 45, only after Sir Rex Roach is dead, or no longer in control of the South East Roach Control Board, that they may know the truth."

Henry was about to ask a question, but Ruth turned and left hurriedly, running straight into Rundell.

She caught her breath, as though ready to cry out.

"I'm so sorry," Rundell said. "I wasn't looking."

Henry said in a reassuring tone, "Ruth, this is Rundell, a former trainee and now my business partner. Are you all right?"

She nodded. "I'm late, that's all. I've got to go."

"I'll see you tomorrow," Henry said as she disappeared down the passage. He turned to Rundell. "What's your hurry?"

"A female came into the shop about an h-unit ago, crying and saying she needed your help. I tried to explain that you wouldn't arrive for quite a while. She said she'd wait, but then she kept getting more and more upset. So I came to get you."

Henry put a stack of parchments and the bundle from Ruth in his satchel and left with Rundell.

"I offered her some tea," Rundell said as they scurried down the lane away from the training facility. "Maybe she'll be calm by the time we get there."

They heard voices as they neared the market stall Rundell had rented.

"I told you, the proprietor will be back in a little while! The sign there tells his prices. Don't you read?"

Rundell hurried in. "What can I do for you?"

The large male turned to him. "This female you have here is an idiot! She won't give me any eggs."

Rundell bowed respectfully. "Please, pardon her. She was only waiting to see Henry. What can I get for you?"

Henry moved around them and guided the female into his work chamber, closing the portal behind him. "I am Henry Roach-Dairier. What can I do for you?"

"You're Henry? I thought you'd be larger. What was in that hot drink he gave me?"

"It was an herbal tea. It helps calm a creature down. Rundell said you were quite distraught. May I have your name, please?"

She looked embarrassed. "My name is Georgette. I'm sorry for the way I acted. I should remember my place, but ... my mate ... he just left ... I have two nymphs. He can't do that, can he? Doesn't he have to send me credit? I don't have anything! What am I going to do? I've heard you're a different kind of counselor ... That you really want to help." She looked about anxiously. "I'm making a fool of myself. I shouldn't have come."

"Slow down. I may be able to help you, but I have to ask you some questions," Henry said.

"Will it cost much?"

"Don't worry about that right now. Did you have a mating contract?" Henry asked.

"Yes," she handed him a wrinkled parchment.

Henry smoothed it out and looked it over. He sighed. "I don't mean to offend you, but do you read?"

She looked at the floor and shook her antennae.

"This is a legal mating contract, but the way it is stated, very little is actually promised in monetary support, not nearly enough for two nymphs, let alone any others you might have later."

Georgette broke down again, sobbing. Henry walked around his work surface and softly patted her back. "Stay here. I'll be right back."

Rundell's customer had left and the outer chamber was quiet. Henry explained the female's situation briefly then said, "Is the tea pot still hot?"

"Yes."

Henry refilled the mug, then looked thoughtfully at Rundell. "We could use a little help around here, couldn't we? Someone to keep things in order when we both have to go out?"

"Henry, what are you thinking?"

"I'll bet she could memorize your prices until she learns to read."

"What are you thinking?"

"Give me your trust, as you did once before," Henry said, returning to the female.

He handed her the mug. "You must listen carefully to what I am going to say."

She took the mug and sipped.

"Did your mate work steadily?"

She nodded.

"Where?"

"On the trade routes, pulling roller-carts."

"Let me keep this copy of your mating contract for a few days. I'll go to his employer and have them deduct the amount stipulated in it from his pay and send it here, since I'm your legal counselor. Do you have good counting skills?"

She nodded.

"Rundell needs someone to help mind the shop when neither of us can be here. He'll help you memorize all his signs. Do you think you can be courteous to those who come in?"

She looked at him incredulously. "You're offering me a job?"

"Yes. Two h-units of each day's pay for half a time frame will cover my fee. Agreed?"

"I can't believe... What will I do with my nymphs?"

"Where are they now?"

"Alone," she hesitated, "but they're in a safety cage ... I wouldn't leave them."

"Georgette, I know you want to take good care of them. Can you carry the cage easily?"

"Yes, I just never really thought this ... you'd be so ... Oh, I don't know what to say."

Henry said calmly, "Be here by eight h-units tomorrow morning. Bring the nymphs with you in the safety cage. There's room for it behind the counter. Be polite to those who come in. Let Rundell teach you what is needed. Now go home to your nymphs."

After she left the shop, Rundell asked, "Now what have you gotten me into?"

*   *   *   *

Late that evening, in the privacy of his sleep chamber, Henry finally opened the bundle Ruth had given him. He found a ragged journal with the name "Gabriel Roach" written inside the front cover. Within a few pages, he realized that Gabriel was the roach mentioned in his great-grandfather, Henry Harvester's, journal, and this was Gabriel's account of the same period of time, when Henry Harvester had been enslaved by Rex Roach.

He spent the next three nights reading, growing more upset at the profusion of lies told to the ants, the awkward position of Gabriel in the middle of it, and the coincidence of receiving the two different viewpoints within such a short time.

Henry spent the next seventhday afternoon discussing it with Rick. "No wonder there's so much distrust. I wonder if it would have turned out as peacefully if South Harvester 45 had known the whole truth at the time."

"Who's to say," Rick replied. "What are you going to do with the journals?"

"Uncle Andrew's letter said that he wished I would write about it, like I did my grandfather's life. Gabriel's journal certainly puts a different slant on it. I still don't feel like I know the whole story."

"I don't think anyone will ever know it all. Maybe the past should stay buried," Rick said.

"No, the roots of today's problems lie in the past. I think I'll do a little research when I have time."

"When do you ever have nothing else to do?" Rick laughed.

For a time frame, Henry found no opportunity at all. Then his training groups settled into a routine and things in Rundell's shop smoothed out with Georgette's help. Rundell spent time teaching her to read. Before long, she was writing out simple messages for Henry from those seeking his advice.

The journals nagged at him. Henry decided he would spend every sixth day counseling those who came to him and let himself have firstday and secondday afternoons for research. He wrote to South Harvester 45 and asked for all public records from that time period. Then he went to The Archives of the Condemned in the governmental section of the city.

*   *   *   *

"How does a creature gain access to the personal records brought here?" Henry asked the thin, frail-looking receiving clerk at the Archives.

"You have to be a Board Member, a legal counselor, or be related to a victim. I'd have to know whose records you wanted and see your credentials."

Henry took out his counseling license.

"Whose records?" the clerk asked.

"The former Sir Rex Roach."

The clerk left for a few moments to check the listings. "That's a long time ago. That container was sealed by the Supreme Executor at that time. Only descendents of victims may have access."

"Master Antony, of New South Dairy 50 was my grandfather. Is that enough?"

"Sorry, I should have known by your name," the clerk said quickly. "Come with me. You can't remove the container from the premises, but you can read all you want and make notes. I'll show you a cubicle you can use whenever you come."

Henry followed him through the maze of passageways and chambers in the lowest level of the building. A musty odor permeated everything. Only a few dim lightning bug lamps lit the passages.

The clerk took a large wooden container from a sagging shelf at the very back of the last chamber. He strained under its weight.

"Let me help," Henry offered.

"Thanks," the clerk said, setting the container on Henry's back. "Follow me."

They left the storage area and the clerk led Henry to a tiny chamber containing a small writing surface, a stool and one lamp. He lifted the container from Henry's back with a groan.

"This will take more than one day. Could the container remain in here when I leave today?"

"I guess so. No sense hauling that thing back and forth too much. As long as I've worked here, nobody else has ever asked to open it," the clerk said, leaving Henry alone.

Henry read through the transcripts of the Formal Inquiry quickly. Nothing new there. Training manuscripts in both Roacheria and The Colonies stated the same facts. He dug deeper into the container and found letters from Rex's Uncle Royal, most of them warning Rex to be careful in whatever he planned and cover himself well.

On his next visit, he read letters from Rex's sisters, Regina and Rolinda, during the season cycles they lived in Sea Edge with Royal. The letters gave him an interesting view of the lives of females in families of power. Several account books lay under the letters, financial records of Rex's business income from two plastic mines and other sources. Then he found it at the very bottom, Rex's personal journal.

A note lay with the journal:

> "Had this evidence been found earlier, the Formal Inquiry might have taken a different stance in sentencing. Rex was turned over to South Harvester Colony 45 on the basis of proven guilt in that incident. Families of other victims never had the proof that lies here."

It was signed by the Chief Enforcer at the time Rex was condemned.

It took Henry many days to read the journal, which sickened him. In graphic detail, Rex Roach had recorded everything about every crime he had ever plotted and carried out, bragging about each. Henry thought of the things his grandfather had told him about Rex's last night of life. Rex had confessed many crimes in the h-units before he died and asked that Antony not make his covering place known. Either Rex had not told it all, or Antony had decided not to tell Henry the details, in favor of stressing the fact that Rex had finally asked for pardon.

The journal revealed a creature totally self-absorbed, without any care for anyone else, and devoid of remorse. He even described how he chose the hiding place for the journal, so it would not be found by enemies and used against him. For many season cycles, it had lain inside the cover of an old Roachstory manuscript, right in the center of the shelf in the parlor of his domicile.

Rex had been investigated several times. Enforcers had searched his sleep chamber, locked credit compartment, work chamber records, even torn out some walls. They never thought to look at the first shelf that met their eyes upon entering Rex's domicile.

Henry made extensive notes from the pages of the journal that related to the season cycle Rex had enslaved his great-grandfather. He knew he had to make the incident public, now that he had the complete picture.

11.

*W*inter arrived. One sixthday morning when he had no appointments, Henry looked carefully at the location chart of the city of Roacheria and the surrounding surface. He looked at the relative locations of the Number 1 and Number 6 plastic mines and re-read the description of the escape of his great-grandfather and the others as related in Gabriel's journal. Research nearly complete, he wanted to walk their probable route and get a feel for what it might have been like.

Gatlin burst into his work area. "Henry, thank you so much. Gabby's father accepted the mating contract you helped me write! He'll bind us in one time frame. I've even found a place for us to live."

"Congratulations! You must have found work then." It had been about a time frame since Gatlin had finished training and had asked Henry to write his mating contract. Henry hadn't seen him since. Every time Gatlin had come by, he had happened to be out.

"Rick helped me get into the communications room at the City Bulletin. I read through and translate everything that comes from The Colonies. Somebody higher up decides which ones are printed. If I do well, I'll get an increase in pay in half a season cycle. I couldn't have gotten this without all that you taught me and Rick's influence. Rick told them that my variety shouldn't make a difference. He implied that you might legally challenge their priorities in granting jobs."

Henry felt a surge of joy. His work and research had paid off again in better opportunities for others.

"What's the location chart for?" Gatlin asked.

"I'm about to take a long hike. Would you like to join me?"

"Sure. Where are we going?"

Henry pointed out the route. "It'll take most of the day," he said.

Gatlin had read Henry's first work in Ant and some of the recent draft Henry had completed.

"Were you able to find out who owns the mines now?" Gatlin asked when they reached the northern rim of the Number 6 mine.

Henry chuckled. "They are getting so used to me at the Archives and the Agency for Document Registration that the clerks just ask, 'What do you want this time, Counselor Henry?' A Board Committee was established and still manages the mines confiscated from Rex. For the first ten season cycles, all the plastic went to The Colonies for restitution under the agreement worked out by my grandfather. After that, they started paying restitution to the families of every victim they could find."

"That Rex. No wonder they banned formal mention of his name. Sure is a pleasant day for the first time frame."

Henry nodded. The pair headed west across the meadows. The grass lay brown and dormant even though they were having a mild winter. They crossed the area north from the Number 1 mine. A few d-units later they skirted a large pond.

"These meadows remind me of home," Henry said. "We're about a d-unit north and east of the trail to South Dairy 50. This would be such a good place have a dairy. Hoppers would thrive here." He pointed out a grove of wood plants at one end of the pond. "That's the kind of wood plants aphids like best. Why doesn't it ever occur to roaches to raise food and hoppers?"

"Why bother when we can get it from The Colonies?" Gatlin retorted.

The two lapsed into silence. Henry knew this must be the pond Gabriel had described. He took in everything around him, imagining it was night, wondering what it had felt like. None of the beauty of the area would have been noticed by three frightened, half-starved ants running for their lives. Their route took them so close to New South 50. But back then, one pair of ants and their one young larva in a tiny, difficult to find mound were all that was there. They'd never have found it in the dark and would have died of exposure lost in the expanse of meadows.

Gatlin's sarcastic question bothered Henry. It made no sense for Roacheria to be so dependent on The Colonies for food when much of their surface was suitable for dairying. Dairying's purpose was to feed, not to produce credit. His mind raced. Did those who controlled the surface area think it wouldn't be profitable enough?

"I'm sorry," he said to Gatlin on their return trip, late in the afternoon. "I haven't been very good company today. I got lost in my thoughts."

Gatlin laughed. "That's nothing new. The only problem with your thinking is that it usually means you're going to drag your friends into some crazy new idea. Next thing you know, you'll be telling Master Riedel he should let you teach dairying."

"Not yet," Henry said.

*   *   *   *

Time frames slipped by. Rundell looked into Henry's office before closing the shop one summer day. "Are you about ready?"

Henry looked up from a parchment. "Almost. I need to finish this formal complaint to the owner of that multi-family unit, the one with the roof about to fall in."

"For the group who came in last sixthday?"

"Yes."

"Do you think it will do any good?"

"The owner isn't likely to fix it, but with this on file, he'll have to pay damages if anyone is injured when it does fall in. I feel so sorry for those creatures. Most of them have no place else to go. I refused to let them pay me."

"I've been meaning to ask you," Rundell said, "have you found out anything more about Ruth, the one who gave you the journal?"

"She's signed up to take a third term in my unit. I've left myself open several times, but she never says anything about herself. Why?"

"Well," Rundell hesitated, "I'd like to talk to her again. I never got a chance to tell her I was sorry for startling her that first day. Is there any way you can find out where she lives?"

"I suppose I could look in the Training Center records." He looked thoughtfully at Rundell. "You wouldn't have something else in mind, would you?"

Rundell looked embarrassed. "I would like to get to know her, properly, of course."

The two of them laughed and left the shop for the night.

*　　　*　　　*　　　*

"I found out where Ruth lives," Henry said to Rundell a few days later, "and more. I think I understand the reason why she is so quiet about herself. The domicile originally belonged to Gabriel."

"The one who wrote the journal? I thought you said the family disappeared?"

"That's what I thought. Records showed that after Gabriel died in the Number 2 mine riot, his mate collected damages and fled. No trace of her was ever found. Rex mentioned 'taking care of the Gabriel problem' in a letter to his uncle, Royal. His journal disclosed several possible ways to kill Gabriel for setting the ants free, along with the statement that it would have to wait until after he no longer needed Gabriel's ability to build mine tunnels in the ant way. Rex instigated the riot in order to get him killed, but no one could prove it. I found out that Ruth's great-grandfather was Gabriel's brother."

Rundell made a whistling noise through his outer mandibles.

"Before you go scampering off to court Ruth, let me visit them, present a copy of my work, now that it's finally complete, and assure them they have nothing more to fear from any of Rex's clan."

*　　　*　　　*　　　*

Henry looked at the domicile, a solid middle-level home, its outer walls made of hardened mud, strong and insulating. The front had one wall opening, with newly painted wooden shutters. He tapped on the front portal. Ruth greeted Henry cheerfully.

He followed her into the parlor where she introduced him to her parents and her grandfather. Henry handed a copy of his manuscript to Ruth's father, Richard, and explained why he had come.

Ruth's grandfather, Gallo, was blind. "You're a roach!" he said after touching Henry.

Henry realized Ruth had not told them anything about him, as she had not told him about herself. He explained. "My father was adopted by ants. My brothers and sister and I were all given ant names. I suppose it is confusing."

"May I get you some ale, Trainer Henry," Ruth's mother, Ginger, asked.

"Yes, please."

"I've heard you also do legal counseling. Is that true?" Richard asked.

Henry nodded. "I teach in the mornings and see clients three afternoons and sixthdays each quarter time frame."

"You have a good income then," Richard commented.

"Not really. The Training Center doesn't pay much. Most of those who come to me for counseling can't pay. I help them because it's what I believe in doing. Many return later with a small amount. Sometimes they offer to work for Rundell for free for a few h-units, in order to return the favor," Henry replied. "In time, it may prove steady enough. I feel that what I'm accomplishing here is more important right now."

Ginger handed him a mug of ale and Henry explained more about his work and his purpose.

"So busy!" Ginger said. "Do you ever get to visit your home?"

"Not as much as I wish I could. I spend Summer Solstice there every season cycle when the Training Center closes for a quarter time frame. I'll be there the day after tomorrow. Ruth, do you remember Rundell? You literally ran into him the day you first gave me the journal."

"Yes, I remember," she said shyly.

"He wanted me to tell you again that he was sorry he startled you. He'd like to tell you that himself, and meet you formally." He turned to Richard. "With your approval, of course."

"Absolutely," said Gallo, answering for Richard, "provided you come with the young male and tell me more about yourself and your family."

*   *   *   *

Henry decided not to take the trail on his journey home two days later. He felt drawn to the surface west of the Number 1 plastic mine. It wasn't much farther that way and he had left extra early. Cutting straight through open meadow from the northwest edge of the city, he reached the area in an h-unit. The lush meadow grass, extra tall from an abundance of sky water, brushed his abdomen as he walked through it. He found several patches of wild berry bushes. Blossoms perfumed the morning air.

Near a small stream he saw mantis tracks and found what remained of a giant cricket. Henry hoped the mantis was no longer hungry and decided he'd better return to the trail. All along, the same thought nagged at him—this could be a dairy.

He crossed the bridge and entered New South 50's eastern surface and increased his speed. Summer Solstice was especially joyful in a dairying colony. Grassfronds from spring planting grew taller each day. Grasshopper nymphs were large enough not to be quite so worrisome and aphids reached their peek of honey dew production. It made a brief time of relaxation; a pause in the ants' hectic routine while crops grew and herds became fat on summer vegetation.

Two d-units away, Henry convinced himself he could smell the whole grasshopper roasting slowly over the huge pile of coals in the pit outside the front entrance of the mound. Summer Solstice was a feast as festive as a mating celebration. The whole colony joined in, one giant family. In New South 50 it was especially true. Although others had joined the colony, the vast majority were descendants of the original five founding families, or relatives of those families who had come later.

He spotted one of his ant cousins, Adeline—or Dell, as she preferred—off the trail to his right, carrying a basket of blossoms.

"Henry," she shouted, seeing him at the same moment and scurrying toward him. "Welcome home!"

He embraced her fondly. "It's good to see you. How is your mother?"

"She's fine, still Head Dairier. Says she has a good many season cycles left."

"Good. I want to spend some time talking to her while I'm home."

Dell's mother, Corina, was the daughter of Henry's grandmother's sister. Corina had originally come to South Dairy 50 during job exploration to spend time trying out archaeology with Henrietta. Instead, she had met and mated Al, son of founding members, Art and Allie, and ended up with dairying for her life's work. Dell followed the family tradition.

"How's your work going?" Dell asked him as they walked toward the colony.

"Teaching is as ever. The number of creatures seeking advice continues to grow. I finished the manuscript."

"Really? Uncle Andrew will be so pleased. He's been ill, you know."

"No, I didn't know. Is it serious?"

"Enough that he retired. Is the manuscript what you wanted to see my mother about?"

"That and something else."

Dell chatted on with the latest colony news. Henry's mind wandered to the intricate relationships of his "family." Dell's grandmother, Hilda, was his grandmother's younger sister. Hilda had mated Corin, the son of Herbert, another of the three ants enslaved by Rex. Both Hilda and Corin had passed on shortly before Uncle Andrew sent Henry the journals.

The two reached the colony's outside common grounds. Dell set the basket of blossoms on one of the eating surfaces already set up. Dozens of colony members swarmed about, basting the roasting grasshopper, carrying honey cakes to the surfaces, setting up more dining areas. Henry lost himself in a sea of familiar faces and embraces. Someone took his satchels, saying they would take them to his parents' home. He found his brothers, and Dorothy, also home for a visit.

The Summer Solstice feast began.

*   *   *   *

Henry found Corina out in the meadow the following morning. Although there were many who could watch the herd, she still liked being there. She greeted him fondly. "Dell said you'd be out this morning. I'm looking forward to reading your work."

"It won't be quite what you're expecting."

"Oh? The journals were fairly straight forward."

"I found out there was a lot more to it, but I hope that when it's read widely, it will help heal, rather than open old wounds," Henry explained. "I wanted to talk to you about something else."

"What is it?"

Henry looked out at the grazing herd and said, "I know we have more surface area here than we need to support large herds of grasshoppers, much more than the colony will ever need. I've been wondering. What is the minimum amount of surface necessary to sustain a small herd of hoppers, say enough to provide the needs of twenty-five or thirty creatures?"

Corina paused before answering. "One adult consumes the equivalent of half a full grown hopper per season cycle, on the average. That would mean a herd of fifteen for consumption. A pair of hoppers hatches about three nymphs each spring. So you'd need maybe six pairs of permanent breeding stock. I'd say a square d-unit would be needed to protect against overgrazing."

"That's less than I thought," Henry said. "What about grassfronds and other foods for the same number?"

"Another square d-unit would be enough. Why?" she asked, shifting position and looking off into the distance. She waved an "all right" signal to the dairier of the far side of the herd.

"There's so much good meadow area in Roacheria, right across the border stream. I've wandered around there a few times. I keep thinking small groups of roaches should learn how to do dairying to provide for themselves. It may not be possible. There are so many obstacles to surface ownership there."

"Aren't you doing enough teaching and counseling?" Corina asked.

"Yes, of course, but I can't help but think there is a better way for the common roaches to live. Some type of a cross between their economic system and ours. If I could form a plan ... maybe ..."

"You never stop, do you?" she interrupted.

Henry smiled at her.

"If I can answer anything else, let me know," she said.

"Thanks. I've got to go. There are many I want to see and I only have five more days."

*   *   *   *

The cost of housing was another obstacle in Henry's idea for a Roacherian dairy. An ant mound was basically free for the digging. He didn't think he would be able to talk many roaches into that idea, considering his own dislike of being underground. Strong buildings of wood and stone were prohibitively expensive. The meadow areas, so good for growing grassfronds, had no Duo Pod ruins to serve as a foundation for new structures. Shanties, built of anything scrounged and left over, fell apart during violent storms.

Henry went to the Duo Pod Research Center to see Master Donna. "Henry," she said when he entered, "how nice to see you. Your father passes your letters around. I'm glad things are going well for you."

"Thank you. Remember when I tried to learn to read the symbols?"

"Who could forget," she said, putting down the manuscript she was translating.

"I remember the images more than anything. I've been thinking of a new project that might help common roaches live better, and I thought I remembered images of many different kinds of dwellings. I'm trying to come up with an idea for less expensive, but strong structures."

"I know the one you mean," she said and went to the shelves for a manuscript that had once been used to teach young Duo Pods to read, and was still used for that purpose, though the creatures learning to read it were quite different now. The images showed Duo Pods living in many different looking structures all over the planet.

Henry leafed carefully through the delicate, old parchment. Perfectly preserved for so long in a vacuum, the manuscripts had begun to deteriorate since their finding. Henry remembered Master Donna telling him about how they were painstakingly making images of every piece of parchment. "Do the words say what they're made out of?" he asked.

"No," she sighed. "It's simple, repetitive phrases like, 'My domicile,' 'Your domicile,' 'Any domicile is a good domicile,' and it's hard to tell from the images. But I could look in some other sources."

A voice in Ant with a heavy Roach accent interrupted them. "Well, Master Donna, I'm back again."

Master Donna turned. "Rafael, how good to see you. Have you met Henry?"

"No, but I've heard plenty," the large, extremely dark brown roach replied.

"Henry, this is Roacheria's Chief Archaeologist, also a Board Member, Rafael."

Henry held out his front pods toward the elderly archaeologist in an Ant greeting. "So how does one address you formally? Master Rafael, Sir Rafael, or Master Sir..."

Rafael laughed and returned Henry's greeting. "In the Board Meeting Chambers, it's 'Sir,' when I'm on a dig it's 'Master,' here with you, 'Rafael,' is enough. I'm pleased to meet you. You are a pretty regular topic of conversation among Board Members, even though you're never on the agenda."

Henry sighed. "I suppose I shouldn't be surprised. Is it all bad?"

Rafael moved over to a near-by floor cushion and made himself comfortable. "Some would like to get rid of you, any way they can. Others say you should be carefully watched. Still others say the time has come to listen to what you are trying to tell us. By the way, your work on Master Antony's life was wonderful. I read it last time I was here."

"Thank you." Henry sat down beside him. "What do you think would happen if I applied for full citizenship? I know that The Board makes all final decisions regarding that, but I haven't checked all the fine points."

Master Donna handed both of them mugs of honey dew. Rafael took a long drink before answering.

"Don't try it very soon. Wait another half a season cycle. Let them get more used to your counseling. Give me time to sound out other Board Members privately. You may have more allies than you think, but your enemies could cause serious problems. Come and see me next winter, right after the new season cycle begins."

Henry nodded. "I'd need that much time anyway. Thank you for the advice. May I ask you something?"

"Of course."

"I know my grandmother trained your father. How did you manage to be appointed to The Board when your training was in Archaeology?"

"So long ago, when my father finished training with your grandmother, he and Master Roland were both converted by the experience. Both felt things needed to change in Roacheria. Master Roland used his credit to help others. My father taught me Ant ways and used his credit to buy influence. He wanted to change the system. He spent everything he had, and used Sir Reginald the Younger's influence to get me on The Board."

"Thank you," Henry said. "I've always been curious."

"You're welcome. Master Donna, have you found any more manuscripts I should look at?" Rafael asked.

"Yes, but I haven't begun to translate them. I found a volume on violent conflict. Henry, Rafael has been doing research on the Duo Pods tendency toward violence. Considering your interest in our present day problems, you'd find it interesting."

Henry sipped from his mug. "Oh?"

Rafael said, "If you think our problems have been bad, theirs were one-hundred, no, one-thousand times worse. They had more horrid ways to kill each other than you can possibly imagine! I'm amazed they lasted as long as they did as a species. Some of what I've found puts a new factor into your grandmother's original hypothesis."

Henry looked at his time piece. "I wish I could stay and hear more. My parents are expecting me for dinner. Another time, perhaps?"

"Of course. I'll be here the rest of this quarter time frame," he said.

"I'll see what else I can find for you," Master Donna added as Henry left.

12.

*H*enry stood in the protected glen where he had become an adult, pods lifted in meditation. Although he often meditated with his grandfather in mind, it felt more special here.

He let his mind wander and spoke out loud, as though his grandfather were present. "I'm doing a lot, but somehow I feel there is more. I think about how Rundell and I are sharing our resources. Maybe it could work. If several of my friends and I put everything we had together and shared it ... a little colony ... just twenty or thirty, counting what young we might all have. If I could get the surface ... If one or two could learn to care for the hoppers, care for the crops ... Others could work as they always have ... I don't know ... There would be so many problems ... But you had problems, and you made it work. Did you dream, too? Did you keep seeing your father in your dreams like I see you? Did you ever feel him pushing you along?"

A soft rustle came from behind. Henry whirled around to see his mother enter the glen. He sighed in relief. "I thought you were a mantis."

"I'm sorry I startled you," she said. "I thought I might find you here. Master Donna said she found something for you."

"She did?" He started toward Genny.

Genny nodded. They both left the glen. Henry ran back toward the colony, leaving his mother behind.

"My mother ... said you ... found something," Henry puffed to Master Donna, still out of breath from the run.

"Actually, Rafael found it. I'll let him explain."

"Henry, look." Rafael beckoned to him from a large work surface, covered with ancient manuscripts.

Henry looked at the image Rafael pointed out, a male and female Duo Pod standing in front of a structure that reminded Henry of the mound his grandfather had grown up in, only smaller. The female appeared to be holding a young one.

"Your building material is beneath your pods," Rafael said. "Quite long before their demise, well before their most advanced technological age, some Duo Pods built things like this. They cut chunks of the thick meadow grass, roots intact, and used them like building blocks. A few wood pieces supported a roof. They left wall openings if they wanted them. The portal was also wood. I read quite a bit about it."

Henry stared at the image.

Rafael went on. "At that point in their time, the vast areas to our north in the middle of this land mass were covered with great meadows, thousands of square d-units. Huge numbers of these extinct four-podded fur creatures roamed freely, eating the grass. The indigenous Duo Pod variety followed the four-podded creatures, killing them for food and using the hairy outer-covering for dwellings. See?" He pointed out another image.

"Then this variety with a lighter outer covering, and more advanced tools and weapons came from another land mass. They seem to have been a greedy lot."

"Like some creatures we know?" Henry interrupted.

"Perhaps. Anyway, the light ones dominated, of course, nearly obliterating the indigenous variety. I won't go into that right now. The point is, not all of these light ones were power driven. Some seem to have been dairiers and saw that the meadows would be good for raising their food grain, a sort of tiny version of grassfrond, perhaps its evolutionary source. They cut through the natural meadow grass, build small homes of it, and planted their food crop in the opened ground. Rather ingenious, wouldn't you say?"

"Yes," Henry agreed, "I bet I could do the same thing. A low structure like that would be quite strong. It would stay fairly even in temperature through out the season cycle, like a mound does. Yet, it would satisfy the desire to be on the surface and have wall openings. The amount of timbers needed for the roofs, wall openings and portals would be very affordable. Reed mats on frames could be used to separate inside chambers for sleep and sanitation."

Master Donna had come over to the surface and joined them about half way through the discussion. "Do you think the roaches you hope will join you in this risky venture will accept living in such antish simplicity?" she asked.

Henry looked at her and said, "If I didn't know you better, I'd think you were being sarcastic. Those I hope will join me have less than this now, or they have already adopted Ant philosophy."

"Have you checked to see who controls surface use the area you're thinking about?" Rafael asked.

"Not yet. But I will as soon as I get back. This and the information I got from Corina have solved my biggest concerns about the possibility," Henry replied, feeling more hopeful than ever.

"Unfortunately, those concerns may have been the easiest," Rafael said. "As I told you the other day, come and see me next winter. We'll see what my pitiful bit of influence can do to gain your full citizenship and the privilege of surface control."

*　　　*　　　*　　　*

The following morning, Henry went through the meadow area again on his way back to Roacheria. He walked slowly around the pond, then a little to the north where he had seen a stream indicated on the location chart. The stream ran clear and sweet, half a d-unit from the pond. He dug into the meadow grass, lifted one chunk.

His mind whirled. The pond for the hoppers and aphids. The stream for everyone else. He pictured tall grassfronds growing off to his right, and next to the stream a cluster of dwellings, one for each family, around a larger community building for meeting, meditation and celebration. It would be a little above-ground colony. Everything would be held in common, their wealth shared according to need. "In common," he said aloud, "here in the meadows ... That's what I'll call it, Meadow Commonwealth."

*　　　*　　　*　　　*

Rick greeted him fondly when he got back. "I can tell you had a good visit. I haven't seen you so relaxed in a long time. There's a gleam in your eyes."

Genelle entered. Henry told them about his new dream.

When he finished, Genelle took Rick's pod in hers and said, "If you are able to do this, we will join you. Won't we, Rick?"

Rick agreed. "I could still keep my job at the City Bulletin. Genelle could work out there. I could sell this domicile to my oldest brother. He's wanted it for a long time. The funds would pay for a lot of wood and other equipment we would need."

"You would give up your father's domicile for my risky dream?"

"My father wanted me to continue to help others and try to bring about change. This could do it. We'll make it work. Then we can show other groups of families how to do the same thing. Remember when you first came and I said it would take young adults with a radically different idea? This concept of yours would blend Ant ways of sharing and caring for all within the Roacherian economic system."

"You aren't afraid of what those with established power could do to us?"

"Of course I'm afraid. Aren't you?"

Henry nodded. He knew most of the risks. He also knew The Board could place obstacles before him he hadn't yet thought of.

Genelle took both their pods in hers. "Then we'll all be afraid together, and together we will give each other the strength we'll need."

Later, when Henry explained it to Rundell, he said, "If you get full citizenship next winter, we could start in the spring. Isn't that when you plant the grassfronds? By the following fall, I might have something to sell in my market stall besides fly eggs. We're sure to produce more food than we need. I know many who will join us."

"Not too many," Henry cautioned. "Two square d-units will only support twenty-five to thirty. We have to start small, support ourselves, then show others what to do."

*　　　　*　　　　*　　　　*

For the first time frame of the new term, Henry had no time to pursue the dream of Meadow Commonwealth. Master Riedel had him teaching three groups every morning and another group of Trade Center workers in the evening.

The workers from the Trade Center made it clear that they disliked this new requirement for keeping their jobs, especially since they had to pay a fee to the training facility. The complaint was the same as each introduced himself.

"I've been working a long time and never had to do this. Why now? My nymphs could have used the plastic instead of what I spent on this place!"

Henry countered. "Don't we all have to do things we would rather not do? But here we are, together, for something that is more important, even if you don't think so now. How many of you remember having to drink a bitter potion at some time in your life to cure an illness?"

Several antennae twitched in acknowledgment.

"Think of the next five time frames in that way. You may not like it, but when it's over, you'll be better for it. Ask someone you know who was here with me last term."

Fortunately, this group began to agree with him much sooner than the previous Trade Center group had. Only one or two continued to resist.

Henry spent every afternoon and all day each sixthday advising those who came to him. He wrote endless numbers of mating contracts, often at the demand of the female involved.

"If he wants me, he'll take legal responsibility," one female said. "I'm not giving myself away to be abandoned like my mother did."

Such comments pleased Henry. Later, he learned that Georgette was the one spreading the word around to the shanty females that they ought to be assertive and look out for themselves, since nobody else did.

Nearly as often, he settled disputes between groups and individuals over living conditions in a structure they occupied for a fee; ownership of some possession of a parent who had died; or who was responsible for some minor damage.

"This isn't counseling," he said to Rundell one day. "It's arbitration."

"It keeps them out of a Formal Inquiry, doesn't it?" Rundell asked. "When you help them settle it, the one who feels offended doesn't resort to crime and end up rotting in the detention facility. Besides, I never lack for help gathering eggs and spreading fly bait, since so many of your clients pay for your services by working for me for a few h-units."

"But your gathering place isn't a secret any more."

"That's all right. Last time frame, some others came to gather. One of your clients informed them that if they did, you would never give them advice. They protect my business, you help them. It all comes out even. See, we are a colony after all."

*   *   *   *

Late in the fall, Henry found a free afternoon to go to the Agency for Document Registration.

"Counselor Henry," the clerk said, "I haven't seen you for quite a while. What do you need today?"

"I need to find out who controls the use of some surface west of the Number 1 Plastic mine."

"Have you got the exact location?"

Henry nodded.

"I'm here by myself today, so I can't leave this station to get it. But I trust you, so I'm going to tell you what chamber to look in and you can find it yourself."

"Thank you," Henry said.

The clerk opened a small portal to their right and said, "Go down this passage-way to the third portal on your left. That's where the surface records are."

When Henry saw the jumble of containers in the chamber, he wondered how anybody knew who controlled anything. No wonder the clerk didn't have time. It took Henry two h-units to figure out which tracts were stored in what containers. For the next three h-units he found no record for the area he wanted and wondered if anyone cared about it at all. He regarded that fact as a good sign. If no one cared about a record, The Board wasn't as likely to object to his taking it over.

The clerk came in. "Counselor, I have to lock up. You can come back another day."

"Five more minutes, please. I'm nearly to the bottom of this container."

"All right. But that's absolutely it."

"Thank you," said Henry as he continued to look at the worn, faded parchments. A smile came to his face as he looked at the last one.

"The Essence is with me," he said to the clerk on his way out.

*   *   *   *

Rundell looked into Henry's sleep chamber at Rick's home. As usual for a seventhday, Henry sat on the bench by the wall opening, deep in meditation. Rundell hated to interrupt.

"Henry," he said quietly, "it's time to go. Ruth's parents are expecting us at four h-units."

Henry turned. He and Rundell had spent every seventhday afternoon with Ruth's family for several time frames. While Henry talked with her parents and grandfather, Rundell and Ruth went off by themselves. "Have you got everything?" Henry asked him.

"Of course. I copied it neatly in my own script, as you said I should."

The two were warmly welcomed when they arrived. Ginger brought them mugs of ale as they sat down with Richard and Gallo. Ruth coaxed her younger brothers, Gallo and Griffin (named for their grandfather and great-grandfather) out of the parlor by promising them crisp fried bee's wings.

"We really don't need to be so formal," Richard said.

"I want it to be formal," Rundell said. "I've worked hard and saved an adequate amount. It's in reserve notes at The Plastic Exchange of Organized Roacheria. Here is my offer to have Ruth as my legal mate." He laid the parchment and a mating cord before Richard.

Richard put his pod in the ink pot and signed it. "I know I don't even have to read this. I could not be happier with your offer for my daughter. When shall I bind you formally?"

"Next spring, after we finish building our home and the other structures at Meadow Commonwealth. We will celebrate the completion of the Common Building with our mating, in an Ant ceremony. Won't we, Henry?"

Henry smiled and said, "I found out two days ago who owns the area. I have an appointment with the owner tomorrow. I don't think it will be a problem."

"I thought you were going to see Ronda tomorrow afternoon," Rundell said.

"That, too," Henry replied.

"Will The Board grant you full privileges?" Gallo asked.

"I don't know. But it doesn't matter. I'll have the surface ownership put in Rick's name for now. I'll continue as a 'Guest Resident,' if I must. Later, we'll find a legal way to list everyone who lives there as an owner, even our slender members. I'll find a way eventually."

Richard rose and called to the other members of his family. "Everyone come in here. I have something to say. Ginger, please bring more ale for everyone, including you and Ruth and the little ones."

Ginger and Ruth came in, carrying platters of fried fly eggs and bee's wings. The two nymphs followed, carrying the jug of ale and more mugs. Ruth seated herself beside Rundell. He took her front pod in his. Henry caught a look between them that reminded him of the way his brother, David, had looked at his Promised One during the time frame before their ceremony. He hoped that one day he would find a female he cared about that much.

"I won't take time for the obvious," Richard said, raising his mug. "We will celebrate a mating in the spring. To Ruth and Rundell."

All of them drank and laughed. Richard continued. "Now, what I really wanted to announce. I've been thinking about this for quite a while. I want my family to join you in your venture, Henry. I went out there one day last time frame. It wouldn't be so far for me to go to my job. I know I can get a fair price for this domicile. The amount will provide for my father's needs. Will you have us?"

Delight flowed through Henry. "Of course," he said. "But there's no need to provide extra for Gallo. We would all take care of him."

"Wait a minute," Gallo said. "I have some pride. You can only take care of me if you find something useful for me to do as well."

Henry reached over and stroked the old male affectionately. "Of course. You know I would never offend you."

"Then let's eat," Richard said, gesturing toward the food.

13.

"***R***onda is out in the garden, Counselor Henry," the thin servant said as she opened the portal.

Henry followed her through the mansion and out into the grounds he had often looked at through the wall openings in Ronda's parlor. Thorn bushes bloomed in abundance in the cool of late fall. The leaves of some wood plants had turned bright red, while others remained green—not all varieties shed their leaves at this time of the season cycle. He found Ronda in the midst of the thorn bushes, cutting the blossoms for a bouquet.

"Henry," she said, "it's good to see you again." She turned to the servant. "Please, bring refreshments at once. We'll sit over there under the largest wood plant. Take these and put them in the parlor."

She handed the blossoms to the servant, who left immediately.

"The garden looks even more beautiful than it did in the summer," Henry said.

"Yes," she replied. "The blossoms don't wilt so quickly when it's cool. How are your plans coming?"

"They'll be much farther along after I leave here today."

"Oh, why is that?"

"I found out who owns the meadow land I want," Henry said as they sat down under the wood plant.

"Who?"

"You do."

"I what!"

Henry explained. "A long time ago, when your grandfather was young, he took an option on a huge parcel west of the Number 1 Plastic Mine, all the way to the border and several d-units to the north. He took it hoping to find more plastic. That never came to be. Gradually, he sold off pieces of it, letting the buyers think there might be plastic. He kept one last tract, about five square d-units."

The servant arrived and served them honey dew and roasted seeds. The offering of traditional ant foods pleased Henry.

"Why did he keep such a large tract of worthless meadow?" Ronda asked as she nibbled the seeds.

Henry drank from his mug of honeydew before answering. "I don't know for certain, but it's common knowledge that your grandfather hated Rex. I found an offer from Rex to buy it that your grandfather rejected. I think your grandfather kept it to spite him, and make him think there was something more than meadow."

Ronda pondered the idea. "Now that you mention it, when I was quite young, my mother told me about a day from her youth. She was listening when she shouldn't have, I guess. Rex came to see my grandfather. There was some argument. My mother said that grandfather shouted, 'When you acknowledge your guilt for my injury, I'll sell you that surface.' It became a family secret after Rex's downfall, when mentioning Rex's name was banned. I never knew what surface they meant."

The two of them laughed at the thought that the same surface would now be controlled by Henry and his group.

"So," Ronda said when she stopped laughing, "what do I need to do or sign to give you control?"

"Actually, it will be better from the legal standpoint if you sell it to Rick. He already has full citizenship privileges. I still don't know if The Board will grant that to me," Henry explained.

"Then Rick may have it at no charge."

"It's better that there is a price."

"Henry, I can't take any credit from you or your friends," she insisted.

"Perhaps you can accept this." Henry drew a small, hexagonal piece of cheap metal, stamped with the seal of Roacheria, the one-hundredth part of a credit unit, from his satchel. "The legal parchments will state it was sold for 'an undisclosed price.'"

"Accepted," she said.

"I took the liberty of writing it up. I have all the necessary parchments with me. We only plan to use a little over two d-units, the area near the pond and the stream, and the meadows around it. That is the portion that touches the border with South Dairy 50. When we are successful, we will turn the eastern half over to another group and show them how to form a commonwealth of their own," Henry said.

He took the parchments and a pot of ink from his satchel. He went over the wording carefully with Ronda, three complete copies of everything: one for her, one for Rick, and one for the Agency for Document Registration. He showed her exactly where to put her signature.

"I sign as legal counselor for Rick," he said, "and Rick will sign here." He pointed to the last blank space.

"It gives me great pleasure to do this for you. You're ... well ... the only family I have."

In all their visits, Henry had never embraced her. He did now, for the first time. She accepted his stroking awkwardly.

"So," she said, returning to her usual coolness, "who will be joining you out there, and when?"

"Hopefully, we will start building domiciles during the first or second time frame, opening the ground. Remember how I told you we would build them?"

She nodded, while munching more seeds.

"Grassfronds must be planted by the middle of the third time frame in the open ground. We'll move when the structures are complete. Rundell and Ruth will have their mating ceremony there, and begin their life together. You'll come for it, won't you?"

"Of course!"

"Ruth's parents, Richard and Ginger, and her younger brothers are joining me. So are Rick and Genelle, Rick's son, Ray, and his mate,

Ramona, my other friends: Rusty, and Gatlin and his mate, Gabby. Georgette and her nymphs will also live with us."

"That's all?"

"For now," Henry said.

She hesitated. "Will you have enough funds for all that you'll need? I could ..."

Henry shook his head. "It wouldn't be good, politically, I mean. Providing the surface is enough for some to be critical. They could say it isn't really an independent venture, that we're still relying on the Roacherian system for support through your wealth. We'll have enough with the sale of Rick's and Richard's domiciles. Rundell and I have managed to save some funds as well, from his business and my occasional counseling fees."

She looked concerned. "What if something goes wrong? You could lose everything."

Henry, more than any of them, knew what was at stake. "All of us are willing to take that risk."

*   *   *   *

In the middle of the thirteenth time frame, Henry came into Rundell's shop as he always did after a morning of teaching.

"Where's Georgette?" Henry asked. She was usually feeding her nymphs when he arrived. They were already asleep.

"I sent her out to make a delivery," said Rundell, in a quiet tone that seemed a warning. Henry noticed that the tea pot was steaming.

"Rundell, is something wrong?" Henry asked.

"I don't know," Rundell said. "You've got one awfully important client waiting to see you. He said he knows you, but I haven't ever seen him around here before. He also said you might need some tea. He's wearing a Board Ornament."

Henry hesitated before he opened the portal to his work chamber. There sat Sir Rafael. Henry breathed an audible sigh of relief. "Sir Rafael, what brings you here? Rundell had me worried for a moment." He held out both pods and greeted Rafael cheerfully.

He turned back to Rundell. "It's all right. This is Sir Rafael, or Master Rafael, as he's known in the world of archaeology. I met him last summer at home. I thought I told you."

Rundell looked puzzled, and then said, "Now, I remember. The one who found the way to build our domiciles. You must have left out the Board Member part." He turned to their guest. "Sir Rafael, I'm sorry I acted so unfriendly. A Board Member coming into this part of the city usually means problems for someone like me."

"I understand. Is the tea ready?"

"Yes," Rundell said, pouring two mugs.

Sir Rafael looked at both of them as he took his mug. "I know you two are close, but I must speak privately with you, Henry."

Henry took the mug Rundell held out. Rundell closed the portal, leaving them alone. Sir Rafael took the client's seat near Henry's work surface. His expression grew serious.

"I thought I was supposed to come to you after the new season cycle begins," Henry said, trying to relieve the growing sense of anxiety he felt.

"I don't know where to begin, or how to say this," Rafael said. "I've been talking to Board Members over the last few time frames. They will hear your plea and grant your request for full citizenship privileges, but," he sighed, "their 'Special Provision Clause' may not be one you can accept."

Henry knew that besides proving purity of line, which he had already done, The Board could make any other request it wanted to, a hefty fee in most cases.

"Have they set the fee at a higher rate than I could possibly manage? Oh, well. We put the surface in Rick's name just in case. I guess I'll have to continue as a 'guest resident.'"

Rafael sighed again. "It's not a fee. They know you have enough friends, or that South 50 would give you some. They also know Ronda would give you anything."

"Then what?"

Rafael drank some of his own tea, and then said, "They want you to completely renounce all ties to New South Dairy 50. You must bring documentation to them stating that New South 50 and your family have banished you. You will never be allowed to go home and no one from your family may visit you. You are formally on the agenda for secondday, the 2nd of the First Time Frame. That's why I came here today. If you really intend to do this, I thought you might like to go home for Last Day. It would, literally, be the last time."

Henry stared at him. He took several gulps of tea. "You were right to tell Rundell I might need tea. I know many hate me but why this?"

"Jealousy. And fear. There are many who see a threat to themselves in what you are trying to accomplish."

"Well, I guess that settles it. I'll be forever as I am, a guest resident."

Rafael's antennae drooped low. He shook his head. "It gets worse. They will not allow you to continue the 'guest resident' status. They want to force you into a choice. Continue here with full privileges, or go home for good, everything or nothing. I managed to keep Arthur's status in trade. He will be able to continue to enter Roacheria on regularly scheduled days. You can be nowhere near the trail or the Trade Center at those times. Believe me, they'll have someone watching both of you closely."

Henry put his head down on his writing surface and groaned. "Who's behind this?" he asked.

"You can't figure it out?"

Henry thought for a moment. "The Head Member of the Legal Counseling Services Committee?"

Rafael nodded. "He is a member of Rex's clan. Even though he has no Board Vote, since The Board decreed that clan could never again have political power when Rex was banished, but he has tremendous influence over several Board Members. There is one bright spot. Although there can be no direct written communications, The Board can't stop others from passing word back and forth. I have to continue my archaeological research in New South 50. They can't legally prevent that. Anyone in your group can write to anyone in New South 50. I'll carry the letters myself, and those back to your group."

Rage and sorrow rose within Henry. He could not speak.

Rafael rose from his seat, came around the writing surface and stroked Henry gently. "I'll have Rundell put me on his delivery list. That will give your members a legitimate reason to come to my domicile on a regular basis. Let me know your decision by fourhday, the 25th of the Thirteenth Time Frame. I have to confirm that you will appear. You will be permitted to address the entire Board. I will schedule myself to speak on your behalf as well."

Henry rose, picked up his mug of tea and dashed it against the wall. He left Sir Rafael standing there and stormed toward the shop portal. "Rundell, notify the Training Center that I have an emergency. Cancel the Trade Center Group. I need to be alone for a while," he said, slamming the portal on his way out.

Henry ran from the city, ran from himself, ran without thought to where he was until exhaustion stopped him. When it did, he found himself near the peaceful pond on the surface he wanted so desperately to turn into a dairy.

He shouted at the sky. "They killed your family, grandfather. They want mine, too. I have no mate to get me through this!" He lay down in the mud at the edge of the pond, half hoping a mantis would come along, and wept.

Sleep claimed him, and with it came a vision so powerful it gave him all the strength he needed for the many battles of the mind that were yet to come. A great many pods seemed to be touching him, stroking him. As each pod slipped gently off the tip of his antennae he saw the faces of those providing such great comfort. He recognized some: his grandfather, one who resembled an image he had seen of his grandmother, Gerry, Renae', other members of his colony who had left the physical world. Many ants as well as roaches he did not know comforted him as well. The creatures moved away from Henry and formed a large, united group. They beckoned to one roach standing off in the distance, refusing to join.

Though he heard no voices, words formed in his mind. "No one can take away your family. They live always within you."

Slowly, the one in the distance turned, and took a step toward the large group who waited to welcome him.

The vision faded and Henry felt himself being stroked by real pods, Rick's. He opened his eyes and raised himself from the mud. Daylight had nearly gone. Behind Rick stood Genelle, Ray and Ramona, Gatlin and Gabby, and Ruth.

"Rundell would be here, but he went to teach your class for you," Rick said. "Sir Rafael told Rundell what they wanted. We all talked it over. You don't need to give up your family. We'll still build Meadow Commonwealth. Nobody can stop us. You began it, but we can finish it.

Go home to those who cherish you. The grassfronds you planted in us will reach maturity."

The others nodded their agreement in silence.

"In spite of the fact that you may lose everything you have?" Henry asked. "In the beginning, you'll be living with less than you're used to. You'll have no cold storage, no good sanitation system. You'll have to do as ants did over one hundred season cycles ago, shovel body waste by pod from collection containers into baskets and carry it to a mulching bin for later use as fertilizer. There won't be any current conveniences or communications systems."

"We believe in your mission," Rick reassured him. "We are prepared to do whatever it takes."

Henry looked at them. "It means a lot to me to hear you say that, but I'll be all right. I'll do what they want. I won't let them have the satisfaction of beating me."

14.

*H*enry celebrated Last Day with his training groups as he usually did at the end of a term. He told them he would be going away to visit his family, but said nothing about his upcoming appearance before The S.E.R.C.B. He left Roacheria for New South Dairy 50 after he finished his Trade Center Group, even though it was late in the evening and already dark. He had all the documents his family and New South Dairy 50's Council had to sign in his satchel.

No reason for banishment was stated other than Henry's request for it. "That way," Sir Rafael had said, "they can't come back on you later and say there was some crime involved."

Henry let out a long, drawn-out sigh as he walked along the trail. Would it be better to tell them right away? No, then the whole visit would be miserable. Better to keep his bad news to himself and enjoy the time as best he could.

A cold wind blew from the north. Clouds covered the stars. Henry knew he was vulnerable, alone on the trail. He didn't care. Let a bandit strike. He had nothing for one to take. Let a predator attack. It would be a graceful way out. Sadness overwhelmed him. He dragged his pods.

A voice came from behind. "Ho there, Trainer Henry, please wait."

Henry turned to see one of the members from his Trade Center Group, a large, middle-aged male who had been a problem the whole term.

"What do you want?" Henry asked, not really wanting to talk to him.

"I decided to try to catch up to you a little while after you left the Training Center," he said. "You know how much I resented having to take your unit. But tonight, when you sang your chant, something happened to me. I can't explain it. I realized so many things. You treated me with respect even though you knew I hated you. Though I followed your requirement and never uttered an insult, at least not out loud, I never said anything kind either. It all hit me, and I wanted to tell you I'm sorry for the way I acted."

Henry was dumbfounded.

The male continued. "I'm going to take all the materials you gave me and study them better, a little at a time. Tomorrow, I'm going to start apologizing to all the creatures I've insulted." He began to laugh. "You know, I feel so much better already, just saying this to you. Does it always feel this good, following your ways?"

Henry found his voice. "Most of the time. Thank you for your kind words. You've done much more tonight than you'll ever realize. I'll be back in a few days. Come and visit sometime." He reached out and took the worker's front pods in friendship.

"I will. You be careful out there."

"You, too," Henry said. He turned to continue his journey and the male ran back down the trail toward the city.

Warm inside now, in spite of the cold wind, Henry quickened his pace toward home.

*   *   *   *

After crossing the bridge, he began to watch for lanterns in the meadows, indicating dairiers on watch with a herd of hoppers. He would stay the night with them and go to the glen at dawn before going home. His parents weren't expecting him until noon.

Not long afterward, he spotted light off to his left. He whistled the friendly approach signal. He was glad to find his cousin Dell on duty with another male dairier.

"Henry," she exclaimed, embracing him, "whatever are you doing traveling at this h-unit?"

Henry returned her affection.

"Have some warm honeydew," said the dairier on duty with Dell, handing Henry a mug.

"Thank you," Henry said, taking the mug and settling himself by their fire.

Dell looked at him. "How is everything?"

"Fine," Henry said quickly. "I left tonight so I could spend some time meditating in the glen before I'm due at home. I was actually watching for someone out here."

Dell gave him a long look. Henry could see he had not fooled her for a moment. She was simply too polite to say anything.

"Are you tired? You can use my coverlet," Dell offered.

"No, actually, I feel wide awake," he replied.

Dell turned to her partner. "Why don't you sleep then? I'll keep watch with Henry."

"Thanks," he replied, curling up beneath the warm thistledown coverlet.

Henry stared into the fire and sipped the warm honeydew.

"Dorothy sent a message that she'd arrive tomorrow. She said you'd contacted her and wanted to be sure she'd be here this season cycle. We all thought maybe you'd found a female you cherished and wanted to announce it, but I see you're alone." She paused, leaving an opening. He saw it in her eyes again. She knew something was wrong. Maybe it would help if he told her. Now he knew how Rafael had felt. He didn't know where to begin, or how to say it either.

"No," he said slowly, "I haven't found a mate."

He finished his honeydew and nibbled some roasted seeds in silence. He looked at her seriously and asked, "If I share something with you, will you promise not to repeat it until I'm ready? You've always been able to see through me. Will you help me to find a way to hide what you see from the others, at least until after Last Day Services? I really want to enjoy this visit and treasure this short time with my family before I have to tell them."

"I'll do the best I can," she said, refilling his mug.

Henry decided to come right to the point. "The Board will grant me full citizenship privileges, under one condition." He stopped and stared into the fire again, unable to look into her eyes as he said, "I must renounce all ties to New South Dairy 50. Our Council and my family must banish me from ever returning. The S.E.R.C.B. will not allow me to continue as a guest resident. I must choose."

Dell remained quiet then finally said, "Oh, Henry ... No wonder you ... But how could you? ... Never mind, I can see you've already made up your mind to do it."

Henry looked up at her. "I'm sorry to burden you with this. I have to. Don't you see? I don't want to, but I must. I know, and I can't explain how, but deep down, I know I will succeed there. I can do much more good for many creatures if I do what they want. If I run, I'll let them destroy all that I've worked so hard to achieve. That's exactly what my enemies on The Board would like to see me do."

She finished drinking her own honey dew and looked deeply into his eyes again. "You're right. You wouldn't be you, if you did anything else."

As the night passed and Dell's partner slept. Henry and Dell talked on and on. Having Dell understand gave Henry the strength he felt he would need to make his visit joyful until time ran out. He finally fell asleep a few h-units before dawn.

$$*\qquad*\qquad*\qquad*$$

Dell shook Henry. "It's nearly nine h-units. If you want to go to the glen, you'd better get going."

Henry roused himself and ate the breakfast Dell offered. He took an image maker from his satchel. "Master Rafael loaned this to me and showed me how to use it. I'd like to get an image of you, Dell."

"Sure," she said, straightening up.

Henry focused the view-finder and operated the device. He wished the image would show the deep purplish black of her exoskeleton, but Rafael had not had enough of the type of materials that showed color.

"Now, let me get one of you, better yet, one of us together. Show my partner how to operate it."

"All right," he replied, showing the other dairier what to do.

"Why the images?" he asked.

"My trainees, and my friends keep asking me what my family looks like," Henry said. "Master Rafael is the only one I know with an image maker. He won't be going back to the ruins for another time frame, so he gave it to me for a while."

Dell gave him a knowing look followed by a reassuring smile.
"Thanks for the food and conversation," Henry said when the image taking ended. "I'll see you later."

He returned the image maker to his satchel and headed off across the meadows. Not long afterward, he entered the quiet glen where he had spent so much time with his grandfather. Even though the branches of the wood plants were bare of foliage and the grass lay brown and dormant, he still felt comfort in the place.

He settled himself in the spot where he had sat and signed his contract so long ago and lifted his pods to meditate. "Oh, Comforting Essence, you sent a vision in my sleep to let me know I can get through this. I don't understand all of what I saw, but I feel the strength I need. Help my family understand. Grandfather, give me the words I need. I would like to feel joy, not sorrow, with my family the next two and a half days. I cannot put a lifetime into it, yet I must hold these days inside me for the rest of my life. And so must they."

Henry listened to the wind in the branches, touched the wood plants and the memorial markers there. He walked to the pond and drank. He picked up some dry foliage from the ground, absorbing the odor. Then he took out the image maker, that he might feast his eyes on the place later.

                    *   *   *   *

Henry's smile was genuine when he embraced his mother. "You look wonderful! I see that little fracture healed."

"Yes," she said, stroking him fondly. "Your father was so worried when I slipped and got that crack. You know him, he worries about me all the time."

Henry was relieved. He had been worried, too, when he heard his mother had hurt herself. She made light of it, but everyone's thoughts had been of critinomalacia. They sat down in the parlor. Henry told her all about his training units, especially about the Trade Center worker. She caught him up on all the colony happenings—who had laid eggs, who was promised ... An h-unit slipped by. "I nearly forgot," his mother said, "your father wanted some tea. Let me reheat it. I might as well send a mug for Drew as well. Will you take it to them?"

Henry nodded. When it was warm, he left for the clinic. He found Drew and his father working together, grinding medicinal herbs and cultivating infection-fighting molds.

"Keeping up your supplies, I see," he said, setting down the mugs. "Do you expect a bad winter?"

Rodger put his pods around his youngest son. "One never knows. You look fine, Henry. I'm glad you chose to come home this season cycle. I know you gather a sizable group for Last Day with Rick, but I like it better when I have all my grown young around me."

"Have you got time to take a walk with me, Dad?"

Rodger turned to Drew. "Will you finish this?"

"Sure."

Henry and his father left the mound. They walked along the stream and through some of the stubble left where the grassfronds had been cut. Their conversation was full of, "Remember when's."

"You're certainly full of nostalgia," Rodger commented as they stopped at the memorial markers of Henry's grandparents.

"Last Day is a time to remember and renew, isn't it?" Henry asked.

Rodger nodded.

"My trainees and friends have been asking what my family looks like. Would you mind if I took an image of you here?" Henry asked, as he had his mother in their home. "Master Rafael let me borrow his image maker."

"Fine, as long as you send me a copy," his father replied.

"Master Rafael will send it. He's the one who will process the exposures."

*　　　　*　　　　*　　　　*

Sixthday and seventhday passed. Henry spent time with each member of his immediate family and his nieces and nephews. He even visited with his basic trainer. They laughed over the escapades of his youth. Everyone commented on how well he looked, praised his accomplishments. Everywhere, he made images, listened, smelled, ate with contentment, embraced those around him. He burned it into his memory.

Dell met him in one of the tunnels seventhday evening. "I'll be with my mother and others tomorrow," she said. "What time will you see our Council on the first?"

"At nine h-units."

"I want to be there," she said.

"I'd appreciate that," he replied. "You've already been more help than you know."

*   *   *   *

"Henry, pass me some more of that sliced grasshopper," David said.

Henry picked up the oval serving tray and handed it to David's oldest nymph, who sat between him and David. He looked around the crowded parlor. His parents smiled at each other. Arthur tended his younger nymph, babbled on about when the new egg would hatch. Drew's middle leg curved around his mate's.

Dorothy, seated on the other side of Henry, prodded him. "I look around at times like this and think perhaps it's time I looked for a mate. What about you?"

"Maybe ... someday."

How could he ask this of them? How could he not? He couldn't put it off any longer. He rose and looked at them. "I have something I have to say while we are all together. And, no, I haven't made a mating promise, except perhaps to my work."

All looked at him expectantly. Even the nymphs fell silent.

"There is another reason Master Rafael let me use his image maker. It isn't only for my friends and trainees. The images are mostly for me, and for you. This is the last time we will all be together."

"What do you mean?" Rodger asked his son.

"I must pay a heavy price for The Board to grant me full citizenship to continue my work in Roacheria."

"Why didn't you say so. The colony will gladly help provide credit," Arthur said.

"Will you really help me pay the price?" Henry asked.

"Of course," they chorused.

Henry looked at his expectant family. "You are the price. Each one of you. Many are jealous of the ties that bind us as a cherishing family. They demand I make a choice. I must give you up, and you must banish me from ever returning here."

A moment of stunned silence was followed by murmurs of, "Why? ... No! ... We can't let them do that."

Rodger's voice rose above the din. "No! I will not give up my son! They cannot make me do that!"

The chamber fell silent again.

Henry said, "Yes, you will. You must, because of everything you believe and everything you were given. All that we are, all that we have come to believe says we must do this. My great-grandfather was willing to give himself up, but another sacrificed himself instead. My grandfather lived in grief and pain, but he didn't give up. He fulfilled his dream in this place and turned sorrow to life and goodness. My grandmother sacrificed her strength and her ability to have young. But she didn't despair. She took you instead, Dad, and made something wonderful happen. Like them, I know there will be sadness from this choice that I make, but I also know that something better will come as a result. Dad, you performed something you found revolting, because of the greater good that would follow."

Support came from a source Henry least expected, his mother. She rose and said, "Yes, Henry, you must. Rodger, when I first met you, I can't describe what I felt. I only knew it was wonderful, so I made our promise. Only much later did I begin to understand what it meant to cherish someone. I only knew the reality; I was getting out of Roacheria! I'd have promised anything for salvation from that life."

Genny directed her pod toward David's, Arthur's and Drew's mates. "You know what I mean. Don't you?"

They nodded.

Genny continued. "Henry can do so much more for so many. He's got more courage than all of us put together." She turned to Henry. "I will miss you terribly, and I will grieve, but I will do what you ask me to do."

David said, "I take back everything I ever said when you were young about your not having a purpose. I don't want to either, but I will."

One by one, the others agreed. Henry read them the banishment document and explained it. He told them how they would communicate with him through Rick. He told Arthur what to expect on scheduled trade days. Last, with tears in his eyes, Rodger signed the parchment.

* * * *

Henry didn't have to explain as much to the Colony Council the following morning. They had heard. It was a quiet formality. Only Henry's roach cousin, Aunt Rayanne's son, spoke. "Like the others, I don't want to do this, Henry," he said. "My mother and my mate echoed your mother's words. They are the only reason I'm doing this."

When all had signed it, Dell and her mate Donald stepped forward. "We want to go with you, Henry. Don't argue with me about it. Our minds are made up. Admit it; you don't really know enough about dairying. Let us teach your friends. Our great-grandfathers taught Roacheria to build mine tunnels. Now we will teach them proper surface management and to provide for themselves in a better way."

Henry stared at his ant cousin and her mate. "You don't know how much it means to hear you say that. I don't know if The Board will allow it."

"We'll wait here for word from Sir Rafael. He'll tell us when to come. If the price is the same as it was for you, our families have already agreed."

Late that afternoon, after long good-byes and extended embraces, Henry put the banishment documents in his satchel and left his family behind.

15.

*H*enry stood in the very center of The Board Meeting Chamber in the S.E.R.C.B. Building, parchments in pod. Since it was still early, few Members had arrived. Henry would be the first to speak that secondday morning. He looked around. The huge chamber rose high above his head. Hundreds of lightning bug lamps hung on strands of braided hemp from wooden beams crisscrossing the ceiling like a spider web. He wondered who had the job of walking the narrow beams to draw the lamps up when they needed to be refueled. He didn't envy that one.

All along the walls of the hexagonal chamber hung portraits of past Supreme Executors and notable long-dead Board Members. He spotted the portrait Ronda had painted of her grandfather, Sir Ronald. Her style was evident in other paintings.

Rows of wooden work surfaces lined each of the six walls. The length of the surfaces decreased toward the center. Six aisles separated the sections of work surfaces. Behind them were padded chairs. Each one's seat and sides looked softer than Henry's sleep mat. Henry watched as several Board Members sat down. Their abdomens protruded from the open backs of the chairs. Most leaned against one side, middle and back pods on the floor in front of them.

The most important Board Members had places in front where they would stare directly at Henry. He would have to turn constantly as he spoke if he wanted to look directly at each. Any of them would consider it offensive if he kept his back to them too long. This was not a group one wanted to offend, and his mere existence offended some of them.

More and more Board Members entered. Sir Rafael passed through the center on the way to his place about midway between the center and the back. He patted Henry's thorax as he passed.

The babble of conversation ceased as Sir Reese, The Supreme Executor, and his son entered and took their places on one side of the center area. Sir Reese placed himself in an especially well padded chair. Elaborate carving decorated the wood trim on its sides.

Young Reese rose from a chair next to his father and announced, "The first regular meeting of The South East Roach Control Board, secondday, day two of the 279th season cycle of Organized Roacheria, has now begun. First item this day will be a request for full citizenship privileges by Henry Roach-Dairier." He sat down.

Sir Reese gestured to Henry and said, "You may speak."

Henry stooped low and spread his front pods out to the sides. He rose to his full height and began. "Esteemed Board Members, I stand alone before you today and ask that you grant me full citizenship privileges. I ask this so that I may continue what I have begun, teaching understanding and tolerance of all creatures, regardless of species or variety. Many of you fear me even though I have no power or credit."

He turned to his right and continued. "I have not asked you for power or credit. All I seek is to show others a better way to live. I don't ask you to give up anything that you have, or change your way of life. Those who want to change will on their own, for the choice to change is within each of us."

As he turned again, he searched the eyes of those closest to him for some sign of favor. He saw sympathy in the eyes of some. "A group of us have gained a small piece of surface. On it, we hope to sustain ourselves, sharing all things in common. You have asked me to choose between carrying out this mission and my family. I have made my choice. I have renounced all ties to my former home. They have banished me at my request. Here are the documents you requested. Let me live and work in peace."

By this time, he had turned full around and handed the parchments to Sir Reese.

"Who else speaks in this one's behalf before we vote?" asked Sir Reese.

"I do," Sir Rafael shouted from his place.

"Advance and be recognized," Young Reese announced.

Sir Rafael moved forward and stood beside Henry.

Young Reese said, "This assembly recognizes Sir Rafael, Chief Archaeologist for Organized Roacheria."

"You may begin," said The Supreme Executor.

"Esteemed colleagues," Sir Rafael began. "I have a lot to say, so I hope you are comfortable. If you don't like my back, that's too bad I will stand in one place. I've been in this chamber a good many season cycles longer than most of you. I've seen more than one Supreme Executor come and go, some wise and some not. I hope this assembly has wisdom similar to those who sat here fifty-eight season cycles ago in the 221st season cycle of Organized Roacheria."

He looked toward the back, where the youngest Board Members sat, and directed his statement at them. "Most of you weren't alive yet. Some of your parents would remember. I was a nymph of ten. That was the season cycle Board Members had the good sense to end hostilities between the Combined Colonies and us. That was the season cycle some had the intelligence to realize that Master Henrietta was correct when she said that the Duo Pods had destroyed their world and poisoned it so completely that they could no longer survive in it. Board Members listened when my father presented Master Henrietta's theory that our own path of technology could result in the same end. Board Members then had the courage to listen to scientists and better plan the use of our environment, not because they cared so much about others, but that they wanted their own posterity to continue to live as they did. So, we abandoned our desire to reproduce the fuels and poisons of a past that destroyed itself. Back then, Board Members chose to learn from the failure of the Duo Pods as a species."

He turned his attention to Sir Reese once again and continued. "You are well aware of my continuing research with Master Donna in New South Dairy 50. As my father learned to read their symbols from Master Henrietta, so he taught me. I, too, became fascinated with Duo Pod culture and demise. For the last several season cycles, I have concentrated on their tendency toward violent conflict. I found another dimension to Master Henrietta's theory.

"They not only laid waste to vast areas of vegetation, poisoned the land and water with chemicals, and the air with fumes from burning fuels, all of which set off changes in the atmosphere and climate. They also made war in such fearful ways that you would not believe it unless you had seen the images I have seen. Their weapons were not mandibles or a fire ant's deadly sting. Their wars, at the end, were not pod to pod struggles, facing one's enemy. No, they killed with explosions and disease over vast distances, wiping out whole cities at once, leaving the craters of devastation we find so often when exploring for plastic. Much of what we assumed to be natural disaster caused by meteors, was instead Duo Pod made disaster."

A ripple of voices went through the chamber. Sir Rafael stopped and waited for it to die down before he continued. "Some of you are wondering, what has all this got to do with us? Plenty! Many of the Duo Pods were motivated by greed and selfishness, as some of you are now. There were several varieties of them, just as there are different types of ants and roaches. But they got so caught up in their differences, in the variations of shade of their outer covering, their particular type of spiritual philosophy, the region in which they lived, or the clan to which they belonged, that they forgot they were all Duo Pods."

He looked directly at one member Henry knew hated ants and slender roaches and said, "Sounds familiar, doesn't it?"

He turned back to the group as a whole. "Their hatred of anyone who was not like their particular type, resulted in the many violent conflicts which destroyed them.

"We have a choice to make today. We can remember that, whether large, small, or mixed roach, or ant, we are all Insecta Sapiens. Or we can continue in our hate, destroying ourselves as they did. What kind of creatures will dig us up and unravel the mystery of our demise many thousands of season cycles from now?

"Master Donna has been studying the various spiritual philosophies of the Duo Pods. She sent me this by special courier yesterday. It's a quote from one of their many books of spiritual guidance:

'Idler, go to the ant. Ponder its ways and grow wise. No one gives her orders, no overseer, no master. Yet all through the summer she makes sure of her food and gathers her supplies at harvest time.'

"It's a shame they didn't listen to their own philosophers. But then, if they had, they might still be here and not us."

Henry saw many members look at each other as Sir Rafael's words sank in. Sir Rafael moved closer to Henry, placed one pod on the back of his thorax.

"All this courageous, selfless young male wants is to show you a better way. He has given up his most precious possession, the cherishing members of his family. Give him his chance. I also ask you to allow two ants, Donald and Dell, from South Dairy 50 to join him. Both are experienced dairiers and would teach the fine points of food production to his group and others. Since they are ants, they are obviously not part of Henry's immediate family, though Dell is distantly related to Master Henrietta, may her Essence rest. They offer to pay the same price that Henry did, if you require it."

He looked at Sir Reese and said, "Esteemed Supreme Executor, may I propose a change in procedure before we vote on this matter?"

"I will listen to your request," Sir Reese replied.

"We all know how this works. Each of us decides whether the personal cost will be greater if we side with enemy or friend. We know many here do not vote what they really feel for fear of reprisal. Let us remove that from this vote and do something we have never done before. Some of the Duo Pods voted in secret when they chose leaders. Let us each take the same kind of parchment, mark it only 'x' if in favor of Henry's plan, including the two ants, 'o' if opposed. We will all put one fold. You may count the parchments. No one need fear the consequences of his choice. That's all I have to say." He smiled at Henry and returned to his place.

Murmurs spread through the chamber. Henry caught snatches from those near him. They echoed real fears in regard to what had happened to Sir Rubin as a result of his support of an earlier controversial vote that failed to pass.

Sir Rubin shouted from the back. "Sir Reese, order it as he suggests, in secret. Too many have paid the price I did, losing a mate and nearly ourselves. Let us not return to the ways some Members used to control others in the past."

The din increased. Sir Reese rose and lifted a pod for silence.

"Enough," he said and pointed to an attendant. "Bring unmarked parchment, enough for all. We will do as Sir Rafael suggests."

The Supreme Executor asked Henry to leave the chamber and wait in the outer court while the voting took place. Henry paced nervously up and down the outer passage for what seemed like a very long time.

Finally, an attendant called him. He returned to the center of the chamber and stood before Sir Reese once more.

Sir Reese said, "Henry Roach-Dairier, you are granted full privileges under the previously stated conditions. The vote was two thirds in your favor. The other two may come as guest residents for one season cycle. Then we will reevaluate their status and listen to their request if they wish to stay longer."

*   *   *   *

Gladness swirled through the conversation in Rick's parlor, as those who would begin Meadow Commonwealth sat in a circle around a woven thistledown cloth covered with food.

"Wonderful feast," Rick said. "Genelle and Ruth, you out-did yourselves."

Genelle said, "You know how much I enjoy preparing food for a group. Maybe we should do this all the time when we've moved out there. Ruth is so good at finding bargains in the markets. We really didn't spend much and she was a great help preparing it."

"Yes," Ruth put in. "You'll all be tired after a day of work and a long walk home. We could prepare a group meal every evening. We could also care for all the nymphs during the day. Could that be our job, Henry?"

"Of course, if that's what you want," Henry said. "I think all of us who already have jobs for credit in the city should stick with those jobs. We'll put all our earnings together to purchase plastic and other necessities for the group as a whole."

"I'm used to working with figures and invoices from my job in the Trade Center," Rusty put in. "I could keep track of our funds. It wouldn't take long in the evenings."

"Good idea," said Rick. "You could plan out what we think we'll need and we could put in our requests."

"Shouldn't we all be part of that process?" Rick's son, Ray asked.

"Of course," Henry said, "but Rusty could set it up for us to discuss. That would save us all a lot of time. If we have a problem with any of it, we will work it out together, remembering our priorities. Plastic and the other needs of the young come first, then basic needs for all of us, extras last. We must remember to keep an emergency fund as well, not that there will be much in it in the beginning."

All agreed. Rick passed the platter of fly eggs around again and Genelle cut pieces of the honey cake Henry had taught her to make when he first came to live with them as a trainee.

"Should I keep working with Rundell in the shop?" Georgette asked.

"You better," Rundell said. "I need you more than ever and you know the delivery route. You won't have to carry your nymphs' safety cage any more. They can stay with Genelle and Ruth. Pass the jug of ale, please."

Gatlin's mate, Gabby, asked, "Henry, when will your two ant cousins arrive? Could they train me to work with the grasshoppers and aphids since I don't have other work?"

"Could I, too?" Rick's mate, Ramona put in, before Henry could answer. "Since Ruth and Genelle offered to take care of all the nymphs."

Henry nodded. "Dell and Donald will be good mentors and both speak fairly good Roach. You'll like them. They'll come in the spring when we have the dwellings built, bringing our starting herds. That about settles our work assignments. We'll all have to help with the grassfronds and other produce on sixthdays. There's one other job, an unpleasant one, removing body waste from the storage receptacles in each dwelling, and carting it to compost bins. This season cycle's waste is next season cycle's fertilizer."

The chamber fell silent.

"Don't all volunteer at once," Henry joked.

"How about drawing lots?" Ray suggested.

"No," Georgette said. "That wouldn't be fair. We all have a lot to do. We should take turns. Then no one is stuck with it all the time."

Positive murmurs rippled through the group.

"Are all of you willing to put in time sixthdays and seventhdays to break the ground and cut blocks of meadow grass? I know none of us can be there all of both days, but we should start building soon. Rick, how long will you be able to live here after your brother gives you the credit for this domicile?"

"He said we can stay here until the first of the fourth time frame," Rick answered. "I can work most of both days."

"I can help both days," Ruth said. "My parents can help on seventhday afternoons, and they'll work however they are needed, but the one who wants our domicile said we have to move out before he gives us the credit. Could we build our home first?"

"No need for that," Rick said. "You and your family move in here. We'll make room. This domicile will hold us all for a short time."

"Thank you," Ruth said. "They'll be glad when I tell them."

"How is your little brother?" Henry asked, knowing that the nymph's illness (an infection of the breathing organs similar to the one Henry's grandmother had died of) had kept Ruth's parents from joining them.

"He's doing better, thanks to the pressure you put on the clinic to give him the mold treatment in spite of our status. And, oh, I almost forgot. Grandpa Gallo says you better find something he can do. I know there isn't much, but he wants to feel needed."

"Do you think he could help weave reed mats with only touch?" Ray asked. "We'll be making a lot of them to separate chambers inside our dwellings. I might be able to teach him how to do that. Even if he does it wrong and someone else does it over, we won't tell him. Agreed?"

Ruth nodded and laughed. Everyone joined her. Major decisions made, they finished the honey cake and meditated together, filled with hope for the new life that lay ahead of them.

16.

*B*y the middle of the third time frame, the members of Meadow Commonwealth had cut all the blocks of sod, completed the Common Building (so all had some shelter in bad weather) and planted grassfronds. Two domiciles stood on one side of the Common Building.

Blocks of grass lay in rows like the synthetic stones of Duo Pod ruins (Master Rafael had told them that was why those old walls had stood so long) rising seven f-units above the ground on one side, five on the other. Wood beams covered with more earth formed slanted roofs on the domiciles. Each had one portal made of a wooden slab and a wall opening on each side. Shutters, which they would decorate later, covered the wall openings.

The Common Building stood twice as tall as the domiciles. Thirty f-units wide, and fifty long, it had four wall openings on each of the longer sides and a wide, double portal in one end. The other end had a narrow portal. They had been able to purchase enough metal slabs for the roof to cover wooden beams placed two f-units apart. A layer of earth covered the metal.

The weather on regular work days always seemed to be good, but constant drizzle stopped their construction several sixthdays and seventhdays. In half a time frame, they would no longer have Rick's domicile. They sat in the Common Building, eating lunch and discussing the situation.

Rundell said, "Since Rick let many us live in his home, he should have one of the finished domiciles now. Henry, you and I could live in the shop for a while."

"Yes, we can," Henry replied. "Richard and Ginger, their nymphs, and Gallo should have the other, even though the inside walls aren't quite finished."

The others nodded.

"I suppose I could stay in my rented chamber a while longer," said Rusty, "but I'll have to continue to keep the fee for it before I give the rest of my credit to the common fund."

Rick looked around the group. "If Ray and Ramona share our quarters until we finish another domicile, there will be fewer in here."

"We've got to dig the underground shelter right away," Henry added.

Rusty protested. "Why? Can't Donald and Dell live in the Common Building like everyone else? Or wait a bit longer to come?"

"It's not simply Dell and Donald," Henry explained. "Larvae are very sensitive to sun light. They must be underground. They can be out for a few h-units, but not all the time. With all the wall openings we put in here, we can't block out enough sunlight for full-time larvae care. In addition, their mound will be our fungus garden and summer storm shelter. The storm season will be upon us before we know it. Dell and Donald must come soon and establish the herd. If we wait any longer, The Board may recant their permission to come. We couldn't help the sky water this winter, Rusty."

Grudgingly, Rusty agreed. They divided into groups. Rick, Ray, Ramona, and Gatlin would begin another domicile. Henry, Rusty, and Richard would start digging. The others would keep weaving chamber dividers.

Two h-units later, Georgette brought honey dew and muffins to the diggers. They plopped down to rest.

Rusty took several large gulps then chewed on a muffin. "I'm tired of hauling baskets."

"I'll trade," Henry offered. "You dig for a while and I'll haul dirt."

"I'm tired of hauling. I'm tired of all of it," Rusty complained. "This isn't what I was expecting! I thought our lives were supposed to get easier. I'm working harder than I ever have in my life. How do I even know I'll like fungus!"

"Do you like the muffin you're eating?" Henry asked.

"What's that got to do with anything?"

"The meal used to make it is dried, ground fungus," Henry replied.

Rusty stared at the muffin and then at Henry.

Richard smiled and looked away.

"Well, we're still working way too much," Rusty said, even more sullenly. "My legs ache all day on firstdays. I can barely do my regular job."

Henry sat silently for a few moments and placed one pod gently on Rusty's thorax. "I told everyone the first season cycle would be difficult. I said it would be better in the long run, not easier. No one is bound to me, Rusty. No one has to stay against their will."

"I didn't say I wanted to leave."

"Then what's really wrong?" Henry asked.

Rusty looked at him angrily. "I lost the female I wanted. Because of this place!"

"What female? You've never said anything."

Richard rose quietly and went back to digging, leaving Henry and Rusty alone.

"I wanted to keep it to myself," Rusty said. "I figured we had enough problems out here for now. I met her at the lunch stand in the Trade Center. She was working there. I got to know her and started to spend my break times with her. I planned to see her father later this spring, take him a proposal maybe in the summer. I told her about being part of this group. Her father acted quickly and bound her to someone else. I never even got a chance to see him." Rusty stared at the ground.

Henry patted the back of his thorax. "I don't know what to say. But I'm sorry."

Rusty pounded the ground with one front pod. "I keep telling myself to forget it. But I can't. It hurts, you know? I never thought anything could hurt me like that." He looked into Henry's face.

Henry met his gaze silently, saw the anger and sorrow there.

Rusty opened his mandibles as if to begin a curse, stopped, then sighed. "That's how you feel all the time, isn't it?"

Henry's antennae twitched and he clenched his mandibles together. He avoided the subject of his family most of the time, reading "Rick's" letters privately and grieving alone. He nodded. The two embraced each other.

*   *   *   *

Enforcers began watching the group the day Dell and Donald arrived. They said it was to insure the proper delivery of the herds purchased from South Dairy 50, since permission had been granted to by-pass the Trade Center. After that, their excuse had been, "We've heard rumors of threats toward your group. You deserve the same protection as those in the city."

Henry knew the real reason. They watched his every move, hoping he would violate his agreement in some small way. He knew his enemies on The Board paid these Enforcers extra to continue their harassing vigil. Henry hoped they would give it up in time.

Spring turned to summer. The grassfronds grew tall. With a bit of sweet bait laid in a trail, a swarm of bees found their way from New South Dairy 50 to a hive Henry and Donald built a quarter d-unit from the border stream.

Dell and Donald enlarged their mound as the fungus patches grew. They also dug several bins to store the fall harvest. By Summer Solstice, the group had accumulated enough extra credit to purchase a sizeable cold storage unit, enabling them to store cooked grasshopper for a longer time. They no longer gorged themselves for five or six days and then went without meat for the rest of the time frame, although they continued to dry some each time they roasted a hopper. Installing the cold storage unit, and its accompanying lightning bug energy fabricator, was the highlight of their first Summer Solstice festival.

Ruth and Rundell's first egg hatched and they celebrated new life. Although all still worked hard, the pace was less hectic and the group looked forward to their first harvest with great expectations.

"I'm headed for the bee hive," Henry said one seventhday.

"Be careful," Rusty said, as he took apart a partition Gallo had done and began to weave it over again. It was the final room divider for the domicile Henry and Rusty shared.

"I will." Henry picked up a small satchel and the honey jug and headed out across the meadow. No one had objected when Henry offered to be the bee keeper. The others could have done it just as easily, but they knew Henry needed the time alone. He appreciated their thoughtfulness.

He remembered the first time his grandfather had taken him to gather honey. "Draw in all your joints," Antony had told the eight season cycle-old nymph, "so your hard plates form solid armor that the bees can't penetrate."

Henry saw the Enforcer as he reached the hive. "Pond scum," he muttered to himself. They had now intruded upon the one activity he had managed to keep private. He filled the honey jug, then stood, gazing westward, debating whether to go on or return home. He decided to go on. They would not take this time from him.

The Enforcer followed, slipping from behind one wood plant or bush to the next.

Henry turned and shouted. "If you must pry into every aspect of my life, do it beside me! I'm tired of your sneaking around behind my thorax."

The surprised Enforcer came closer. "What?"

"I know why you're here," Henry said bluntly. "You want to see if I'm about to violate my agreement with The Board. Well, I'm tired of pretending I don't know you're there. So quit sneaking along behind me and come with me openly."

He walked briskly right to the edge of the border stream. The Enforcer scuttled along, slightly behind.

"Sit down," Henry commanded. "I could go down the bank if I wanted. I could even go half way across the stream, but the bank satisfies me."

He set down the honey jug and took the images of his family from his satchel, and laid them in front of himself. "I took these before the banishment," he explained, "and there is nothing you or those who sent you can do to prevent me from sitting here, looking at them and meditating whenever I choose to. So sit beside me and listen. You might surprise yourself and learn something."

The stunned Enforcer did as Henry told him.

Henry touched each image gently. He closed his eyes and imagined his parents. In silence, he reached out and embraced air in the shape of their bodies. He imagined he was stroking them, and they him. He let his tears flow freely, for he knew that each time he emptied himself of the longing, it took less time to do so. The emptiness grew easier to bear. He knew that if he persisted, peace would come.

When he had no more tears, he lifted his front pods toward the sky and meditated out loud. "Essence of Wisdom, You sent the vision again last night as I slept. I still do not understand all of it. Who are all of the faces that I see in the dream? I only recognize a few. Have they all gone before me? Or are there some who have yet to come? I recognize more than before, because I have searched for images in the Archives. Now, I have no access to antstoric images. Essence, tell me who they are somehow. Let me understand the purpose of the one who stands apart. Is he past or future?"

Henry remained silent for several minutes. He breathed deeply and opened his eyes. He looked steadily across to the opposite bank. Each seventhday, he wished someone from New South Dairy 50 would happen to be there. He knew it would not happen. That would violate the agreement. He had told Sir Rafael very specifically where he would sit and at what time, so he could relay to all members of the colony that they should never be within sight when Henry came here to meditate.

Henry spoke in meditation again. "Essence, comfort my family as You comfort me. Let them see me in dreams, as I see them. Guide my choices and help me continue to prosper here. Let my openness touch others with understanding, that hatred may end and friendship grow in its place."

Henry lowered his pods, picked up the images and returned them to his satchel. He looked into the eyes of the Enforcer. "Tell those who sent you that Henry Roach-Dairier knows how to follow regulations and keeps agreements. Tell them there is no need to intrude upon his private meditation."

He turned and walked home, leaving the stunned Enforcer sitting on the bank of the border stream.

*   *   *   *

The storm hit in the middle of harvest time. Many season cycles had passed without a major storm hitting their area. This season, several had occurred in other parts of Roacheria along the sea coast to their east and south. The Board had sent credit, but only to rebuild government structures.

Henry was sitting with a client when he felt the tingling sensation throughout his body about mid-afternoon. He remembered it from a storm during his youth. Everyone in the colony had scrambled to bring as many hoppers and aphids underground as possible. Most of the creatures left to fend for themselves outside the mound had been lost.

"Go home quickly," Henry said to his client. "Take shelter in some ruin. Don't stay in your flimsy domicile."

The young female stared at him, not understanding.

"Don't you feel it?"

She nodded.

"That tingling means we'll be hit with a severe storm within the next two h-units. Leave now! Find shelter for your family," he repeated.

She dashed out the door.

Rundell was out collecting eggs. Henry hoped he would head straight for home.

"Georgette," he shouted. "Help me bolt the shutters quickly. Hopefully, they will prevent major damage to the shop, if it stands up to the wind."

The two of them finished in a few moments.

"Henry, I'm afraid. What about the others? Do we have time to get back home?"

"I think so, if we run our fastest. Donald and Dell will have directed the others already. Everyone should be underground when we get there. Hopefully, those who work in the city will head straight home, as we are."

Sky water began falling in torrents before they reached Meadow Commonwealth. Georgette slipped several times and panicked. Henry pulled her along. "Keep moving! Take my pod! It's only a little further."

Slipping and stumbling in the blinding wind and sky water, they continued toward the safety of the underground shelter. They had to crawl the last quarter d-unit.

Still tugging on the now hysterical Georgette, Henry banged on the portal. A gust of wind plastered them against the portal. Henry pulled both of them to the edge, so their friends inside could open it and let them in.

"Give me your pod!" he heard Donald shout as the portal opened a crack.

Henry shoved Georgette toward the opening. Donald grabbed her and pulled her inside while Ramona and Gabby pushed against the portal to keep it open. Another gust of wind blew it shut, catching Georgette's back pod. She screamed as the heavy wood crushed the tip of her pod. Henry held on to the latch with all his strength as the next gust came on a slight angle. He fought to keep the wind from sweeping him away.

Genelle joined Ramona and Gabby. With their combined strength, they managed to hold the portal against the wind long enough for Donald to pull Henry inside.

"Is everyone else here?" Henry panted as he picked himself up.

Donald shook his head. "You two are the only ones back from the city so far. We can only hope they make it, or have found good shelter somewhere. We got all the breeding pairs in, but not the rest of the herds. All of us who were out here are safe."

"Donald, where is the plaster? Georgette's pod isn't too bad," Dell called to him. "I can set and plaster it if you help me."

"It's in the storage cupboard in our sanitation area. I'll get it. Have someone make tea and put extra sleeping herbs in it. Get her calmed down first." He left Henry and hurried across the large open chamber.

Genelle and Gabby hovered over the injured Georgette. Ramona rejoined Genelle and Gallo as they tried to keep all the nymphs calm. Ginger and Ruth pushed the hoppers and aphids back into their pen. Three had jumped out when the portal opened.

Henry heard a faint yell and hurried to the portal. Pushing against the wind once more, Henry, Ginger, Ruth, and Ramona managed to rescue Rick and Gatlin before the wind swept them away from the mound. Both were exhausted but uninjured. Only Ray, Rusty and Rundell remained unaccounted for.

"The thistledown plant is very strong," Ramona rationalized. "Ray probably decided it would be better to stay there."

"Rundell was out collecting," Henry said. "He'll find shelter somewhere. He's good at thinking quickly. As a nymph in the last storm, he dragged his mother into an old Duo Pod tunnel."

"What about Rusty?" Richard asked. "The Trade Center is so open."

"Yes," Rick said, "but they close it quickly whenever there is any threat of a bad storm. I think they require the workers to stay in a shelter near it, so they can come out as soon as a storm passes and guard what goods are left in the Center. All we can do is wait."

As the storm raged on, they took turns calming the nymphs into a fitful sleep, quieting the aphids and hoppers, watching over Georgette, lifting up thoughts for the safety of the others, and trying to rest. A little after midnight, the roaring stopped. An eerie quiet replaced it.

"Is it over?" Ruth asked.

Rick shook his antennae. "Only half has passed. It will be calm for a while, perhaps even an h-unit. Then the winds will begin again in full furry from the other direction. Sometimes the second half is worse than the first."

"Maybe we could go and search for Ray and the others," Ramona suggested, twisting her front pods over and over each other.

Richard and Ginger moved close to comfort her.

"No," Richard said. "In the darkness, it would be hard to say when the calm might end. It's far better for us all to stay here, where we're dry and safe."

Dell handed Ruth a cup of tea, then carried a second mug to Ramona. "I'm sure all of them are fine. Drink this and try to sleep."

The two worried females had almost dropped off to sleep when Henry heard the thumping and muffled cries for help. He scuttled to the portal and opened it. Ray and Rusty staggered in.

"Praise The Essence! It's dry in here!" Ray burst out.

Ramona wrapped herself around her mate. The others brought them woven thistledown coverlets and handed them steaming mugs of honey dew.

"You took an awful chance traveling in the lull," Richard said, "but thank goodness you're both all right."

"Did you see Rundell anywhere?" Ruth asked.

Ray shook his antennae. "As soon as the lull hit, I left the weaving plant. I'd timed the storm from the start. I guessed that if the quiet area was about the same as other recorded storms, and it moved the way others have, I could make it here, if I ran my fastest. I had to swim through several low areas."

Rusty pulled the cloth tighter around himself. "The overseers at the Trade Center didn't want anyone to leave when the lull began. Finally, since I'm not large enough to help in defending the trade goods— whatever might be left—from marauders, they let me leave."

As suddenly as it had stopped, the roaring began again. Ruth, beside herself with anxiety for her mate, wept. Near dawn, her mother finally got her to sleep.

By morning, the worst was over, though sky water still fell steadily. Dell, Donald, and Henry told the others to remain inside while they assessed the damage. The two ants headed into the meadows to see how many hoppers and aphids had survived and the condition of the crops. Henry headed for their domiciles.

He picked up a shutter that had blown off the Common Building and headed there first. All the shutters were gone. Sky water had blown in the openings, leaving much of the inside soggy, but the structure stood sound. He could see a few other portals and shutters across the meadows and wondered how many they would actually find. The last two domiciles built (Henry and Rusty's, and Ruth and Rundell's) had flatter roofs than the others did. Sky water had saturated them instead of running off. Both roofs had fallen in. The other domiciles stood firm, though things inside dripped where sky water had blown in through wall openings.

Henry looked up to see Rundell plodding toward him. He ran to embrace his friend.

"I was so worried about you. Ruth was hysterical. Where did you find shelter?" Henry asked.

"In the Duo Pod ruin near the refuse piles. Is everyone all right? Did the others make it back here? Things look pretty good here. The city is a shambles. Low areas are all flooded."

"Georgette broke her back pod when the wind blew the portal shut on it, but Dell plastered it. She'll be fine. Dell and Donald are out in the meadows. They only managed to get the breeding pairs underground. As you can see, we've got a lot of damage, but it's repairable." Henry supported the exhausted Rundell as they entered the mound. He woke Ruth and sent the reunited pair into Dell and Donald's sleep chamber, knowing the two ants wouldn't mind.

Dell and Donald returned a little while later. "It will be a long winter and spring with no meat, and little honey dew," Dell reported. "Only three hoppers and two aphids survived. The others are crushed beneath fallen wood plants where they must have tried to shelter themselves."

"Can we salvage any of the meat?" Henry asked. "The cold storage unit and other equipment in the Common Building are fine. We could roast a lot now and dry some."

Donald shook his head. "Maybe a little, but most of it's only fit for fertilizer. Our crop of grassfronds is ruined as well. We might be able to dry some of the seed, but I'm afraid a lot will mold if we don't get it gathered immediately. We must preserve some for next spring's planting. I don't know about the bees. We didn't go that far."

A long sigh rippled through the group.

Henry reported the damage to the buildings and then said, "We should lift up our thoughts in meditation and be thankful we're all safe and the damage to our homes is light. We'll pull together and be fine."

"Be fine! Be thankful?" Rusty yelled. "We've no food! I don't want to live in this stinking hole in the ground! We have practically no credit in reserve! I can't take this any more. I'm leaving. You're all crazy if you stay here." He stormed out of the mound before anyone could stop him.

Henry looked around at the others. "If anyone else feels the same, I'll understand. If you think I've wronged you, take any recourse you must, but choose now. As for me, I've nothing else. I will rebuild here, or die trying."

Rick looked at Henry. "I may have fewer possessions, but I've known more peace of mind in the last several time frames than I ever had in my life. I'm with you, Henry. I always will be."

The others nodded in agreement.

Henry looked at Dell and Donald. "What should we do first to salvage the most?" he asked.

Dell responded. "Two of you come with me. Bring baskets and we'll get as much of the meat as we can. Donald, you and one other stay here to care for Georgette, our larvae, and the nymphs. The rest, get baskets and gather grassfrond seeds."

17.

*T*he more prestigious dwellings in the city of Roacheria stood on higher ground, well away from areas that flooded. During the second portion of the storm, within one of them, a young, adult female lay writhing in her mother's pods. Her screams rose above the howling wind.

A large male leaned over the injured female. "Rebecca, you've got to hold her still. I must pull the broken parts of her back appendage apart to set it. She's making it worse moving. I don't have the proper equipment here, and there's no getting it now."

"Regina, you must lie still. Your father is the best physician in the city, but he can't help you if you keep squirming," Rebecca said to her frightened daughter.

In all her sixteen, sheltered season cycles, Regina had never imagined such pain was possible. She gripped her mother's thorax, shrieking in an effort to do as her mother asked. She heard a snap and lost consciousness.

When she opened her eyes again, light streamed through the wall opening. Her eyes met her mother's.

"Drink this potion," Rebecca said to her daughter. "It has herbs for the pain. It was probably best you passed out. The plaster is already dry. You're going to be fine. Your father says you'll be dancing by Last Night."

Regina emptied the mug and looked around. She lay on a padded parlor bench that had been pushed against an inside wall. Across the chamber, pieces of shattered shutters and shreds of the cloth that had adorned the wall openings littered soggy, woven floor mats. She looked fearfully at her mother.

"It's all right now," her mother assured her. "The storm is over."

Her father entered the chamber. "Rebecca, your brother is at the front entrance. He wants to see you."

Rebecca gave her mate a shocked look and rose from the stool beside Regina. "I'll be right back," she said, patting Regina's thorax.

Regina slumped back onto the cushion as her father came near. He reached out awkwardly and touched the top of her head. "Are you feeling better?" he asked.

Regina nodded weakly.

"You should have stayed away from the wall opening. I tried to tell you."

"I'm sorry."

"Never mind." Regina's father paced the chamber, muttering curses as he looked at the damage.

Rebecca ran in sobbing. "My father is dead. My mother is injured. Please, just this once, Robert, help my mother. Go with my brother and bring her here. Please! Just this once. Both my brothers' domiciles are ruined. In all these season cycles, I've never asked you for anything for them."

Regina watched her mother lower herself in humility before her father. Her mother had taught her from early nymphood that this was the way a proper female asked her mate for anything.

Robert let out a disgusted sigh. "All right, I'll go with him. They can stay here with the servants in the lower level, but only for a few days. Then they must make other arrangements. I have my reputation to consider. I don't want it getting out that I'm sheltering skinnies. Make sure they keep out of sight."

Rebecca pressed herself against her mate's back pods. "Thank you," she whispered.

"I'll be going straight to the clinic after that. There will be a lot of business. This sort of thing is actually good for me. I'll request Enforcers for you since I probably won't be home much for several days. Keep Regina here in this chamber the rest of today. Give her more of the pain potion every three or four h-units. Make sure she's never alone, especially after I have workers sent to fix this mess. I don't want some vagabond worker getting eyes for her. You can move her to the back parlor tomorrow. I'll put your mother there, too. Make sure none of the workers ever see her. Get up."

Rebecca rose slowly.

Robert strode from the chamber. "Don't let anyone go up to the second level. The whole roof has caved in."

"You told me your family was dead," Regina said to her mother when they were alone.

Rebecca sighed. "I don't want to go into it, but I'll tell you this much. My mother is slender. My father was very large and I got most of his size. I always passed for large. Your father hates slenders and mixes. You were never supposed to know about them."

Regina stared at her mother. "But if he hates ... and you are ... then why?"

Rebecca cut off the conversation. Her voice was sharp. "I told you, I don't want to go into it! Now drink this. You need to sleep."

*   *   *   *

Regina slept a long time. When she woke, she found someone had moved her into the back parlor, which had escaped storm damage. Her mother stood across the chamber, her back to Regina, tending someone else.

"You're strong, mother," Rebecca said, "very strong for your age. You're going to be fine. Robert says the fracture in your abdomen is small. He only used a little plaster. I'll get your domicile fixed. I have some funds of my own I've put aside. He won't even know."

"Don't fret over me. I'll get by. I always have. How I will miss your father, though." Her voice trailed off.

Rebecca leaned over her mother and started crying. Regina lay very still and watched. The ancient female lying on the cushion (which Regina now realized was the grandmother she had not known existed) did something Regina had never seen before. Although she was much smaller and more slender than Regina's mother, she encircled Rebecca with her front pods and swept them slowly upward over the back of her thorax and on up to the very tip of Rebecca's antennae. Over and over she repeated the movement until Regina's mother stopped crying.

"I'm sorry. I should be the one helping you, but here you are, touching me in the wonderful way you did when I was only a nymph. I'd forgotten how it felt," Regina heard her mother say.

Rebecca turned. Regina closed her eyes quickly and pretended to be asleep.

"I suppose you never passed that on to my granddaughter, either?"

Regina's mother was silent.

"I thought so," the old one said. "Sometimes I regret binding you to him."

"Don't say that, mother. Robert has been a very decent mate. Much better than some. He's never violated the contract. I'm sorry he treats you so badly, and won't let you be a part of our lives, but he can be quite decent when he wants to. You did deceive him, after all. In spite of it, he's never abused me or Regina."

"He wouldn't dare," the old one said. "That was the best part of what you refer to as deceit. We did it to protect you. It worked, too. You should be glad of it. It got you a good life." The voice dropped to a whisper. "And settled an old score."

"What?" Rebecca asked.

"Nothing. My old mind rambles." She changed the subject. "When may I finally meet Regina?"

"I'll wake her now. Please, don't tell her why ... at least not yet."

Regina lay very still. When her mother shook her, she sighed and opened her eyes slowly. "What time is it?" she asked.

"Late afternoon. The potion worked well. You never even flinched when the servants moved you in here. Let me push the rolling couch over here. I want you to meet your grandmother."

Rebecca rolled Regina's bed several f-units across the chamber. "Regina, this is your grandmother. She's lived far away all these season cycles. That's why you've never seen her before. She only arrived the day before the storm and hadn't gotten a chance to come here, yet."

Regina accepted the flimsy excuse. She looked at her grandmother. Her exoskeleton was lined with age, yet there was a spark of mystery in her eyes. She lay on a floor cushion placed on top of a low table. A narrow patch of white plaster covered perhaps an f-unit on the back of her abdomen. Regina nodded politely. "I'm glad to know you. I'm sorry I can't bow properly right now."

"Never mind that," said her grandmother. "I never thought I'd see this day. You are even lovelier than your mother was at your age."

The conversation of stilted pleasantries continued, with Regina concealing what she'd overheard, determined to find out the truth.

*   *   *   *

Rebecca insisted on tending her mother and her daughter herself, not allowing the servants to enter. The following morning, Robert finally returned to his family. He strode into the chamber and greeted his mate formally.

"Workers will arrive tomorrow to begin the repairs," he said. "Keep doing as you are, not allowing anyone in here. Where are your brothers?"

"They went back to see about repairing their own places," Rebecca replied.

"Good. The less I see of them the better." He turned his attention to Regina. "You should be able to move about now. It's not easy, but you should be able to get around on five legs. Roll over. I'm going to bind the injured appendage up against your thorax."

Regina did as instructed. Her father finished binding her leg and helped her off her bed. She stood helplessly.

"Put your front pods down," he directed.

"Use my front pods on the floor?"

"No, on the wall, silly female, put them down!"

Regina had never used her front pods for anything but eating, writing, or sculpting with her tutors. The floor felt strange. "Ouch!" she cried as the tip of her right-front pod touched a rough spot on the wood floor.

Robert gave her an exasperated look. "Stay on the floor covering then," he said. "Rebecca, you've spoiled her completely."

"She's of high rank. You'll find her a good mate and she'll never have to worry about anything but looking pretty," Rebecca said.

Robert turned away from his daughter and approached Rebecca's mother. He examined her quickly and asked, "Are you feeling better, Rochelle?"

"Yes, thank you, Master Robert. I appreciate your kindness after all I . . ."

He cut her off. "That's gone by. Don't speak of it."

Rochelle nodded. "Very well. Shall I try to move about?"

"Yes." He helped the old female onto her pods. "Be careful. Don't twist your abdomen in any way."

When she had walked across the chamber and back, he helped her onto the pallet once more. "Exercise a little each day," he said, then turned to his mate. "Make sure you help her, Rebecca."

Rebecca tipped her antennae.

"When will I be able to leave?" Rochelle asked.

"Any time you want, as long as someone stays with you and you have decent shelter. Come to my clinic in two time frames and I'll remove the plaster. But," he paused, "you can stay here until then if you'd rather."

Regina caught a look of gladness in her mother's eye and one of relief in her grandmother's. Robert turned to leave.

"I've got to go back to the clinic. I must have plastered two hundred fractures in the last two days. I have a couple of trainees helping tend them, but it's not enough."

"Where are all the medical attendants?" Rebecca asked.

"The roof and one outer wall of the main medical facility collapsed. Several were killed. Be glad you can stay here, sheltered. This has been the worst storm in seventy-five season cycles."

Rebecca put her pods to her mandibles. "Oh, Robert ..."

"Quit worrying over others. I'll be twice as rich when this is over."

*   *   *   *

Henry and Rick struggled to remove the broken roof support from Henry's domicile. The group had salvaged all the food they could.

Grassfrond seeds lay all over the floor of the Common Building, drying before being stored. Dell and Donald had recommended leaving the wettest seeds in the fields, in hopes that they would germinate voluntarily in the spring. Their sodden belongings lay over strands of twisted hemp strung between their homes, drying in the sun.

"It's too heavy, Henry," Rick said. "We need more help."

"Everyone else is busy reattaching shutters."

A voice came from behind. "I'll help."

Henry and Rick turned. There stood Rusty. They stared at him.

"I insulted you and everyone. I was wrong," Rusty said. "Please, forgive me. I'd like to come back, if you'll still have me." He stood awkwardly.

Henry would have reached out to him immediately, but Rick spoke first. "Why the change of heart? Suddenly we're not crazy anymore?"

"I don't blame you if you feel that way. I spoke in frustration and anger. I left thinking I'd find everything all right in the city. I found out we fared much better here. Hundreds were killed, hundreds more are injured. The city is in chaos."

Rick glared. "We've heard. Enforcers came not long after you left to inform us that all regular business and job activity would be suspended for at least a quarter time frame. We were instructed to remain here until further notice. How were you able to come back?"

"I know how to get around when I have to. Please, will you take me back?"

"Grab the end of this beam with us," Henry said. "We have to pull it all down before rebuilding. Then we'll make one wall higher so the roof has a better pitch, like the others that didn't fall in."

By sundown, all the debris had been cleared. Rusty apologized to the entire group at supper. They were glad to have him back.

*   *   *   *

Regina reassured her mother. "I'll be fine for a little while. You can check on the repair workers if you like."

Rebecca hesitated. "Are you sure? I may be gone for an h-unit. Is there anything you need?"

"No, we have food and drink," Rochelle said. "Go on. Don't worry. It'll give Regina and me a chance to get to know each other."

Rebecca finally left the chamber. "Don't let anyone in," she reminded them, closing the portal behind her.

Regina limped across the chamber and bolted the portal. She returned to her bed and looked at her grandmother. She hesitated before speaking. "I don't know what I'm supposed to call you."

"I'd be pleased if you'd call me Grammy, but don't ever let your father hear it. Use 'Rochelle' when he's around."

Regina looked at the floor as she spoke. "I probably shouldn't pry, but would you please tell me why my father hates you? I confess, I heard a little of what my mother said the day they brought you here."

"I will tell you, but keep it to yourself. Agreed?"

Regina nodded.

"Where to start ... I guess I should tell you how your grandfather and I mated. I was working as a clerk for a Board Member. He was the Board Member's personal security warrior. Our employer was a fairly decent male. He would not allow his male employees to take females whenever they felt like it against our will, like so many did back then. I was vulnerable, since I'm of thin variety."

"What do you mean? Take you?" Regina asked.

Rochelle looked at her granddaughter. "You really have been sheltered, haven't you? Out there, in a world you've obviously never seen, some males think they can force themselves in mating on a slender or mixed female whenever they feel like it. Then the female is left to raise the nymphs alone, or forced to give herself to anyone all the time to get enough credit to provide for them."

"Oh."

"Would you get me some water, please?"

Regina reached out for the mug and pitcher on the surface near her and poured water for her grandmother.

Rochelle drank and resumed her tale. "Your grandfather didn't care about variety. He was interested in me and wanted to be honorable. He asked if he could see my father. My father died when I was about six season cycles old, but I didn't want him to know that and spoil my only change at a legal mating. I told him I would take his offer. I took it to my employer instead. He told me he was pleased, that it was time for things to change. He not only signed your grandfather's offer, he was the one who bound us."

Regina reached for a fried fly's egg from the serving tray on the surface near her and asked, "Who was he?"

"His name was Sir Rogue. Because your grandfather was important in his staff, we lived in one of the better parts of the city. I stayed in the background, content to raise my sons and your mother, grateful that they had inherited his size and no one questioned their variety when they entered training and later work."

"So how did my father ..."

"I'm getting to that. Hand me a couple of eggs."

Regina did as requested, trying to be patient as her grandmother ate.

"Your father had quite a reputation as a young male. He liked to have a female around, but not as a legal mate. Many an eligible female would have liked to catch him, a good physician with plenty of credit. Many season cycles went by without his taking a legal mate, even though no one would have complained about his clan's unsavory past."

"What unsavory past?"

"Come, Regina, you must have had some Roachstory with all those expensive tutors."

"Oh," said Regina quietly. "You mean my great-great-uncle? But my father says the evidence was forged."

"Never mind," Rochelle sighed. "I won't go into that. Anyway, when your father began to follow your mother around, after seeing her in the market one day, I insisted that my sons escort her everywhere. I didn't want anyone taking her without a proper mating contract. Robert had a passion for your mother, even though he was much older, because of her beauty. He approached many times. Whenever he did, my sons would say, 'If you want our sister so much, come and make a proposal to our father.' I knew a lot about your father and his clan. I'll say one good thing of them, they never hid their hatred of thins and mixes. I was quite surprised when Robert actually called on my mate formally. I knew that if he had one look at me, any chance of a contract for your mother was gone. I stayed well hidden."

Regina changed her position on her couch. "Is that why he says you deceived him?"

Rochelle shifted too. "Partly. Your father actually called on your mother formally several times. My mate would watch from a crack in the door. He'd say to me, 'He really wants her. There's something in his eyes that says it's more than lust.'

"I told him, 'Take advantage of that. It would be a good step up for her, if he offers a contract. But when he sees me, he may take his wrath out on her. Don't give her to him unless he agrees in the contract that he can never abuse her, or take another female. Make him face dire consequences, give her half of all he owns if he violates the contract,' I insisted."

"I listened at the portal when Robert negotiated for your mother. I could tell from his voice he didn't like the terms, but his desire was more powerful. My mate kept saying, 'If you want her, these are my terms. There are others willing to agree to these conditions.' There weren't, but the ploy worked. He signed it."

"So that's why."

"Yes. Your father never saw me until the binding day. When he did, the anger in his eyes frightened me. I faced him quietly and said, 'Remember your passion and what you have signed.'

"I'll never forget what he said then. 'I will abide by the terms, you deceiving piece of fly bait. But you will pay a price as well. In order that others never know your shame, you will never see your daughter again. Your whole family will cease to exist for her. Her nymphs will be able to call themselves pure because they will never be allowed to know you.'"

Tears came to Rochelle's eyes. "My mate bound them then. Your father took your mother from our home, and he kept his word—all of it."

18.

A full time frame passed before life returned to some semblance of normal in the city of Roacheria. The main activities were repairing bodies and buildings. Creatures skilled in repair work had more credit than they knew what to do with, at least from those who had credit to pay out. Ordinary citizens had nothing coming in from their regular jobs, and none to have their domiciles repaired.

Rundell's shop fared well. Refuse from the storm attracted flies in droves, laying eggs abundantly. Rundell collected what was needed for his regular paying customers in the better parts of the city, fed his own group and gave the rest away.

Those at Meadow Commonwealth acted with compassion when their own repairs were completed. They went into various hard-hit neighborhoods and simply did what was needed. Grateful recipients followed their lead, and turned to help still others. In spite of the misery, grief, and lack of food and other goods, the mood of the common roach expressed hope. Enforcers had much less violence and theft to deal with than they had feared might occur.

Dell tapped on Henry's portal one evening. When he invited her in, she handed him a letter. "This is the strangest letter I've ever had from my mother. It doesn't make a bit of sense."

Henry read the letter:

"We were sorry to hear you suffered such losses in your stock during the storm. We were very fortunate. South Harvester 45 notified us as soon as they knew it was coming. That gave us extra time and all herds were brought safely underground. We lost a lot of grassfronds, but we had plenty stored from last year's abundant crop. We have been grazing the hoppers in the eastern meadows lately, watching them closely. You never know when one of those stupid creatures might take a notion to follow the bees and perish in the stream. Give our care to everyone, Corina."

"Hoppers certainly aren't stupid in that sense, and why would they follow bees?" Dell asked.

Henry began to laugh. "Remember when Sir Rafael told us to watch what we say because we'll never know when, or if, letters are being read before they are brought to us, unless Sir Rafael brings them himself?"

"Yes, but..."

"Remember how we lured the bees? This is your mother's way of telling us that they will send us a hopper to eat now and again. They know I'm at the bank of the stream every seventhday. When I see one, I'll have one of you retrieve it. We wouldn't want our Enforcer friends to think I'd gone too far."

Dell smiled for the first time since the storm. "Too bad grassfronds can't grow legs and walk."

"You worry too much. We have eggs and fungus. We'll get by somehow. You'll see," Henry said, stroking his cousin affectionately.

*   *   *   *

Regina watched the Enforcer enter her father's private study in their home. Staying on the soft floor covering she limped closer to the portal and listened, shaking like a leaf dropping from one of the wood plants in the garden.

"Well? What have you to report?" she heard her father ask.

"Nothing new, Master Robert. He never steps one particle of an f-unit off that bank. Even that seventhday when he saw a hopper tangled at the bottom of the stream bed in the brush, he had one of the others get it."

"Whose side was the hopper on?"

"Theirs."

"Theirs as in ants?"

"No, theirs as in whatever they call that place."

"Meadow Commonwealth, need I remind you?" Regina heard irritation in her father's voice. "What did they do with the hopper?"

"Roasted it. What would you do? It smelled so good. I had all I could do to stay in my watching place."

"You better make sure you do stay there! How'd the hopper get there?"

"Apparently the creatures are very stupid. They bound off before the ants can catch them and fall down the bank. Then the ants can't retrieve them because they're on our side. Lots of citizens have found them all up and down the border stream lately, all the way down to South Harvester 45. I've been listening in on the talk in the Trade Center. The ants say that all the herds are skittish since the storm, bound off at the slightest noise. They say it's their loss and the finder's good fortune."

"Keep listening! There's something peculiar going on. I know it! That bunch fares too well on their piddling amount of credit. They've got to be doing something illegal! That surface should have belonged to my clan two generations ago. That piece of fly bait, Sir Ronald, stole it from my great uncle. And that Ronda as much as gave it to them to spite me. I'll bet they've found plastic somewhere. That must be how they rebuilt so fast and had more to pass on to shanty grudge."

"Begging your pardon, Master Robert, but they rebuilt with grassfrond pole-stems from their own harvest and more of those blocks of meadow grass. They gave away the poles they didn't need. I watched."

Regina heard a crash. Her father had broken several things in anger since the storm. She wondered which sculpture he had thrown down this time and hoped it wasn't something she had made.

"Don't tell me what I know!" her father shouted. "You find out what they're doing! Get going and don't come back till you do."

Regina retreated as quickly as she could. The portal banged open and the Enforcer scurried out. Robert caught sight of her.

"Regina! What are you doing here?"

Regina stooped as well as she could. "Excuse me ... You said I ... Today was the day you were to remove the plaster."

Robert sighed loudly. "That's right. Go wait for me in the back parlor."

Regina nodded. "Shall I tell Gra ... Rochelle?"

Another loud sigh. "Yes."

*   *   *   *

Robert removed the wet packs from the plaster on Regina's leg while Rebecca looked on. He had already finished with Rochelle. The moisture had done its work and he broke away chunks of damp plaster easily. He examined the healed fracture and said, "Well healed. You should have no other problems. The scar hardly shows. Get up now."

Regina did as instructed. She was tired of her front pods being sore from use against the floor. It felt good to raise her head and thorax to walk normally.

"Fine," her father said, "with the life you lead, you never need to worry about re-cracking." He turned to Rochelle. "Please leave before dawn tomorrow. Use the servants' entrance. Disappear from my life again so you don't spoil your granddaughter's chances at a good mating. Rebecca, sweep up here, would you?"

"As you wish, Master Robert," Rochelle said. "Thank you for what you have done for me. I won't forget this kindness."

"Nor I," echoed Regina's mother.

Robert turned and left the chamber without another word. Rebecca began to sweep up the plaster.

"I'm going to miss you, Grammy," Regina said. "Isn't there some way I can see you again?"

"No, it's best you don't cross your father. You never know; he may regret his actions someday and let you see me, hopefully not before I leave this world. If you sneak around, he'll find out. He and his clan have their ways ... I will always treasure the memories of these two time frames."

Rebecca nodded in agreement. "Perhaps you will have a mate who will understand and allow you to see your uncles and cousins, Regina. Times change. Not all are like your father." She turned to Rochelle. "Will you be all right when you leave?"

"Yes, don't worry about me. I'll live with your oldest brother. Watch for him in the markets. By chance, we may have word of each other, as we've had a few times over the season cycles."

*   *   *   *

"I'm not all that hungry this evening," Henry said. "Let the nymphs have my portion of hopper. Two fungus muffins are enough for me."

"They can have mine, too," added Rundell.

Genelle smiled and divided the meat among the nymphs. All of them had said the same thing over the last several days. Without even a signal, they took turns ignoring their hunger pangs and watching the young devour every scrap.

Rick looked at Rusty. "Has our fund got anything available for a small Last Night Festival?"

Rusty laughed. "What fund? We went through what little there was the first time frame after the storm when none of us were working for credit. Since the cut-backs, we earn about enough each quarter time frame for plastic and that's it."

Donald came into the Common Building from the mound. "I hate to bring more bad news, but the grassfrond seeds are getting spoiled in spite of the way we dried them. The whole bin smells like ale."

Everyone groaned. There wasn't anything else they could cut back on. Several hoppers sent down the stream bank had been found by others even more desperate than they were. The Combined Colonies had sent Roacheria an offer of help, but The Board had been too stubborn to accept.

"Ale! That's it!" Henry shouted. "We'll make ale out of the whole mess and sell it. Will there be time before Last Night, Donald? Rundell could offer it to his egg regulars. Ronda will buy some, too. She always sponsors a big affair. She'd give us credit outright if she could."

"Many of my egg customers will buy some," Rundell said. "Sir Rafael has been giving me more than the standard price lately, you know."

Donald smiled broadly. "There's exactly enough time. Come help me, Henry. We'll start it right now."

*   *   *   *

"Regina," her mother called. "Come to the back parlor right away!"

Regina hurried down the ramp from her recently repaired and redecorated sleep chamber. She wondered why her mother sounded so excited.

Rebecca beamed. "I must teach you the Last Night dance steps. Your father said he's planning a large gathering. He wants it to be for you. He said several prominent citizens with eligible sons have accepted his invitation! Even the Supreme Executor! You must look and dance your best. Many of them will call afterward, I'm sure. Your father will have a good choice of mates for you."

Regina had spent all her life within the walls of her home, trained by tutors. When her father's family came to visit, she socialized with them, and very occasionally others had called, but she had never been in a large group. She stood rooted to the floor in front of her mother.

"What's wrong?" her mother asked.

"I ... don't think I know what I should do."

"Nonsense. You've had good training. Be polite as you are when we have other guests. Speak when you're asked to and look as lovely as you are. Your father will present you to everyone. Just tip your antennae respectfully and smile a lot. When the young males ask you to dance, do the steps correctly, as I'll show you. Let the males tell you all about themselves. Don't interrupt. Be interested in what they have to say. You're well informed on many subjects. If they ask about you, tell them your interests in reading and making pottery figurines. But, please, don't mention your grandmother."

So, I'm to be deceitful, too?"

"Don't put it that way. You needn't be deceitful. Simply don't mention it. When your father has a good offer for you, and the bond is tied, you can let it out. I'll try to influence him toward one I think might be more accepting. Now, we must concentrate on your dance lessons. We've only half a time frame to get ready!"

*   *   *   *

In answer to Meadow Commonwealth's hopes, a hopper appeared, tangled in the brush at the bottom of the stream the day before Last Day. Since the holiday didn't begin until the third h-unit after noon in Roacheria, those who worked in the city were not free until then. They had decided to combine the Ant and Roach celebrations. They would complete the Last Day ritual as soon as everyone was back. Then they would feast with the little they had and celebrate moderately in Roach fashion.

"Hold the gate, Gabby," Dell said, "while I prod the aphids in."

Ramona stood on the far side of the pen, holding out a few leaves to lure them in. Every night since the storm, they had cooped up what was left of their herds in the domed enclosure. They couldn't afford to lose any more. Dell, Donald, Gabby, and Ramona took turns with night watch.

"I don't like restricting them like this," Dell remarked.

"But it's much easier to prevent theft," Ramona said as the last creature crawled inside. "How did you and Henry come up with this idea anyway?"

Dell explained. "When Henry went to South Harvester 45 for Job Exploration, he liked going to the leisure centers. They have small domed enclosures like this one for one or two young hoppers. Young adults take turns trying to stay on their backs as they bound around. This dome is, of course, much larger."

Ramona and Dell left the enclosure and Gabby secured the gate.

"Well, it works," Ramona said, looking up at the structure. Three twenty-five f-unit grassfrond stems had been bound together to form an arc, anchored in the ground at each end. Twenty-four such arcs, about two f-units apart formed a dome approximately fifteen f-units in diameter. Other stems were lashed to the upright ones in concentric horizontal rings.

Dell nodded. "Yes, but I wish it weren't necessary. Now that we're done, you go on ahead to the Common Building. I need to help Donald feed our larvae before we join the rest of you."

"Aren't you bringing up the coop? It's cloudy and will be dark soon."

"Yes, we just want to settle them first, so we can relax."

Gabby and Ramona entered the Common Building. Rick and Henry were arranging floor cushions in a circle around three lightning bug lamps for their ceremony. The others were busy preparing their meager feast. The nymphs scurried around excitedly. A few moments later, Ray came in carrying his cricket leg viola. Donald and Dell arrived with the larva coop containing their two young ones. Donald also had his pea pod shakers.

"If you can play the tune, I'll keep the beat," Donald said.

Just before they began their ceremony, Henry went to the portal. He opened it wide and called out. "I know you're out there. Since you're stuck out here watching us, you might as well come in and watch more closely."

Reluctantly, the Enforcer came out of the shadows and into their presence. He remained by the portal throughout their ceremony. When they began the feast Henry filled a bowl and walked over to the Enforcer.

"We can't stand to see you hungry while we eat," Henry said.

"I'm on duty. I can't."

"I'm not offering you ale, only a little food," Henry repeated, holding out the dish.

"Is this the hopper you found yesterday?"

Henry nodded.

"What's this other stuff?" the Enforcer asked.

"Fried fungus and a fungus muffin."

"Fungus?"

"Yes, we grow it underground. It's the one thing we have plenty of, and it's very nourishing."

"I'll try it, thank you," the Enforcer said, taking the bowl.

*   *   *   *

Gaiety filled Master Robert's domicile. Ale flowed freely and banquet surfaces overflowed with food. Several Board Members, their mates, and adult young dined on fly eggs, fried bees wings, imported grasshopper, and a variety of sweets. Musicians strummed on cricket leg violas, tapped on hollow reeds of varying length, and whistled through their mandibles.

Rebecca sat at the front of the main parlor with Regina beside her. As the guests arrived, Robert said the same thing to each. "You know my lovely mate. May I present my daughter, Regina, of age, well trained, and ready to join society."

Regina tipped her antennae the way her mother had instructed her. She looked about between introductions, eager to get this part over with and move on to the dancing and food.

"May I eat now?" she whispered to her mother.

"Be patient. The Supreme Executor has not arrived yet. He promised he'd come. It wouldn't be fitting to start before you're introduced."

Sir Reese strutted into the chamber. Everyone stood aside for him. Young Reese followed him, then Sir Reese's mate. Robert rose, stooped, and swept his front pods out to the sides. "I'm delighted you could come and grace out home, Sir Reese. May I present my mate, Rebecca, and my daughter, Regina."

Rebecca and Regina stooped as Robert had.

Sir Reese tipped his antennae slightly. "Pleased to meet you. Pardon our lateness. This is my son, Reese the second. Master Robert, you've kept your lovely daughter to yourself much too long." He nudged Young Reese.

"May I?" asked the young male, holding out a pod toward Regina.

Regina looked at her father, who beamed and nodded. Regina stepped away from her chair and allowed Young Reese to lead her toward the banquet surface. He picked up a large bowl and she began to fill it with generous portions of each dish. She handed him a large mug of ale to go with the food.

"You should get yourself something too," Reese said. "Sit with me."

She nodded, served herself and followed him to a bench near a wall opening. She waited until he ate before touching her own food.

"It's quite mild for Last Night, isn't it?" she said casually.

"Yes, it's nice to have the shutters opened. Last year, my father had to keep ours shut. It was much colder and drizzled."

"Tell me what it's like to work with your father."

"Some days it's interesting. He explains each proposal to me before it's presented to The Board. Other times, I just sit there, not saying a word, while he meets with one Member after another, convincing them to vote in favor of an item or not."

"That sounds interesting."

"I will take over his position someday."

"When will that be?" Regina asked.

"When my father retires, but I didn't come to talk politics. Would you care to dance?"

Regina nodded and the two rose from the bench and joined the circle of dancers. Filled with the elation from the newness of her first social experience, Regina glowed. She performed the steps flawlessly. Late into the night, she swayed and swirled among the guests. Though several young males took her front pods in turn, it was Reese who commanded her attention.

19.

*R*egina's life changed after Last Night. Before then, her training had been handled by tutors. She had learned to read, studied Roacherian literature and poetry, Roachstory befitting her station, and art. She had shown an interest in pottery and her father had brought in an expert in the craft to instruct her.

Now, her mother took over training. She taught Regina the fine points of handling the household and their servants. Robert chose his most trusted security warrior to be Regina's official escort whenever she left their home with her mother. He told Regina she had nothing to fear as long as she remained with her escort. Any male applying for work as an escort to an unmated female of high rank had to be a well trained warrior. They had to prove they already had a legal mate and nymphs and then submit to surgical removal of their sex organs. Regina's father had done the procedure himself.

Regina began to see a side of Roacheria she had never known before. She cringed when her escort shouted at scrawny workers pulling heavy loads in roller carts to get out of their way, and then struck them when they didn't move fast enough. Although they stayed in the better parts of the city and routes were carefully chosen, she saw a driveling, plastic depraved adult pounded by an Enforcer for no reason as he crawled down a narrow space between two market stalls.

When she asked why, her mother only said, "Don't pay any attention to things like that. They aren't of your station. You've no need to concern yourself with such matters."

She thought about her grandmother and grew restless.

Reese called on her several times. At first, Regina enjoyed his attentiveness. Her mother was all aflutter every time he came. "What a wonderful catch he would be," she kept saying. "Imagine, you could be the legal mate of the future Supreme Executor!"

After the first few times, Regina found Reese boring. He went on and on about himself, and how important he would be one day. He talked openly about his father's various mistresses, letting it be known that fidelity to a mate was not important to his father and wouldn't be to him.

As they sat in the garden, with her escort watching from a distance, Regina grew bold and asked, "What do you think of thins and mixes?"

"What do you mean?" Reese asked.

"Well, I mean, what do you think about them? Do they deserve to be treated like us?"

Reese laughed. "Why should you worry about that? They're far beneath either of us."

Regina hesitated. "I don't worry about them. I just wondered what you felt, working with your father and all. Have you ever known any, besides servants?"

Reese's expression changed.

"I'm sorry ... I shouldn't have," she stammered.

"No, it's all right. I don't mind them, as long as they stay where they should. I had to tolerate a few when I was in training, had one for an instructor at my father's insistence. I came to respect him. Like my father, I never formally associate with any now."

She had heard enough and changed the subject. "The weather's grown so warm. Look how the new plants are sprouting up around the base of this wood plant."

Their conversation drifted on. Regina knew she must continue to play the part. If Reese made a proposal, her father was certain to accept it. Her mother had said over and over what a wonderful step up it would be for her and her future young. Her mother's family would never be a part of her life. Regina despaired. She didn't know what she wanted from life, but she knew Reese wasn't it.

*   *   *   *

The two males, both obviously mixes, sat in Henry's client chairs and looked anxiously at him. The larger one spoke. "We actually represent a larger group, six families. We all live in a boarding building. I work in the thistledown factory. Ray is my overseer. You couldn't ask for a better supervisor. Anyway, sometimes at lunch he sits with us and talks about all of you at Meadow Commonwealth. We got to thinking maybe we could do something like that in our building, but we don't know how to start."

Henry had never thought about groups within the city sharing resources among themselves, but he saw the possibilities immediately. "How many adults did you say you had?" he asked.

"Six mated pairs. We're close in age and all in about the same circumstances."

"How many nymphs?"

"The youngest family only has one. I have three. Together we have ten, so far."

"All the males are working?"

"Yes, and one female. My mate takes care of her nymph for her."

"That's good," Henry said. "You already have the basic idea of cooperating with each other. How much formal training has each of you had?"

"I think I've had the most. I got one season cycle above my basics. All of those working have finished basics, and I think one of the other females finished her basics, but the other females don't even read. Do we have a chance at trying this?" he asked. "How much will it cost for your advice?"

Henry looked into his worried face and answered, "Let me talk to our members about how best to help you. My advice will be free if your group agrees to two conditions."

"What conditions?"

"First, make a two-season-cycle commitment to learning this new way of life, and then promise to give the same help that you receive to some other group when they want to learn from you."

The two males smiled at each other. "I think we can do that," the larger one said.

"Good! Give me your location. I'd like to meet with all of you. How about this seventhday afternoon?"

The larger male wrote down where they lived and they left, talking about their plans. Rundell smiled when Henry explained their request as he and Henry walked home.

When they neared the Common Building, Gabby came running up to them shouting. "Henry, The Essence is truly with us! Remember how we left the wettest seed after the storm? It's growing! All over that area little shoots are coming up. They've shot up four tenths of an f-unit just today! Come and see."

Henry followed her, Rundell behind him. They stood at the edge of the open ground. What had seemed empty and dead all winter, a constant reminder of their loss and hunger, was now luminous with pale green shoots. Henry stepped carefully into the meadow and walked slowly through it.

"We can roast the seed we saved," he exclaimed. "There will be a huge crop here without further planting."

The entire group rejoiced that evening. Henry told them about the group in the city and all agreed to help in any way they could. Ruth and Genelle even offered to help their females learn reading and other basics if they would come out to Meadow Commonwealth two or three evenings each quarter time frame.

*   *   *   *

Regina looked down on the Enforcer from the wall opening in her sleep chamber as he knocked on the front portal. It opened and one of the servants led him inside. She knew he was here to see her father again. She slipped quietly down the ramp and watched him enter her father's private study. Then she crept to the portal and listened.

"Still nothing?" she heard her father ask.

"Master Robert, you're wasting your credit with my continued spying. Nothing illegal is going on at Meadow Commonwealth. Even The Board has recalled their Enforcers."

"That Henry is smart. He knows how to fool you, that's all."

"No, I've even been invited into their Common Building to inspect. They are simply a group of very generous individuals trying to make a living."

"Inside! When?"

"Last Night. Henry called out that I might as well watch from inside. So I did. Later they offered me food, even though they had little enough for themselves."

"You took a bribe?"

"No, I politely accepted a meal. It's a good thing I did, because that's how I found out what they live on. They survive because they share everything. They still have a food supply, fungus that they grow underground all season cycle. It looked rather strange, but was quite tasty. I tell you, there is nothing illegal. From the way everything's growing in this warm spring sun, they'll have a huge crop. I never knew grassfronds grew that fast. The shoots are over an f-unit tall already. Last seventhday, I followed Henry to a meeting in the city. He was telling a group of families in a boarding building how to start a commonwealth group there. Two females from Meadow Commonwealth, the ones that take care of all their young, are even training some of them to read."

Regina heard her father pounding on his writing surface. His voice rose. "They can't. It's not possible! There must be something! He's a clever one, that Henry is."

"Well, you find it yourself. I won't harass them any more. I quit!"

Regina scooted away from the portal and up the ramp before being seen. A plan began to form in her mind.

*   *   *   *

Regina found her mother in the pantry making a market list for another social gathering. "Oh, here you are. Am I to go with you again today?"

"Yes," her mother replied.

"I was wondering," Regina said innocently. "Could we stop at the research center on the way back? The last time Reese came to see me, he talked about some things I wasn't familiar with. I felt so stupid. I thought maybe if I read up on it a little, I could impress him."

Rebecca beamed. "What subject? Maybe I could tell you what you need."

Regina searched her mind for something her mother knew nothing about. "A science project The Board is considering funding. There was an article about it in last time frame's City Bulletin."

"You know science doesn't interest me. We can stop for a while I guess. Do you think you could find it quickly?"

"I'm not sure. Couldn't you leave me at the research center and go on to the market with my escort? I'm sure I'd be through by the time you came back for me," Regina said.

Rebecca hesitated. "I hate to leave you alone there."

"Oh, mother, what can happen in the research center?"

*   *   *   *

Free of formal supervision for the first time in her life, and unsure of herself, Regina entered the Research Center. She approached the clerk uncertainly.

"May I help you?" the clerk asked.

"I ... think I need to see back issues of the *City Bulletin*."

"How far back?"

"A bit over a season cycle, I think."

"This way. Are you one of those female students from the Advanced Training Center for the Professions?"

Regina nodded as she followed the clerk to the back of the research center. He led her to a large chamber and pointed to some shelves.

"You'll find all the City Bulletins in order from the first day of each season cycle."

"Thank you," she said as the clerk left her alone.

Luck was with her. She found the item she was looking for almost immediately.

"Board Action Today: passed: Petition by Henry Roach-Dairier for full citizenship in Roacheria, following formal banishment by New South Dairy Colony 50. Henry, proven member of the clan of long deceased Board Member, Sir Ronald, teaches Ant language at the Advanced Training Center for the Professions and holds a legal counselor's certificate. He and several others were granted control of a few d-units of surface northwest of the city for an experimental community."

The article brought up more questions than it answered. Why had he been banished? If The Board had given up, why was her father so convinced he was doing something wrong? Did it have to do with the banishment? Unfortunately, she could find no other information in the City Bulletin. However, as she searched, she refined her plan. She remembered something she had learned about South Dairy Colony 50 and returned to the clerk.

"May I see the city directory, please?"

"Of course. It's on that shelf right over there."

Regina crossed the chamber to where he had pointed and looked up Henry's counseling service. She knew she didn't have much time.

*   *   *   *

Regina tapped lightly at her father's portal. Her mother had fixed his favorite foods and he talked about having had a good day. Hopefully, he would listen to her.

"Who is it?" she heard from within.

"It's Regina. May I speak with you, Father?"

"Of course."

She entered and stood before him, wondering if she should actually stoop down to make her request, or approach the subject in a straight-forward manner, like others who came to see him.

"Well," Robert said, "What is it?"

"I have a confession, sort of... and an idea for you."

He looked at her curiously. "And?"

Regina took a deep breath. "A few days ago, when that Enforcer came to see you, I was very curious and I listened to your conversation."

Robert's expression changed. Regina continued quickly. "I know I shouldn't have done that, and I'm sorry, but please, listen to me. I got to thinking that somebody like me might be able to get closer to that one you hate than your Enforcer could. I might be able to find out what you want to know."

Robert glared at his daughter. She could almost see his mind working, exactly the way she wanted it to.

"You haven't the faintest idea about what's going on," he said, "and why should you care about my problems?"

"I know that this Henry Roach-Dairier is from New South Dairy 50 and that you hate that place because its founder was responsible for your great-uncle's downfall. I heard enough between you and that Enforcer to know you still believe there is something illegal going on out there. If I can charm Reese, I can surely get to him. He is a male after all, and not mated."

Robert's expression changed to a sly smile. "I believe you could."

"So what will you give me if I do?"

"What do you want?"

"I want to choose my own mate, not take whomever you pick for me."

"Now wait just a minute!"

"No," she interrupted, "hear me out. You wanted mother so much that you agreed to conditions in your mating contract that were unheard of then. And you stuck to it! You have always been good to mother and me. You've remained loyal to her when many males keep others on the side. I want someone who wants me that much. Don't you want that for me, too?"

Irritation crept into Robert's voice. "You spent too much time with Rochelle. I should never have allowed that."

"But you did, because you still want mother that much. I'm not blind, and I'm not stupid. I want what my mother has, someone who will be as good to me as you are to her."

"And you don't think Reese will be?"

Regina chose her words carefully. "I don't know if he will or not. I just want to be part of the negotiating, so I can have conditions put in about loyalty and possible abuse. Is that too much to ask for the possibility of getting rid of an enemy?"

"You're something of a schemer, aren't you?"

Regina smiled. "Maybe it's an inherited trait."

"How do you plan to get close to Henry Roach-Dairier?"

"I know where he does his counseling. I could go to him and say I'd gotten in trouble with my family and needed legal advice. I'd say I had no place to live. I'd cry a lot. If he's really like what that Enforcer said, he'll take me into his community. Then I can find out what you want.

When anyone asks where I am, you could say I went to Sea Edge to visit my cousins. That's what mother should think too."

Robert tapped one front pod on his writing surface. Regina remained quiet.

"I'll give you two time frames," he said.

"And no matter what I find, I may choose my own mate?"

Robert tipped one antenna.

Regina fell at his pods. "Thank you, Father!"

"Pack two satchels to convince your mother, but leave them somewhere. Take nothing with you when you meet Henry. I'll send your escort with you when you leave here. He'll take you within sight of that miserable egg stall. Then you're on you own."

20.

*H*enry returned to Rundell's shop. He had been at The Detention Center talking with a client about how they would establish his innocence. As usual for sixthday, Rundell was out collecting and Georgette was painting new lettering on a sign.

"A lovely young female is waiting to see you," Georgette said. "She's in a worse state that I was the day I first walked in here. She wouldn't talk to me at all. I fixed tea. She's fairly calm now."

"Thank you, Georgette."

Henry entered his work chamber. Her back was toward him, a solid, rich earthen brown, no markings at all. He rattled the portal to alert her. She turned, holding the mug of tea. Something about her face reminded him of Ruth the first time he had seen her in his training unit.

"I'm Henry Roach-Dairier," he said. "What can I do for you?"

She tried to set the mug down, but it slipped from her trembling pod, spilling the last of the tea onto Henry's writing surface. "Oh ... no ..." she gasped. "I'm so sorry ..."

"Never mind," Henry said gently. "This surface has seen many spills." He opened a compartment and took out a cloth. "What can I do for you?" he asked, wiping off the surface.

"I had a terrible argument with my father," she began. "He cursed at me ... then he ..." She looked about, twitching.

"Forced you to leave your home?" Henry asked.

She nodded. "Can he do that? Just send me out with nowhere to go?"

"Under some conditions, yes. What's your name?"

"Regina."

"Well, Regina, I need to ask you some things before I can determine how to help you."

"Wh ... What do you need to know?"

"How old are you?"

Regina hesitated. "Sixteen season cycles."

"Have you had any formal training?"

"What difference does it make?"

"A male head of household may send a son or daughter away after a certain age, or if some training has been provided. His legal obligation under a mating contract is considered fulfilled. Are your parents legally mated?"

"Yes, they are, and I have completed my basics. I suppose that means you can't make him take me back?"

Henry nodded.

"What am I going to do?" she wailed.

Henry could see from her mannerisms that she came from a well-to-do family. He knew how sheltered such females were. They had no idea how to take care of themselves. Usually, the training they had was not helpful in finding work.

Henry called Georgette. When she entered, he described Regina's problem briefly, then asked, "Do you know anyone who might have an extra chamber?"

Georgette started to shake her antennae then stopped. "She reminds me of myself. You were so kind to me, Henry. I have room in my domicile. Let me take responsibility for her, and return to another what was so freely given to me."

Regina stared at Georgette.

"It's probably not the kind of life you're accustomed to," Henry apologized. "But I don't want to think about someone like you wandering in the city alone."

Regina looked startled. "What makes you think you know my life style, or what I would accept?"

"Forgive me, I didn't mean to offend you. Your mannerisms indicate a certain station in society. Please, accept our offer. It's the only help we can give you. Perhaps in time, I can help you reconcile things with your father. We often say and do things in anger that we later regret."

*   *   *   *

Regina walked toward Meadow Commonwealth with Henry and Georgette. Excitement had filled her when she embraced her mother and left home with two satchels, soon tossed in a refuse bin. Her escort had pointed toward Rundell's shop and left her standing there. That was when the terror had hit.

What was she doing?

The day before, she had wondered how to work up tears. Standing in the shop, the tears had been very real. Planning this and carrying it out were quite different.

Regina forced herself to concentrate. She must remember what she had already said and not contradict herself. This was for her freedom. Freedom? She thought again. She didn't even know what she wanted. Her pods ached. She had never walked so far.

Henry's voice broke into her thoughts. "Regina, are you all right?"

"Yes, just a little tired," she replied.

"I can imagine it's been quite a day. We're nearly there."

Ahead of her, Regina saw the oddest looking structures, crude things of dirt, grass actually growing from their roofs. One in the middle stood taller than the rest. "What are those?" She asked.

Georgette said, "That's our community. My domicile is the one over on the far right. Come with me. We'll freshen up before dinner."

"I'll see you in a little while," Henry said, turning toward the other end of the group of buildings.

Regina followed her guide. Would she really be able to tolerate living in this squalor? Was the freedom to choose her mate worth it? She thought about her grandmother. Had she grown up like this? If so, no wonder she had done what she did to get Regina's mother out of it. Regina considered running back to the city as fast as her pods could carry her.

Georgette opened the wooden portal. The interior surprised Regina. Colorful woven strips adorned a wall opening. The woven reed mats forming walls were quite attractive. Two comfortable looking floor cushions sat along one outer wall, which she now saw was made of blocks of earth. It felt strangely welcoming.

"This season cycle, we hope to paint images on the reed mat dividers," she heard Georgette say. "My nymphs sleep in this chamber." Georgette pointed. "You'll share my chamber and sleep cushion. It's plenty large enough."

"Share your mattress? But your mate ..." Regina's voice dropped to a course whisper. She slumped to the floor and burst into tears.

Regina felt herself surrounded by Georgette. Georgette's pods stroked her. A warm, wonderful sensation filled the shaking Regina.

"I have no mate now. I have no idea what you've been through," Georgette's soft voice crooned. "But you're not alone. Henry saved me one day about two season cycles ago when my mate deserted my nymphs and me. I was scared to death. I couldn't even read. Others had told me about Henry and I went to him for help. It turned out my mating contract wasn't worth the parchment it was written on. Henry gave me a job and my dignity. I've been working with him and Rundell ever since."

Regina looked up at her. "I'm sorry," she said. "I'm acting like a fool."

"Never mind. Come, take a cloth and wash a little. Here is a jug of water and a bowl."

Amazed at the kindness of these strangers, Regina rose and accepted the soft woven cloth, dipped her front pods in the water and splashed it onto her face. "Where did you get such a strange cloth?" she asked, then corrected herself as she dried her face. "I don't mean that to sound like an insult. I've never seen anything like it before."

"Ray is an overseer in the weaving plant. He brings home all the scraps that would be thrown away. We sew them together and use them." She pointed to the strips around the wall opening. "That's how we made those, too."

"They're rather pretty," Regina said. "I would never have thought of that."

"Are you ready? It's dinner time."

When they reached the larger building, Henry was standing outside waiting for them. For the first time, Regina looked at his features. She was slightly larger than he, and a shade darker brown. His eyes seemed to look into her very soul with a softness she had never experienced. She looked down quickly.

"Are you feeling better?" he asked.

"Yes, thank you."

He took her front pod in his, led her inside, and directed her to a place next to him at a large eating surface. He introduced everyone to her, even the nymphs. She concentrated so she would remember all the names. Then he said simply, "Everyone, this is Regina. She'll be staying with us for a while."

No one asked any awkward questions. Bowls of food were passed around. To her amazement, Henry served her. She was too dazed by everything to pay full attention, but she remembered snatches of the conversation later. Two of the female hoppers had laid three eggs each. More were sure to come. There were blossoms on the berry bushes by the pond. They needed to build a second bee hive—something about swarming season. Things were back to normal in the Trade Center. Somebody named Gatlin had been given a small bonus for good work. What was their greatest need for its use?

Several times she stopped herself from staring at the two ants seated across from her. They were the first she had ever seen, and not what she had expected. When she was a nymph, the servants had filled her with stories of the strange creatures—huge mandibles, always slashing, and watch out for that point at the end of their abdomen, red as the sunrise. These two were a deep purplish-black. Their mandibles were smaller than hers, and their abdomens rounded. She liked the strange way they spoke Roach words and the few things they said in Ant, which she didn't understand, sounded comforting.

After the meal, someone guided her back to the small dwelling, said something about how she needed to sleep now. She felt herself lifted, covered, then stroked into oblivion.

*   *   *   *

A pod touched the back of Regina's thorax. "Regina, wake up. How are you this morning?"

Regina rolled over to see four little eyes staring at her, Georgette's two nymphs. Georgette stood behind them.

"What time is it?" Regina asked.

"Mid-morning. I thought it would be best to let you sleep a bit longer, since it's seventhday. Henry said he'd come by soon and show you around."

Regina climbed off the cushion, remembering everything and her purpose. "I'd better get ready then," she said.

Henry arrived as she finished a breakfast of roasted seeds.

"Good morning," he said cheerfully. "Did you sleep well?"

"Yes, very. It's been many days since I've slept that long," she said truthfully.

"Come, let me show you around and we'll talk about your role with us," Henry said, taking her pod in his and leading her out into the warm spring sun.

"My role?"

"I don't mean to offend you, but I don't think you've ever done any serious work."

Regina looked down.

Henry continued. "No one is on holiday here. We all do what we can to help. Even Gallo, the old blind one who sat on the other side of you. You'd be amazed what he can weave by touch. It took him a while to learn, but he needed to feel useful. So we kept helping him. Now, it's as though he were ten season cycles younger."

He led her into the meadow. She breathed in the fragrance of spring and decided to be as honest as possible.

"You're right. I've never worked," she admitted.

They walked in silence for a while. Henry showed her the pond and the wood plants where the aphids climbed to eat the tender new leaves and suck sap. He explained a little about the care they needed. He pointed to Dell off the distance with their grasshopper herd.

"In a little while," he explained, "Gabby will come and take over for her."

He showed her their herb garden and the grassfronds, now two f-units tall. "You can almost watch them grow this time of the season cycle," he said. "By fall, when we harvest, they'll be twenty-five to thirty f-units tall, and each stalk will fill a basket with its seed. This crop is a gift from the earth. Last fall, the storm destroyed almost everything. We went hungry many days during the winter. But see? The earth returns what it took, and ten times more."

Regina looked at the shoots. "I don't know anything about any of this."

"That's all right. You'll learn," he said, taking both her front pods in his. "This is an ant greeting of friendship. We take both pods because neither of us is above the other." Then he said the word for friendship in Ant.

Regina repeated it shyly. She felt as free as a new butterfly. After she had seen everything, Henry suggested, "Perhaps the best thing would be for you to spend a quarter time frame in each of the work areas here to see what suits you best."

"Perhaps," she repeated absently, and then remembered she did have a job of her own. Her father had said he was convinced the creatures here had found plastic. His Enforcer had never been able to go into Dell and Donald's mound. "Could I start with whatever it is they do in that place underground?"

"Sure. It's as good a place to start as any. But now, why don't you head back to Georgette's home? I have something I need to do."

"May I come along?"

"I guess so, but let me warn you. It's not pleasant."

He headed for the Common Building where he took a large basket and a shovel from a storage bin. Then he went to the outside wall of one of the domiciles and opened a portal about two f-units across. The odor made Regina gag. She backed up. Henry began shoveling body waste from its storage compartment under the domicile's sanitation area into the basket.

Regina coughed. "What are you doing?"

"It's my turn to empty these. This is next season cycle's fertilizer. I warned you it wasn't pleasant."

"But why you? You're the leader here!"

Henry stopped a moment and looked at her. "No one is the leader here. Besides, a true leader would never ask others to do something he would not do himself. If you decide to stay with us permanently, your turn will come."

"What if I refuse?"

"If you can't accept our way of life, I suggest you think about reconciling things with your father."

Regina said no more. She watched in fascinated horror as Henry finished filling the basket, carried it to a large bin on one side of the yard, and began the process again at the next domicile. When he had finished them all, he covered the dumped loads with a layer of dirt and dry grass. Then he took the basket and the shovel to the pond and cleaned them thoroughly before returning them to their storage place.

*   *   *   *

Georgette woke Regina early firstday morning. "I've got to leave to get to the egg stall," she said. "Go on over to the mound whenever you're ready. Dell will probably be out with the herd. Donald will be waiting for you." She turned to her nymphs. "Come on, time to go to the Common Building for the day."

Regina watched them walk across the community yard. She saw Georgette stroke her nymphs affectionately and realized that it was the same thing she had seen her grandmother do to her mother the first day after the storm. Where had Rochelle learned to do that? Why had her grandmother been critical when she found out Rebecca had not passed it on to her?

Regina closed the portal and headed for the mound. Its portal stood open. Unsure about walking in unannounced, she called out, "Donald, I'm here."

"Come on down."

Regina let her eyes adjust to the dimness. The earthen ramp sloped down to a large open chamber with smaller chambers around it, all empty. Was this where they dug plastic?

Donald held a wiggling white thing. "Excuse me for a moment," he said. "I've got to finish feeding my son."

Regina stared in curiosity and then apologized. "Pardon me for being so rude. I've never seen a young ant before. Actually, I never met any ants at all until I met you and Dell."

"It's all right. That's part of the reason Dell and I chose to come here with Henry. Learning to understand each other is what Meadow Commonwealth is all about."

He went on to explain the ant life-cycle. By the time he had finished, the larva had fallen asleep. Regina followed him as he entered the chambers he and Dell lived in and laid the young one in his larva coop. He picked up his larger daughter from the coop next to it and proceeded to feed and care for her.

Regina looked around. The smooth, curved walls felt comforting, like the stroking she had received from Georgette. She watched, amazed, as Donald dipped his pod into a mug of something over and over again. Each time the larva lapped the sticky looking liquid from his pod.

"We grind the plastic finely and mix it with honey dew since larvae have no mandibles," Donald explained.

"Oh. Do you always care for your young?"

"Most of the time. It was my choice. Dell has always liked the surface. I'm better at growing fungus anyway." He laid the second larva down. "Now I can show you around."

They returned to the large chamber. "Those bins are for storing grassfrond seed. The spaces along this wall where you see the gates are for those times when we must bring the herds underground."

"When do you do that?"

"We did during last fall's storm. It was pretty crowded in here that night. We expect an even greater harvest this fall, so I'm enlarging some of the storage bins. I work at it whenever our larvae sleep. Right now, I need to fertilize the fungus."

Regina followed him out of the mound and across the yard to a bin right next to the one where Henry had dumped the body waste the day before. He picked up a basket and a shovel near it and dug into the mixture. Regina noticed that the odor in this one was not strong at all.

"This mixture of organic waste, dry leaves and grass has been sitting here all winter. Now it's ready for use."

He filled the basket and returned to the mound. He led Regina into another underground chamber and began to mix the contents of the basket with loosened earth on the floor. From the other side of the chamber, he picked some gray tufts. "These are spore pods. I break them open and spread it in this newly prepared area for more fungus to grow. In a time frame, we'll be eating this. Some of the spore pods will be planted in that third area. The first area will be fertilized and prepared again. From one to two to three," he pointed to each area again, "giving us food all through the season cycle."

Regina's fascination with all she had observed outweighed her disappointment at not seeing any plastic. That afternoon, she helped feed the larvae. The next day she let go of her pride and filled the fertilizer basket. She tried to help dig the storage bin, but her muscles, unused to such labor, rebelled. Her legs ached for a whole day. Henry brought her a pain potion in the evening and messaged her aching joints.

"When did you get this fracture?" he asked, seeing her scar.

"Last fall, in the storm."

"It's healed well, but you shouldn't do any of the heavier work here. You could re-crack it."

Glad of an excuse, she asked, "How do you know so much about such things?"

"My father is a physician. I spent a mandatory time frame with him. We're all taught some basic emergency procedures."

"Oh ... well ... I feel much better now," she smiled at him, and then looked away quickly. Every time she looked at him, her heart began to beat faster. The softness of his gaze both frightened and excited her.

*   *   *   *

The following seventhday, Regina started to follow Henry as he left for the bee hives. Rundell stopped her.

"We all leave Henry alone when he goes to the hives," he said.

"What does he do there?" Regina asked, her thoughts returning to her search for something illegal.

Rundell looked carefully at her. "You really don't know much do you?"

Regina looked down and twitched her antennae. "I'd like to learn."

"Come with me." Rundell led Regina to Henry's domicile. He took out the copies of Henry's writings. "I know you don't speak Ant and we haven't had time to translate these, so I'll explain."

Rundell spent two h-units giving Regina her first lesson in Antstory. When he finished, he handed her the copies of the banishment documents which were written in Roach. Regina was not the same creature when she returned to Georgette's domicile that evening.

21.

*R*egina spent her second quarter time frame in the meadows with Dell, Ramona and Gabby. She didn't like watching the herds or caring for aphids, but found the three females fascinating. The two roaches had grown up in different circumstances, but they never criticized her and were open about themselves. Regina found herself thinking about her grandmother again and felt she had a better idea of what her grandmother's life and her mother's early season cycles had been like.

Dell's stories about early adulthood in an ant colony captivated Regina. She especially enjoyed hearing about Henry. "Was he really all that terrible?" she asked.

Dell laughed. "He was quite a rascal as a nymph, but now you couldn't find a more compassionate creature anywhere. He'd sacrifice himself in a moment for any of us. Already has."

Each evening at dinner, Henry sat next to Regina. As the days went by, she looked forward to seeing him more and more. They always spent sixthday evening together. They would walk in the meadows and then sit by the pond and watch the moon rise. Regina's original purpose slipped farther and farther from her mind.

In her next work experiment, she began to help Ruth and Genelle care for the nymphs. She readily admitted absolute ignorance. They were patient with her.

One morning Ruth asked, "Would you mind helping my brothers with their lessons? Genelle and I have so much to do with the tiny ones, that they don't get the attention they need."

"I'll try," Regina replied. "I remember how my tutors worked with me."

"I wish we had more supplies," Ruth said. "We only have a few training books, and no extra parchment. We filled two trays with damp soil. They practice writing their symbols in it."

Regina had always been told that those of thin variety were not as intelligent as others were, so she prepared herself to be patient.

"I can read these first two," Griffen said, pointing to the first training books. "Gallo is still learning to name the symbols."

By the third day, they had fallen into a routine. Regina would have Gallo practice tracing the symbols in the soil while she worked with Griffen in the third book. Then she would write questions in Griffin's soil tray. He would write the answers while she practiced the symbols with Gallo and helped him learn to form them into simple words.

Regina had always thought of herself as fairly bright, but these two learned more quickly than she had. The longer she stayed at Meadow Commonwealth, the more she realized that everything she had been taught about thins and mixes was wrong.

One morning Griffen asked her, "Regina, will you please stay with us forever?"

It took her by surprise. "I'm not sure, Griffen. Why?"

"Because I like having you teach me. You see, I want to learn a lot so I can finish my basics after I make my final molt next season cycle. Someday, I'm going to be a famous chemist and discover what it is about plastic that we need. I plan to go to the Advanced Training Center for the Sciences. Then, if The Board will let me, I'm going to study with Henry's sister, Dorothy, in South Harvester 45. Dell and Donald are already teaching me how to speak Ant."

Regina smiled at his youthful dreams and the reality of his surroundings. "How will you get the credit to go to that center?"

"I'll have a sponsorship. When my sister and Rundell had their mating ceremony, Henry's cousin, Ronda, came. Those with power won't let her give us things directly, but she said she will sponsor all the nymphs here for training when we come of age. See? So with you to teach me my basics, I can get there a lot faster."

"You have your life well planned for someone so young."

"Henry says that it's good to plan. He says I should never stop dreaming, but I have to make it happen. Don't you have any dreams for your life?"

Regina sighed. "Not really. I've been very confused for a long time."

"That's another reason why you should stay here. You like us, don't you? And you make Henry smile."

"Griffen ..."

"I'm sorry," he said quickly. "My mom always says it's rude to get personal. When I first met Henry, I was much younger, but I saw he was happy. When we all moved out here, he acted like he was happy, but I knew better. Since you came, he smiles again. He looks at you like my sister looks at Rundell."

Regina shifted uneasily. "You notice too much. Now, let's get back to your lesson."

*   *   *   *

Henry stared at the wall, then looked down and splashed water over his face from the wash bowl early one sixthday morning. He gazed into the water for a while before he reached for a cloth. He looked up to see Rusty. "Sorry I took so long," he said. "I was thinking about the meeting I have this morning with that group trying to form a commonwealth in the city. They have to learn how to budget better."

Rusty smiled. "You weren't thinking about them. When we have our next group discussion, I think we should propose building another domicile."

"Why? I thought we were getting on well sharing quarters."

"Oh, we are. I just think it might get a bit crowded when one of us has a mate."

"A mate? Rusty, congratulations! I didn't know you'd met someone."

"You really are smitten." Rusty laughed. "Not me. You and Regina. Admit it. You look at her. She looks at you. And neither of you knows your antennae from your abdomen. Don't let her get away, Henry. She's good for you. You even hum when you're lugging fertilizer out to the grassfronds."

"I ..."

Rusty put a pod on Henry's thorax. "You and I have come a long way together. Don't be offended. Somebody had to make you see what's as plain as the mandibles on your face to everybody else here." Rusty turned and left the domicile.

   *   *   *   *

Seventhday morning, Regina sat next to Georgette when the group gathered to meditate. It was Henry's turn to lead them as they sang "Web of Life," an Ant song about the wholeness of the earth and their connection to it.

Henry began, "I am but a strand in an infinite web
But without me, the web is broken."

The others joined in the verse:

"I am a part of the sun
Its energy flowed to the plant
The green world soaked it in
To become food for all creatures
The sun is a part of me"

Regina looked at Henry as he sang the refrain again:

"I am but a strand in an infinite web
But without me, the web is broken"

His eyes were fixed on her. He smiled. Regina looked away, embarrassed. Her voice faltered and the others sang the next verse without her:

"I am a part of the earth
Of the same elements all are created

Simple to complex, one to ninety-two

Essence of Ardor infused her life
The earth is a part of me"

Henry's voice resonated with the refrain once more:
"I am but a strand in an infinite web
But without me, the web is broken"

And Regina thought of the evening before. As they had talked, and she had told him how she liked teaching Gallo and Griffen, he had pulled her toward him and stroked her softly. She had never felt more at peace with herself. She joined the others as they sang:

"Break a strand
The web lies wounded
All of it feeling the pain
Essence of Ardor as Araneida
Must come and repair it again"

Regina smiled back at Henry as he chanted:

"I am but a strand in an infinite web
But without me, the web is broken"

After meditation, while they sat eating dinner, she stretched out her middle pod and wrapped it around Henry's beneath the table as he was passing around a basket of fungus muffins. His pod slipped and he dropped the basket.

"I'm sorry," he said to the group, gathering up the muffins that rolled about in front of him. "I don't know what came over me."

"I do," said Griffen.

Griffen's mother cut him off. "Go fetch the jug of honey dew from the cold storage unit."

Rusty said something about the good weather they had been having and the conversation moved on.

At the end of the meal, Henry said, "Well, I'm headed for the hives," and left the Common Building.

Regina stayed to help clean up, and then said she thought she would take a walk. She wandered off toward the pond, thinking about Henry and Georgette and the others who had been so kind to her. She sat in the shade of one of the wood plants, listened to the aphids sucking sap above her, watched as a wild cricket satisfied its thirst on the opposite side of the pond. Everything about life here felt so right.

Not paying attention to direction, she rose and wandered on, filled with the warmth of the sun and the fragrance of blossoms. She reached out and plucked one, then spotted another color further on, and on. When a giant butterfly glided past her, she realized that nothing looked familiar. She whirled around in panic, but a soft sound caught her attention. She stopped still and listened. Yes, it was a voice, singing a mournful tune. It came from beyond a little rise and she headed for it.

Moments later, she found its source—Henry—seated on the bank of the border stream, images on parchment before him and front pods raised toward the sky. Regina stopped and stared. Had she walked so far without realizing it? She remembered Rundell's explanation of Henry's trips to the bee hives and felt ashamed that she had intruded upon his privacy, yet something drew her on. With the blossoms she had picked still firmly in one front pod, she approached him from behind.

She touched the back of his thorax to announce her presence. He turned, his eyes filled with sorrow. Awkwardly, she wrapped herself around him and began to stroke him. "You have freed me of all my fears and confusion. Please, let me try to fill your emptiness."

Henry shook slightly as he leaned against her. Gradually, she felt him relax as she continued to slide her front pods up the back of his thorax, over his head and on to the tips of his antennae. Several minutes passed. Finally, he eased away from her embrace.

"I," she hesitated, "I didn't mean to intrude. Actually, I walked farther than I intended and got lost. I was afraid. Then I heard you singing."

"It's all right. I'm glad you did ... not got lost, I mean ... but found me ... I come here ..."

"I know. Rundell told me."

Regina looked at the ground, not sure what to say next. Henry reached out and gathered his images from the ground then said, "This is my family. Would you like to see?"

He handed her the images one at a time. "This is my mother in our domicile in New South Dairy 50 ... and my father ... Behind him is the tiny mound where my grandfather once lived ... My brother, David, and his mate ... These are David's nymphs ..."

Regina gazed in awe at Henry's slender mother and his huge father. She caught herself before saying out loud her surprise that Henry was of mixed variety, and that all of his brothers had mated slender females. She thought about the members of Meadow Commonwealth: some large, some slender, some mixed. None of that mattered here. Maybe Henry could help her locate her grandmother and the rest of her mother's family.

She listened and looked as Henry showed her all the images, including the one he had taken in the glen where he had become an adult. She looked at him intently as he told her about his final molt.

Henry looked directly into her eyes. "Regina, I can never give you the life you're accustomed to, but I know that I cherish you. Will you have me as your mate?"

Regina looked at him, taken aback by the way he worded it since she had been taught that it was she who should give herself into his service, if a legal mating was offered. Then she remembered that in Ant culture, it was just the opposite. She thought about Henry's gentleness as opposed to Reese's pompous attitude; the loyalty she knew went with Henry's beliefs and the flagrant lack of fidelity of most wealthy male roaches; the uselessness of luxury and the simplicity of life at Meadow Commonwealth.

"Yes. I cherish you, too," she said. "I don't want the life I had any more. I want to stay here."

She listened as he recited the words of an Ant mating promise, and described the ceremony they would have in a time frame or so, as soon as a new domicile could be built. Then she rose with him, lifted her front pods with his and recited, "I promise myself to you as your mate, to cherish and support, no matter what joys or sorrows may occur. I will nurture with joy all new life that may come from our union. I promise this freely as long as we both live in this world."

"We are morally bound to each other now," Henry said, "though we will wait for physical union. I would like to make it legal as well. Is there any chance your father would sign a mating contract?"

The mention of her father brought Regina back to reality. What if Henry found out her original reason for coming to him? How could she ever explain it? Would he understand how differently she felt about everything now? What would her father do when he knew that Henry was Regina's choice?

"No," she said quickly, "he ... no ... that would be a very bad idea. We don't have to do that, do we?" She remembered what Rochelle had said about her employer having bound her and her mate. "Couldn't someone else bind us?"

"I suppose we could ask Rick to complete that portion of the ceremony, but I'll still write a contract, sign it myself, and formally register it. I wouldn't want any of our nymphs to go through what I did to gain full privileges."

"What do you mean?"

Henry explained the arguments he had made before the Legal Counseling Services Committee and how he had proved his "purity of variety."

"Do you mean that a so-called mix disappears when one legally mates into a pure clan?"

Henry nodded.

"And all this time, he was worried because ..." she cut herself off.

"What?" Henry asked.

"Nothing," Regina said quickly. She decided she would never hurt Henry with the truth. She would never return home to her father.

22.

*B*asking in their happiness, Henry and Regina returned to the community. They didn't have to say anything. Everyone knew by looking at them. Donald said that since they didn't want to enlarge the grassfrond field at that time, they should cut blocks of meadow grass from around the pond where it would grow back quickly. Those who remained in the community during regular work days began cutting blocks whenever they had spare time.

Griffen looked up from his lessons on thirdday and said, "Can we take a break after lunch? We could cut some more grass blocks."

"Only if you have this memorized by then," Regina replied.

Griffen immediately returned to his task and Regina turned back to Gallo. By noon, both had finished their lessons perfectly.

"Stay out of the mud," Ruth called after her brothers as they scampered toward the pond ahead of Regina, tools in their pods.

Grass grew to the edge on the north side of the pond, which was full from late spring sky water. Before long, Griffen had cut two good chunks. Gallo pushed the tool into the soft earth but the tool slipped from his pod and fell into the water. He splashed in after it.

"Gallo," Regina said, "you did that on purpose, and your sister told you not to."

"No I didn't," he said, putting both pods in the water and groping around. "I can't find the tool!"

Regina moved closer and looked into the water, clouded by Gallo's efforts. She reached in at the edge and began to feel around. "The bottom is so firm here," she noted. "Ah, here it is." She pulled up the tool.

"Oooo, it's all yucky!" Gallo said.

Regina began to put it back into the water to clean it off and then stopped. She scraped a bit of the muck off with one front pod and looked at it. Then she reached into the pond again and dug at the bottom.

"Look who's playing in the mud," Gallo giggled.

Regina worked her other front pod into the blob she pulled up. "This isn't ordinary mud," she explained. "It's clay, pretty good clay, too."

"What's clay?" Griffen asked.

"It's mud you can make things with, like statues, or vases. It can be shaped any way you want it, then baked till it's hard."

"We could put blossoms in vases. But what would we do with statues?" Griffen asked. "Can you make anything useful, like bowls and mugs? Do you know to do it? We really need some bowls and mugs."

Regina smiled. Finally, there was something she knew, and could do well, which would benefit all of them. "Yes," replied, "and I'll show you how to help."

*   *   *   *

Henry leaned over a law manuscript, flipping the pages, searching for the reference he needed to help a client. He heard someone enter the shop.

Georgette's pleasant voice greeted the visitor. "Good day. What can I do for you?"

"I'm looking for information."

Henry rose and came out into the main part of the shop. "What kind of information? I might be able to help you," he said. He looked carefully at the large male. Something about him set Henry on edge.

"Are you the counselor?"

"Yes."

"I'm looking for a young female who disappeared."

"You're an Enforcer?" Henry asked, his suspicions rising. He gave Georgette a quick signal not to speak.

"Sort of. I do search work privately. My client is looking for his daughter. They had an argument and he kicked her out. Now, he regrets it. I've been following leads for over a time frame, all of them yielding nothing. Early this morning, a female in the shanties said maybe she came in here. She said she's referred several to you for legal help."

Henry immediately thought of Regina. He had brought up the subject of her family several times, but each time she had emphasized that she didn't want to go home. He remained wary. "What was the female's name?" he asked. "I've counseled many on family matters."

"You would remember this one," he said drawing out an image. "Her name is Regina."

Henry didn't need the image, but he looked anyway. He replied cautiously, "Yes, she did come in about two time frames ago. She was frantic. Not physically hurt, but emotionally bruised. She nearly went to pieces when I told her she was of age and I couldn't force her father to take her back."

"Do you know where she is now?"

"I might be able to locate her. What if she doesn't want to return home?"

"Her father knows she may bear him ill will. He told me he treated her shamefully. He wrote a letter to her. I have it with me. Would you be able to deliver it to her? I'll return tomorrow for her reply. Perhaps, since you're a counselor, you could help him work things out."

The male looked around the shop. "He would pay well. Looks like you could use it."

Henry was far more interested in Regina's welfare than in any credit offered. He nodded slowly and said, "I'll accept the letter. I know you could follow me when I leave, but I ask you not to. Like you, I have an obligation to protect a client's confidential matters."

"Agreed," he said, taking a letter from a satchel and handing it to Henry. Then he left the shop.

"Henry," Georgette said, "I don't know whether to be happy or not. Every time I've hoped Regina would open up about her family, she says she doesn't want to discuss it."

Henry nodded. "There's something about all of this. I know I've seen that male somewhere before with some Enforcers."

Regina, Gallo and Griffen were covered with clay to the second joints of their front pods when Henry walked into the Common Building late that afternoon.

"Look!" Regina called to him. "We found clay on the north side of the pond. Lots of it! We've already formed several mugs. Gallo's are a bit odd shaped, but he's learning quickly. Later, I could even make some things to sell."

Henry greeted her affectionately. "That's wonderful. Let's go for a walk before dinner."

"Of course. Let me clean up. Gallo and Griffen, we'll stop for today. Cover everything that's not finished with damp cloths."

Regina went to the food preparation area and washed the clay from her front pods in the tub they used to clean serving bowls. Henry led her out of the Common Building and into the meadow. He didn't speak until they were quite far from all the community buildings.

"I know you don't want to talk about your family, but a male came in to see me today saying he had been searching for you on behalf of your father. He said your father regrets what happened and wants you to come home. I didn't tell him where you were. He asked me to give you this letter from your father."

Regina stiffened. She took the letter slowly, broke the seal and read the message to herself:

"We made a bargain for two time frames. It's up. Reese has made an offer for you. I have not seen any evidence."

Regina tore the letter to shreds and slumped to the ground. Henry surrounded her with his pods. "Whatever it is, we can get through it together. But you must tell me what's going on."

"In the beginning ... oh ... I thought I could forget it ... Please, believe me, I wouldn't hurt you for anything. That's why I didn't want to tell you. Everything's so different now. I really do cherish you. I want to be your mate and I never want to leave here. Do you believe that?"

"Of course." Henry stroked her.

"I don't know how to say this," she said, tears coming to her eyes. "I want you to know that I'd be willing to take every turn at hauling body waste, if that would convince you that I don't want any harm to come to you or anyone here. But it didn't start out that way."

"Regina, you're not making a bit of sense. Don't you know I'd do anything for you? Whatever is wrong, I'll stand by you, even to death."

Regina sighed. "I never told you any lies. I just didn't tell you all of the truth. The first day I came to you, I really was afraid, but not for the reason you thought. I was afraid about what I was doing. Was the male who came in very large, so dark brown he seemed black, with a scar on the side of his thorax?"

"Yes! Do you know him?"

"He works for my father as my official escort and he's known all along I've been here. He only said what he did to keep up appearances. My father hates you and I knew that. He wants to bind me in mating to someone I don't like. I made a bargain with my father that if I could find something illegal going on out here, he would let me choose my own mate."

Henry sat quietly.

"By the end of the first quarter time frame, I knew there was nothing illegal going on. Everyone was so kind to me and I got so interested in knowing more about you, I wanted to stay. I wanted to forget all about my father. I really meant what I said when I made our Promise."

It was Henry's turn to sigh. "Well, that answers why no Enforcers have been spying on us for a while."

Regina looked sadly at Henry. "They wouldn't have anyway. The Board recalled theirs and the one working for my father quit. I overheard him telling my father. That's when I got the idea. I've made a huge mess and will end up hurting you anyway. Can you to forgive me?"

Henry embraced her again. "How could I not forgive you?"

"Is there any way out of this except for me to go home and be bound to someone else?"

"Let's walk. I have to think as your counselor now."

They walked several paces in silence, then Henry asked, "When you made the bargain with your father, had any male actually made an offer?"

"Not when I left. That's why I did it. I wanted to get the chance to choose before someone did. Now he has an offer."

"Did you have to find something illegal or just look for it?"

Regina smiled. "That's it! I said, 'No matter what I find, I can have my choice,' and he agreed. My father acts out hatred, but deep inside he's not so bad." Regina told Henry about her grandmother. "He's done right for my mother and me all this time, and he did take care of my grandmother. He doesn't understand about you, that's all. I'll go home tomorrow. I'll tell him there isn't anything wrong out here. He never goes back on his word." Regina felt a surge of confidence she had never known before.

"Maybe I should come with you," Henry said.

"No, I've learned how to be myself here. I'm not afraid anymore."

"Are you sure?" Henry asked, stopping their stroll and taking her front pods in his. "I don't want to lose you."

"Yes, I'm sure. You won't lose me. I made a Promise and I'm going to keep it."

Regina explained everything to Rundell and Georgette on their way to the shop the next morning. Her escort arrived an h-unit later. "Regina, he found you!"

Regina rose from behind the counter where she had been helping package fly eggs. "Forget the act. I've told them. Don't take me home. Take me to my father's clinic. I will talk to him there."

Rundell put a pod on her thorax. "Would you like me to come with you?"

"No thank you, I'll be fine. Tell Henry I'll see him later this afternoon."

Regina followed her escort. Neither of them said a word as they proceeded through the market section of the city and to the area beyond it, where those of high rank conducted their professions. Regina had never been there before and looked about with curiosity. Most buildings had two levels, large portals, and many shuttered wall openings. The exteriors were quite impressive, unlike other parts of the city where some buildings still lacked repairs from the previous fall's storm.

Regina's escort led her up the ramp and through the portal of a mid-sized structure. He took her to a comfortable inner chamber and said,

"This is your father's private study. Wait here for him. I'll bring you refreshments."

Regina looked around the chamber. Shelves of medical books lined two walls in neat rows. A large, well-stuffed cushion sat behind a polished wooden writing surface. Another padded bench lay in front of a wall opening. Regina opened the shutters and sat down on the bench. Her father came in before the refreshments arrived. Her escort was with him. The escort remained standing at the portal.

Robert walked around the writing surface and sat down in the cushion. He came right to the point. "Well, where's my evidence?"

"There isn't any. Your Enforcer was right. You're all wrong about them, father. There is nothing illegal going on out there. They ..."

Robert cut her off. "Then I will bind you to Reese next sixthday as planned."

"As planned? What do you mean? You said I could have my choice no matter what I found!"

"I said no such thing."

Regina's voice rose. "Yes, you did. I said, 'No matter what I find I can have my choice,' and you twitched your antennae and gave me two time frames!"

"I never agreed to that. I had an itch," Robert said calmly. "I'd signed an agreement with Young Sir Reese before you ever approached me. I only let you go to get this foolishness out of your head, and rid myself of that upstart as a bonus."

Regina's voice shook. "You'd already signed? Why didn't you tell me?"

"You didn't ask," he laughed. "You see, Regina, scheming isn't an inherited trait; it's an art. And you'll never have it."

Regina broke down. "No! No! You can't. I don't want to be Resse's mate. He doesn't care about me. He won't be loyal. That's not what I want for my life. I want to stay at Meadow Commonwealth. They know how to live there. They know what it means to care. I wasn't even planning to come home! I want to be Henry's mate."

Robert rose from the cushion and slammed his pod on the writing surface. "Don't you tell me what you want! You don't own yourself! I'll bind you to whomever I please."

In desperation Regina cried, "You can't! I've made a Promise! I've already given myself to Henry."

Robert's tone of voice changed abruptly. "You what? You'd choose that poor, half-thin over the son of the Supreme Executor? Tell me you haven't already..."

"Yes," Regina said. If her father thought she and Henry had already mated, he would have to allow her to return to Henry. Her father stared at her in silence. Her escort stood mute.

Then her father smiled strangely. "Well, if that's the case, then I guess we'd better get him here and make it legal." He turned to Regina's escort. "Go back to Counselor Henry's place and insist he come here immediately."

"Yes, Master Robert. The sign on the shop says he doesn't arrive there until noon. Shall I fetch him at the Training Center?"

Robert tapped his front pod on the surface. "No, we'll keep this quiet. Bring him as soon as he arrives at the egg shop."

The escort nodded and left.

Robert shook his front pod at his daughter. "If you really want him and not Reese, you will remain in this chamber." Then he walked out and slammed the portal.

*   *   *   *

A strange feeling nagged at Henry all morning. He went through the motions of his training units. He had never asked Regina for any names. He had plenty of enemies. It didn't matter which. Why would someone who hated him send his daughter on such an errand if someone were seriously courting her? A large bribe to some shanty female would have made more sense. Regina had said The Board had recalled their Enforcers, and he believed her. What had her father hoped to find? Was it something personal against him, or Meadow Commonwealth in general?

Regina was so innocent. That was what had attracted him to her in the first place. Was her father using her and she didn't even know it? The thought of her going home alone worried him. What if he never saw her again? He didn't really know who she was. His emotions had blurred his judgment. He should have been more careful. Had he already placed her or himself in jeopardy?

He left the Training Center at noon and headed for the egg shop. An Enforcer followed at a discreet distance. The sight of Regina's escort outside the egg shop increased his anxiety.

The escort smiled. "Regina's father was most glad to see her. They worked everything out splendidly. He wishes you to come with me that he might reward you personally."

The Enforcer following him was still there and he spotted a second between two other shops down the lane from Rundell's. Now Henry was certain of a conspiracy.

"One moment, please," Henry said. "I must leave a message with my partner. I'm expecting a client soon."

Henry entered the shop. Rundell said nothing, but there was a worried look in his eyes. "It seems Regina's father wants to see me," Henry said. "If I'm not back in two h-units, go to Master Robin. His location is on a note in my Legal Counseling Services folder. I might need his services."

Rundell nodded.

Henry poked his head out of the portal and spoke to the escort. "Excuse me. My partner needs to know where I might be located in an emergency. I make it a point not to ask more than is needed of any client. Regina didn't mention who her father is. Where are we going?"

"Master Surgeon Robert's clinic."

Henry's heart sank. He and Rundell exchanged glances. "I'll go as soon as Georgette gets back," Rundell said.

Knowing it was far too late to do anything else, Henry left the shop and followed Regina's escort. The two Enforcers no longer hid themselves. One walked in front, the other behind. When they reached the clinic, the Enforcers entered as well. Anxiety filled Henry as he walked into the chamber and saw Regina. He saw joy in her eyes and then dismay at the sight of The Enforcers.

"Henry, he ..." Regina began.

Robert stood and thundered at his daughter. "Silence!" He turned to the Enforcers. "This miserable mix has seduced and violated my daughter and I had already signed a mating contract with a young male of high rank. Take my daughter into your protective custody. Keep her escort with her at all times. Take this criminal to the Detention Center, but keep it quiet. I won't have my daughter's reputation soiled. She's to be bound to her intended in three days."

Henry thought his joints would cave in under him. His mind whirled.

He heard Regina cry. "No! Father, no! He didn't! We didn't! You lied to me. You lied! How could you? Henry, I cherish you! I do."

Robert laughed. "Things worked out after all. Your own words will condemn him, Regina."

Henry could hear her crying as the two Enforcers dragged him away.

23.

*I*n the lower levels of the Justice Structure, the portal slammed behind Henry and its bolt slid into place. Henry waited as his eyes adjusted to the dim light in the detention cell. No one ever stayed here long. Inquiries were conducted immediately in Roacheria. Enforcers weren't interested in the truth, but in quick disposal of those accused.

Two other thin roaches sat against the far wall of the bare chamber. Their faces dripped life juice from where their mandibles had been cut off, probably that morning. One groaned in pain. Tomorrow, they would be pushed into the mantis compound. Henry shuddered. He might be in the same position soon. He slumped to the floor. The joints in his legs were swelled and aching. Life juice oozed from the main support joints of his back legs. Several Enforcers had bent each joint backward as they "questioned" him upon his arrival.

He wondered if Master Robin would come. Since he had first encountered the middle-aged counselor while proving his "purity," the two had formed a professional friendship. They did not meet often, but corresponded through letters.

Henry forced self-pity from his mind and concentrated on the search for a strategy. His emotions had gotten him into this, but only his knowledge of the law could get him out, maybe. If Master Robin didn't

come, he would speak for himself as best he could. H-units dragged by. His stomach complained in hunger and his mouth puffed with thirst. The chamber didn't even have a body waste pot. He lost track of time.

Pods clicked down the passage, followed by a familiar voice. Henry sighed in relief. The bolt slid back, the portal opened and light entered the chamber.

"Get my client out of this dung hole! Now! I'll cover the fees for better quarters."

Henry tried to rise but fell back. It took all his strength not to cry out. Master Robin took hold of his front pods and assisted him. "Thank you," Henry rasped.

"You know you shouldn't speak until we're alone," Master Robin replied.

The Enforcers led them to an isolation chamber. Its furnishings consisted of a small bench, a stool and an open pot for body waste. Master Robin helped Henry to sit down and handed him a jug of water. Henry took it and sipped slowly.

"Will this be satisfactory, Counselor?" the Enforcer asked Master Robin.

"No! And I will report this completely unnecessary and excessive abuse," Master Robin said, setting his satchel down on the floor of the chamber. "I want a decent sleep cushion brought in, a writing surface and another lamp. Don't feed him the slop you offer here. I'll have food sent in for my client. Leave us and don't hang around listening."

"Call when you're ready to leave," the Enforcer said.

"I'm sorry I don't have any pain potion with me," Master Robin soaked a cloth with water and washed Henry's injuries. "That's the best I can do. Not even my influence will get you a physician." Then he handed

Henry a small sack filled with slices of grasshopper and a couple of fungus muffins. "From Rundell," he said.

"I'm sorry it took me so long to get here, Henry. Rundell came to me shortly after noon, but I kept getting interrupted. You've got yourself in one very tough situation. Master Robert's accusation papers don't paint a pretty scene. Rundell filled me in on a lot of background, which helped me understand what's going on, but it won't demonstrate innocence."

"First," Henry said, between bites, "let me say how grateful I am. Especially since I've no private funds."

"Forget my fees, Counselor Henry. You have more friends than you thought. I could have gotten paid several times for you. Rundell said to give them till harvest time. I told him not to worry. Then your cousin Ronda sent word that she'd pay. I sent back a message saying I'd been paid. After that, a male came saying he represented a group of former clients. He handed me a sack full of small credit units they'd collected on your behalf. I told him to use it to buy plastic for the nymphs of those who gave it. Sir Rafael offered to pay, too. I told him that counseling you would be for the pleasure of beating Master Robert. I have no affection for that piece of fly bate. Let's get down to business. Did you physically mate with Regina?"

"No."

"According to the accusation papers, she told her father she 'gave herself to you.' Would you mind explaining?"

"Regina and I made a Mating Promise," Henry replied, and described the Ant custom and what he had said to Regina about belonging to each other from that moment on. He also told Master Robin every word he and Regina had said to each other the evening before. "If I had known who her father was, I would have handled things quite differently."

"What's Master Robert got against you, besides that case you won forcing physicians to provide infection-fighting molds to all, regardless of variety?" Master Robin asked.

Henry spent quite a while explaining the intricacies of his family history, his grandfather's relationship with Robert's great-uncle, Rex, and the earlier conflict between Rex and Ronda's grandfather over the surface now occupied by Meadow Commonwealth. "There's something else, too," he continued. "Master Robert and my father were in medical training at the same time. There was an incident where my father went against regulations and obtained infection-fighting molds for a shanty female's nymph. Master Robert found out about it. Later, my father didn't want to participate for moral reasons when his turn came to de-mandible the condemned. Master Robert threatened to expose him and the others involved in the mold incident if he didn't. My father went through with his part at the Center for the Condemned to protect those around him."

"And now you and Master Robert's daughter fall for each other." Master Robin tapped his pod on the wall and whistled softly through his mandibles. "You certainly know how to make enemies."

"Where have they taken Regina? I'm worried about her. She doesn't understand what's happening. Her father tricked her and used her to get to me. I'm sure she thinks this is all her fault. Will they let you see her?"

"No, they won't let me talk to her until I question her during The Inquiry. She's locked in a comfortable chamber up on the third level. Three warriors stand outside the portal and her official escort is inside with her."

"When you question her during The Inquiry, please, let her know somehow that I still cherish her and I don't blame her."

Master Robin nodded and continued. "Apparently, Master Robert's plan was to get rid of you quietly and bind Regina to her intended one before he found out about you. That didn't work. The whole city seems to know you are accused of violating her."

"Do they think I'm guilty?"

"No, but that doesn't help you. We both know that only time will prove your innocence, and that, my friend, we don't have. Robert has demanded that The Inquiry take place tomorrow morning at nine h-units. He says the male with the contract won't accept 'a damaged female.' Master Robert wants you condemned immediately, since he wasn't able to keep your involvement quiet. But whoever the male is, he's got more power. Those who know won't say who he is."

Henry shifted on the stool, trying to find a more comfortable position. "There's got to be a way to get some time. Before you came, I kept trying to think. My mind kept going back to when I did all that research to prove my purity. Remember that?"

"How could I forget? But reminiscing won't get you anywhere." Master Robin began pacing the cell.

"I remember reading about an old custom where a female went into isolation for a certain amount of time before she was bound in mating. It seems that, back then, females wanted to show that they were chaste mates. I don't remember the details."

"Have you still got that text?" Master Robin asked.

Henry nodded. "It's with my other law manuscripts in my work chamber at the egg shop."

"I'd better get over there and start reading. I've got exactly fourteen h-units to find a way to keep you alive."

"Master Robin, have you got any extra parchment and ink with you?"

"Yes, why?"

"I'd like to write some letters to my family, in case ..."

Master Robin tipped his antennae. "I'll deliver them personally, and assure them of your innocence." He took several sheets of parchment and an ink pot from his satchel and handed them to Henry. Then he called out to the guards that he was ready to leave. "Remember," he added, "not one word from you during the proceedings tomorrow. I'm the counselor this time."

*   *   *   *

Regina threw herself onto the cushion in her confinement chamber wailing, "You lied to me! Everything you said was a lie! How can you do this to me?"

Master Robert spoke to his daughter. "Regina, what's done is done. You should talk about lies. You went out there with the intention of finding something illegal. I found a different method, that's all."

"I hate you. I hate everything you stand for. And I won't be Reese's mate. I'd rather jump out of that wall opening and crush myself."

Robert turned to the Enforcers standing by. "She's foolish enough to try it. See that the openings are bolted from the outside, or move her to another chamber with no openings."

"Right away, Master Robert. There is an outside ledge at this level. I'll send guards right now to secure the shutters." He pointed to one Enforcer who left.

Robert turned back to his daughter. "Listen to me, if you want me to spare your precious Henry's life," he sneered. "Henry's counselor, and somehow he's managed to get a good one, will question you tomorrow. If you say anything to discredit me, or mention Young Sir Reese's name, I'll make sure you watch as Henry is pushed into the mantis compound. Keep quiet, and I'll request banishment instead. Remember, the Chief Enforcer will believe the words of a male over a female every time."

*   *   *   *

Henry had a restless night. The sleep cushion brought to him was thin and did little to relieve the pain in his legs. Meditation finally brought sleep a few h-units before morning. The vision of ants and roaches united came to him again, but this time he stood between the united group and the roach who stood apart. In his dream, he walked toward the assembly of ants and roaches. Again they stroked and strengthened him. Henry stood with them beckoning to the lone roach. He was too far off to see his features clearly. Slowly, so slowly, he came toward them. When he was almost close enough to recognize, Henry awoke.

The portal of his confinement chamber banged open and three Enforcers entered. "Time to go," the first said, holding out hemp binding cords. He had often been present when Henry came there as a counselor.

"You know me," Henry said. "The restraints won't be necessary."

"They're required. Your counselor hasn't arrived yet to guarantee you. Submit."

Henry spread his middle and back pods and held out his front appendages. The degrading procedure began. The second Enforcer tied the cords from one pod to the next. Henry stooped, allowing them to lift the plate of his exoskeleton behind the back of his head, pass the final cord under and secure it in front. The second Enforcer gave a tug on it to lead him out. Barely able to breathe, holding the letters he had written, Henry limped down the passage and up the ramps leading to the public chambers of the Justice Structure where Formal Inquiries took place.

Master Robin came scuttling toward them as they reached their destination, pods filled with parchments and the ragged manuscript from Henry's work chamber in the egg shop. He gave the Enforcers a stern look. "You couldn't wait five minutes! Get these humiliating restraints off my client. Now! I won't enter this Inquiry with Henry in this condition."

Henry gave Master Robin a look of gratitude and held out the letters. Master Robin put them safely in his satchel.

*   *   *   *

Regina sat on the bench in the victim's chamber, giving her father an icy stare as he told her once more what she should say and not say when questioned. She hated him and she hated herself for what she had done. She hated what she would have to do in a few moments. But if it would save Henry's life, she would do it. More than anything, she wished she could turn back the days and do things differently.

An Enforcer opened the portal and gestured for them to enter the public chamber for The Inquiry. The Chief Enforcer sat on a high bench at the front. Henry and his counselor stood before him. Georgette and Rundell sat on a plain wooden bench on the opposite side of the chamber. A roach she did not recognize sat on another. Other benches for the public were filled to capacity.

Henry's eyes were fixed on her, full of the same caring he had always shown her. She wanted to weep at the sight of his injured legs. She wanted to shout her sorrow and guilt, say she would trade places with him or die with him, but restrained herself remembering her father's words. She tried to tell him with her own gaze how much she cared as she lowered herself onto the softly padded victim's bench. Her father and her escort sat down on either side of her.

The Chief Enforcer addressed Master Robert. "You may come forward and state your case in the matter of Henry Roach-Dairier's guilt."

"Lord Chief Enforcer, a young male of high rank has been courting my daughter since Last Night, always in the presence of her escort. My daughter was always with her escort when away from our domicile. I signed a mating contract with the young male, who deserves his privacy in this degrading affair, over two time frames ago. My daughter requested to visit her cousins in Sea Edge. She packed her things and I sent her with her escort. When they stopped at a food booth for refreshment, my foolish daughter took it into her mind to run away. She told her escort she needed to go to a sanitation area and slipped away from him."

Robert lowered his head and shook his antennae, as if recalling great anxiety, then continued. "It took us so long to locate her, only to learn that this miserable piece of fly bait," he gestured toward Henry, "had taken advantage of her innocence, seduced, and violated her. She told me plainly that she had given herself to him." Robert drooped again as though about to weep. Then he looked up at the Chief Enforcer. "He deserves to be punished to the maximum extent of the law."

"Thank you for your statement," the Chief Enforcer said. "Do you wish to examine Master Robert in defense?" he asked Henry's counselor.

Regina's anger burned at her father's blatant lies. She looked at Henry, who still gazed at her sadly, not uttering a sound.

Master Robin addressed the Chief Enforcer. "I see no point in allowing him to spew more lies. I have better creatures to defend my client."

Murmurs rippled through the public area. Robert returned to his place beside Regina.

"You may examine them now," the Chief Enforcer said to Master Robin.

Master Robin called for Georgette.

Regina looked hopefully at Georgette. Georgette stood before the Chief Enforcer and described the day Regina had come to the egg shop. She told how Regina stayed in her home.

"Did Henry ever spend time alone with Regina?" the Chief Enforcer asked Georgette.

Georgette lowered her head. "Yes."

When his turn came, Rundell told how many training units he had taken from Henry, their personal friendship and his belief that Henry could not have violated Regina because of his integrity and his dedication to Ant ways. A soft hissing of approval spread among those watching the proceedings. Regina was grateful that neither Rundell nor Georgette had told why she had actually gone to Meadow Commonwealth.

Master Robin called the roach Regina did not know. "This is the senior interpreter for the S.E.R.C.B. He will now, as an expert in Ant culture and with no personal connection to my client, explain what Regina meant when she told her father she had 'given' herself to Henry in a Promise."

"Proceed," the Chief Enforcer said.

"Among ants," the interpreter began, "it is usually, but not always, the female who proposes mating. The couple makes a verbal promise giving themselves to each other. By their tradition, they are morally bound from that moment on. Generally, however, physical mating does not take place until after a formal ceremony. The young female," he indicated Regina, "could have been referring to that tradition when she said she gave herself."

The Chief Enforcer asked him, "What happens to a couple who do mate physically before such a ceremony?"

"It simply doesn't happen, Lord Chief Enforcer. Their beliefs are very strong."

"But, supposing passion overcame a couple. Are there any consequences under their laws for such an act?"

"No, not if they are promised to each other."

"Thank you for this information. You are excused," the Chief Enforcer said.

Regina rejoiced that someone outside the circle of Henry's friends understood what she meant. Still, she knew she had deliberately planted the idea in her father's mind that she and Henry had physically mated.

"Counselor," the Chief Enforcer said to Master Robin, "your defense is terribly weak. Though it proposes the possibility of innocence, it does not prove it. Have you anyone else you wish to examine?"

Several creatures in the public area twanged their mandibles in disapproval of what the Chief Enforcer said.

"Silence!" he commanded.

Master Robin addressed him. "Yes, Lord Chief Enforcer. I would like to examine Regina in some depth. I ask you to grant me a bit of latitude in this, since she deserves great respect and dignity for her rank and as a supposed victim. I request that you allow me to explain some points of law to her that she may not understand."

Regina's pods began to shake. She cast an anguished look toward Henry. His eyes remained steady.

"Such as?" the Chief Enforcer asked.

Master Robin picked up the tattered manuscripts from the small stand near him. "These, some of which are so old and seldom used that you may benefit from the explanations as well. I assure you, they are valid and still in force."

The Chief Enforcer tapped one front pod on his bench in thought. Regina looked up at him, trying not to shake. Whatever Master Robin wanted of her, it was to help Henry. The Chief Enforcer stared down at her. She looked away, afraid she would lose control, and fixed her eyes on Henry again. Master Robin put his pod on Henry's thorax. She felt her father grip her back pod in his where no one could see, a final warning.

"Agreed," the Chief Enforcer stated. "Regina, come forward."

Regina rose slowly from her place and walked to the area in front of the Chief Enforcer. She stooped low and spread her front pods out to the sides as she had been instructed. Then she turned and faced Master Robin.

Master Robin approached her calmly. "Regina, the things I will say and ask at first I do not want you to answer. I intend for these comments to help you decide what you should and should not say. I know you are terribly frightened of all this and I want you to understand that I know you are completely innocent of all wrong-doing in this matter."

Regina nodded weakly.

"It is forbidden for Henry to speak to you today. I want you to think of my words as his. You do not have to offer to take any turns at shoveling body waste for us to know that none of this is your fault in even the smallest way."

Regina started at the reference to what she had said privately to Henry. She looked at him. He moved one middle pod very slightly.

Master Robin continued. "It is very probable that you are afraid answer my questions honestly. You may have been told what you should say. You may have been threatened. I don't want you to say if you have, or have not, been so instructed. I do want you to think carefully about everything you were told by anyone before you went to Meadow Commonwealth, while you were there, and since your return. Think about who told you the truth and who didn't. Trust those who told you the truth."

Regina thought about all the lies her father had told her. Had he lied about what she should say as well? She had heard him ask for maximum punishment only a few minutes before.

She nodded.

"Regina, I want you to answer my questions simply and honestly. Don't give me a reason unless I ask for it and then keep it as simple as possible. That is the best way for you to help me today."

Master Robin looked at her with gentleness and she nodded once more. Perhaps he would not ask her to discredit her father or say Reese's name.

"Did Henry seduce and violate you?"

"No, he didn't."

"What did you mean, then, when you told your father you had given yourself to Henry?"

Tears came to her eyes. "It's Henry that I cherish. I want to be his mate, as I promised him. I don't want to be ... someone else's mate. I thought that if I said that, my father would let me be with Henry. I swear; I didn't know this could happen."

Hopeful words quietly passed through the crowd. For the first time, Regina looked at them. There in the center, sat her grandmother, smiling at her. She dared not look at her father.

"Lord Chief Enforcer, may I now explain the point of law I referred to earlier?" Master Robin asked.

"You may."

Master Robin addressed the assembly. "Many generations ago, when South Roacheria combined with East Roacheria, mating codes were rewritten to include East Roacheria's customs. They demanded more of their females than South Roacheria did at the time. Among those properly mated, it was common for a female to ask to be confined and protected for a period of three time frames after a mating contract had been signed, so that she could prove to her intended that she was chaste. If by the end of that confinement, the female had laid no egg, her intended male had no doubt about his responsibilities toward any eggs laid after he took her."

Master Robin turned to Regina. "Let me be precise about how this applies to you at this time. It may not seem at first like the best way for you to clear up this misunderstanding between you and your father, but believe me, it is the only way Henry can prove his innocence so you can be with him as you stated you wanted to earlier."

Regina looked steadily at him. "Please, explain this to me."

"Wait a moment!" Robert shouted angrily from his place.

The Chief Enforcer glared at him. "You've had your say. Be quiet." He nodded to Master Robin to continue.

"If you request the Chief Enforcer to allow you to demonstrate your chastity, you and Henry will both be confined for a set period of time. You will not be allowed to see each other or communicate in any way, although both of you may have other visitors under the supervision of Enforcers and as determined by the Chief Enforcer here today. When the time is up, one of several things will take place. If you produce an egg, your father or your intended may take action. Your father can only request that Henry be banished. He has no authority to order him condemned to death. Only your intended, if he steps forward publicly, can condemn

Henry. If you lay no egg, thereby proving your chastity and Henry's innocence, Henry will go free. Your intended may then claim you as his, or, if he chooses not to appear, Henry will claim you. If you are unclear about any of this, now is the time to ask."

"Must I name my intended?" Regina whispered, thinking that perhaps if she didn't embarrass Reese or his father by bringing them into the picture, he would show mercy as well and not show up to claim her.

"No," Master Robin stated. "It's up to him to come forward."

Regina turned to the Chief Enforcer and smiled for the first time. "I want to do this. I want to be confined and show that Henry didn't seduce me. Please."

"I won't allow it!" Master Robert yelled. "She still belongs to my household."

"Quiet! It's no longer up to you," the Chief Enforcer told him. Then he asked, "Master Robin, would you give me that text that I might be certain we document this properly?"

Master Robin approached and extended the manuscript, opened to the proper page, toward the Chief Enforcer. The chamber remained silent as he read it. Regina looked toward Henry and they smiled at each other. Master Robin rubbed the back of Henry's thorax. She glanced toward her grandmother who silently mouthed the words, "I will visit you." She could feel her father's anger.

Several minutes later, the Chief Enforcer stated, "I will grant Regina's request. Allowing for the advance in our knowledge of the female reproductive system since these were written, but in order to satisfy all present, I will set the period of confinement at two and one half time frames. Regina will be confined where she remained last night. I will personally interview the Enforcers who will guard her, in order insure that no other male may molest her while under my jurisdiction. All requests for supplies and permission to visit either of them will be approved by me. This Formal Inquiry will reconvene in seventy days."

The Chief Enforcer climbed down from his bench, handed the manuscript back to Master Robin, and left the chamber by his own exit, ending the proceedings. Regina's father stormed out of the chamber. The crowd pounded their pods on the floor in approval as Enforcers led Henry and Regina to their confinement chambers.

24.

"*T*hank you," Henry said to Master Robin when they were finally alone in his cell.

"It was your manuscript that did it. I was sure Regina would agree, but I was afraid the Chief Enforcer would not accept it. You can be sure I will reread all those old codes. I might be able to use them in future cases. I'll request everything I can think of to make this period more tolerable. What's most important to you, so I can bargain?"

Henry looked around at the tiny underground chamber and its bare synthetic stone walls. Could he stand two and one-half time frames without seeing the surface? "I'd like a lot of parchment and ink. It looks like I'll finally have time to translate my writings into Roach. I'd like to have my journal and the images of my family. Rundell will get all of that for you. Plenty to read and one of my cousin Ronda's wall-sized images of the surface would be nice."

"I don't think any of that will be a problem. I'll order a better sleep cushion too. I'll try to stop by and see you every time I'm here on business."

"Will they allow you to see Regina?" Henry asked.

"Probably not. To mollify Master Robert somewhat, The Chief Enforcer isn't likely to allow anyone you know to see her."

Henry sighed.

"I'll bring you a calendar and I'll continue to have decent food sent in," Master Robin said as he turned to leave.

*   *   *   *

Regina looked out the wall opening of her confinement chamber, resenting the tether on her back pod, but glad that she had been able to compromise with her escort. The Chief Enforcer had installed a bolt on her side of the portal. She had sworn to use it after her escort left each evening and the shutters were secured. She was grateful that she had been given the choice to refuse any visitor approved by the Chief Enforcer. It gave her untold pleasure to refuse to speak to her father. She crossed off another day—forty-five left.

She heard a tap on the portal. Her escort opened a small peephole. "It's your mother and some other thin, old female."

Regina turned. "Let them in!"

Bolts on both sides of the portal slid back. Rebecca and Rochelle entered. Regina rushed to them. "Mother! Grammy! How are you able to come together?" she asked, knowing from her mother's pervious visits that Rochelle had been denied the privilege.

Rochelle stroked her. Regina basked in her touch, wishing it could be Henry's.

"I've left your father," Rebecca said. "Master Robin said he couldn't counsel me because of his connection to Henry, but he recommended another and that one finally got The Chief Enforcer to grant permission for your grandmother to come."

Regina stared at her mother. "You left?"

"I got a little courage from you," Rebecca said. "I decided it wasn't worth it any more. It's not final yet, and I'll have nothing when it is. The private fund I had went for the counseling. I'm staying with my oldest brother and your grandmother."

"But ..."

Rochelle interrupted Regina. "I'm proud of you! Don't you worry about any of us. You spoke for so many females when you said you didn't want to be mated to another, but to one who cared for you. You lifted us all. Be strong now and finish this. We'll all be together on the day you and Henry have your ceremony."

Worry crept into Regina's mind. "But what if Reese claims me?"

"Let's not worry about that, now," Rebecca said.

The three females talked for an h-unit and then Rochelle whispered, "I have another surprise for you. When your mother's counselor argued for me to visit you, he didn't use my name. On my own, I secured permission to see Henry. What message shall I give him from you?"

Regina glanced at her escort, who had not been paying much attention to them, then whispered back, "Tell him how much I cherish him. Tell him about how I refuse to speak to my father and that I long for the day when we will be together."

Rochelle nodded and she and Rebecca rose to leave.

*   *   *   *

The portal of Henry's confinement chamber banged open. "You have another visitor," the Enforcer said.

Henry looked up from his parchments at the thin, elderly female who entered. He waited for the portal to close, listened to the pods retreating, then said, "You bear a striking resemblance to one I see in my dreams. I feel as if I know you."

"We are connected," she replied. "Are we quite alone?"

Henry rose and listened at the portal. "Yes."

"I am Regina's grandmother. She wants me to tell you that she cherishes you very much. She refuses to talk to her father and counts the days until you will be together," she said, extending her front pods in an ant greeting.

Henry took her front pods and looked at her carefully. "I won't ask how you got permission to see me. If you are permitted to see Regina again, tell her I cherish her more than life itself, and I'm counting the days too." He still held both her front pods. "Did Regina teach you this greeting?"

"No, I learned it as a tiny nymph. Let's sit down. I haven't been well lately, and you must know the secrets of my heart in case I leave this world before your confinement ends."

Henry was confused. He directed her to sit on his sleep cushion.

"I am called Rochelle, but that is not the name I was given when I hatched. My mother changed her name, my sister's, and mine to protect us. I read your notices a few season cycles ago. You were searching for the decedents of one named Gabriel. I am Riley, his younger daughter."

Henry was dumfounded. So often, old Gallo had spoken of his lost cousins, wondered whether they lived or not, longed to know. That was the reason he had posted notices after completing the story of his great-grandfather. "Why didn't you come forward? Does Regina know? Will you ..."

The elderly female interrupted him. "One thing at a time, quietly, please. The walls in this place listen. Rebecca and Regina do not know this for their own protection. You are the first creature I have ever told. If Master Robert still has enough hate to use his own daughter to try to destroy you, what do you think he would do to me, or to them? Has Regina told you anything about me?"

"She told me about how you tricked Robert when he mated Rebecca, how he wouldn't allow you to know her, but then took care of you after the storm."

"Ah, yes," Rochelle sighed, "giving my daughter to Robert was my attempt at quiet revenge for my father's death. I shouldn't have. Revenge is never productive. Rebecca finally left him because of all of this. She's living with my oldest son and me. Robert must never know as long as he holds his hatred. I have told you because I trust you, as my father trusted the one whose name you bear. You and Regina will one day bind all those old wounds. It's so right that you should join with her because of who you are."

Henry took her front pods in his again. "I've been finishing the translation of what I wrote about your father. My cousin, Ronda, has promised the funds to publish it. I still have his journal from Ruth. Gallo speaks often of you. But I will promise not to say anything, if that is your wish."

"It is," she reaffirmed.

"Will you tell me what you remember of Gabriel? What happened to your mother and your sister? The day will come when it can, and should, be known. My dream tells me that."

"What dream?"

Henry described his recurring dream of the unity of ants and roaches.

"I remember my father well," she began. "I always knew him as a gentle and caring creature. Before his death, I didn't realize that not all male roaches were like he was. He helped my mother care for my sister and me. He was faithful to her. Inside our home, he lived the ways of ants he learned from your great-grandfather. I remember the night he set your great-grandfather free. My parents thought I was sleeping, but I heard all of it. I didn't fully understand the whole thing until many season cycles later, but I was struck with terror when Rex's chief of security came for my father."

She shook slightly and Henry comforted her.

"He was never the same after that day," she continued. "He lived with constant pain from Rex's punishment, but he always cared for us. Many season cycles later, I realized that he knew his days were numbered. He lived every day as though it might be his last. He caressed each of us when he left in the morning, and rejoiced each evening when he returned home. Then the day came when Rex no longer needed him, and he didn't come home."

"And no one explained why to a nymph who needed to grieve."

"Oh, I grieved, Henry. I got all that out ages ago. But the fear never left. My mother said very little, to protect me, I suppose. I kept listening, though. I remember when my uncle found the journal. He helped my mother pack a few of the most important things, and the credit she'd gotten. We left the city that night.

"For the next several season cycles, we wandered from one community to the next, never staying in any more than a few time frames. We lived as though we were destitute, but my mother always saw to it that we got enough plastic. She would take my sister and me to the edge of the markets and tell us to wait for her. Then she would pretend to be the servant of some rich family so no one would wonder why she had credit for plastic."

"What happened to your sister?"

Rochelle looked down. "The first winter, Gabrielle, whom my mother had renamed Genette, got an infection. My mother took her to a clinic, but they wouldn't give her the infection-fighting molds because we were thin. My mother offered twice the amount of credit. Still they refused. My sister died a few days later. The day after that, renegades killed a female and two nymphs who lived very close to us. Her name had been the same as my mother's before she changed hers. We fled again."

"When did you finally come back to the city?"

"Not until after I reached adulthood. My mother finally settled in Nauroach. She'd had good training, so she applied for work as a tutor. She was accepted by a member of that community's local Board. I got my basic training along with his nymphs. When I was of age, she gave me the rest of the credit from my father. She told me to get whatever training I could, find a good mate, remember who I really was, but never tell it, and separate myself from her for my own safety."

"You didn't feel safe after Rex was banished?"

She shook her head. "I sat quietly in the back of the public area at his Inquiry. It was never reported, but his clan swore vengeance. I knew how far their pods could reach, still do. Look at you."

Henry remembered Ruth's shyness at first. "I will keep your secret," he said, "as long as it's necessary. You and your family are welcome at Meadow Commonwealth, if you wish to live with us."

"Thank you, but do you think you could live that close and not reveal this secret? The hardest part, all these season cycles, was knowing where my cousin was, watching his family grow, watching Ruth and her brothers from a distance, never being able to tell them."

"I'm accustomed to keeping things from others. It's part of my job. Regina will be my mate, I hope, but I will not tell her. Don't let it keep you from accepting my offer."

"I'm not sure about my sons, but Rebecca and I may take you up on it. I'd better go. These guards might wonder why an old female takes so much of your time."

Henry embraced her, and then called for her to be let out.

A few days after Rochelle came, Henry had another unexpected visitor. He heard no warning tapping of pods on the passage floor, only a soft sound as the bolt slid back. The latch turned and Young Sir Reese stood before him.

Henry rose from his translating. "To what do I owe this honor?"

Reese paced nervously. "My father doesn't know I'm here, or that I've been to see the Chief Enforcer privately. This visit never took place, but I had to tell you."

"Tell me what?"

"That I had nothing to do with Master Robert's plans. As a matter of fact, I was on my way to Sea Edge to visit her the day you were taken."

Henry's mind reeled. "You are Regina's intended?"

"She didn't tell you?"

"No, not even me."

Reese slumped down onto Henry's cushion. Henry remained silent.

"You've no idea how glad I am that she kept my name out of it," he said. "You can't imagine what I've been through since. I went to Sea Edge, believing she was there. I returned to find everything staring at me in the City Bulletin! My father managed to keep me out of it. He told me not to go near you, or her, and especially not to show up at The Inquiry. Can you understand how I felt? I thought she was fond of me."

Henry glanced around his cell. He stifled several sarcastic remarks about his own circumstances.

Reese continued. "After the first few days, I got over the anger. I began to think more about you and what I learned from you. It began to wear on me. I couldn't sit back entirely."

Henry nodded, now glad he had remained quiet a few moments before.

"I went to the Chief Enforcer privately a little while ago, to renounce my claim on Regina. I know I didn't have to, staying away would have done it, but I didn't want you to think I'd been part of it. I never liked you much during training, but I won't be the one to condemn you."

"Do you believe I'm guilty?" Henry asked, looking directly into Reese's eyes.

Reese rose and moved toward the portal. "I am not my father. I am what I am outwardly because, for now, I must be. When my father leaves this world, things will change. My father made a mistake when he sent me to your training unit. No one spends a term with you and remains the same. No, Trainer Henry, I do not believe you are guilty, and I will not take Regina from you."

Henry rose and stooped in respect. "I appreciate your coming more than you'll ever know. What you have told me today will remain confidential as long as I live."

Reese slipped out as quietly as he had entered.

*   *   *   *

The days plodded by. Henry finished his translating work, read several manuscripts, stared at the surface image by Ronda that he had finally been granted permission to have. Another seventhday arrived. Rundell came for his usual visit.

"Only four days left, Henry!" he said. "We finished your new domicile, the inside, too. Sir Rafael said to tell you that he got hold of one of those special rocks you wanted for your symbolic gift. Rebecca seems happier and Rochelle is doing well. They said to send you greetings."

"Is Rochelle feeling better with the herbs?"

"Yes, that's one feisty old female. She's determined to live until you and Regina are together."

Henry laughed, and then grew serious. "Rundell, tell Rochelle that when I am asked what I want from Master Robert in restitution for the insult, not to be either surprised or disappointed at my request. Remind her what she told me about vengeance."

"I don't understand."

"It doesn't matter if you don't. She will."

*   *   *   *

Henry awakened very early. All the parchments were packed into their containers and Ronda's painted image was carefully rolled and bound. Master Robin arrived ahead of schedule. The enforcers made no mention of bindings. "Guess we won't be seeing you any more," one said to Henry as they escorted him to the Inquiry.

"Oh, you'll be seeing me plenty," Henry replied, "but not from this side of it."

The public area was once again jammed. As Henry strode confidently into the chamber, carrying two of the containers of parchment, their pods drummed the floor. Most of the members of Meadow Commonwealth sat in front. Henry also saw several of those forming the group in the city and many former clients. Master Robert stood in front of the Chief Enforcer's raised bench, flanked by two Enforcers. Regina sat beaming on the victim's bench, her escort was still beside her.

Henry and Master Robin took their place. Henry set down the containers. They waited for the Chief Enforcer to arrive.

All rose when the Chief Enforcer entered, stooped low and spread their front pods to the sides as the he took his place. "Henry Roach-Dairier," he announced, "it having been proven that you are innocent of the accusation made against you, this Formal Inquiry sets you free. Before you leave, what would you like these two Enforcers to do with Master Robert for this grievous insult to you?"

Henry looked at Master Robert. He wondered if his own eyes had ever shown such a look of desperation. "My requests are simple, Lord Chief Enforcer. I want Regina for my legal mate. I want my good name back, through a public statement of my innocence in the City Bulletin. I want no more harassment or spying on any member of Meadow Commonwealth, or any other similar group that may form in the future. I want Master Robert to be required to read these translated copies of my works about my grandfather and great-grandfather, and my personal journal," he pointed to the containers of parchment. "Then he must be taken to the Archives of the Condemned and supervised as he reads his great-uncle's journal for himself. Perhaps then he will understand. If he chooses to, I would be pleased if he would tie the mating cord between Regina and myself this coming sixthday at noon."

The chamber remained silent. The Chief Enforcer looked surprised.

"That's all? No revenge for what you've been through? No credit for your anguish?"

Henry spoke softly in reply. "Vengeance is not productive. I never sought credit. You do not have the authority to grant what I really want."

"So ordered," the Chief Enforcer announced. He turned to Regina's escort. "Your services as official escort are no longer needed here, though I will recommend you to many. The female now belongs to Henry. This Formal Inquiry has ended."

The sound of drumming pods resounded through the chamber. Henry ran to Regina and embraced her. The Enforcers picked up the containers of parchment and escorted Master Robert out.

25.

"*H*old still, Regina," Georgette said. "I'm not through oiling the back of your thorax."

"I'm sorry. I'm nervous."

"Who wouldn't be on their mating day."

Regina sat as quietly as she could. "I'm not as nervous about the ceremony as I am what I'll do if my father actually shows up. Half of me wants him to come and admit he's wrong, while the other half never wants to see him again."

Georgette stopped rubbing in the oil and stroked her instead. "I know what you mean. I feel the same way about my former mate. I finally decided that if he ever does show up, I won't lower myself to his level. I'll tell the jerk he's forgiven. But he'd have to make some major changes before I'd take him back."

Regina turned and smiled. "Thanks."

"Don't let him spoil your day."

"I won't."

*   *   *   *

"Are you ready, Henry?" Rusty called as he looked out the wall opening. "I can see Rebecca and her brothers standing outside Georgette's domicile with the basket. Rick and Genelle are on their way here with

yours. It's a good thing the sky is clear. We'd never fit everyone into the Common Building."

"I'm almost ready," Henry called from his sleep chamber. "Do you think we'll have enough food and ale?"

Rusty laughed. "Donald made more ale than you can imagine. Said we'd sell it later if we didn't need it all. Everyone coming up the path now is carrying a bundle of food. All the surfaces we set up are covered with serving bowls."

Henry came out of his sleep chamber. "Is he here?"

Rusty hesitated. "Not yet."

Henry sighed.

"You can't make someone change, Henry."

"I know. I was just hoping."

Rick opened the portal. "They're waiting for our signal. Regina's ready."

Henry put thoughts of Robert out of his mind. "So am I."

He picked up a round rock, the mating cord, and the contract and climbed into the basket. Rick and Genelle lifted it and carried him toward the center of the community. At the same moment, Regina climbed into hers, carried by her mother and her uncles. Rochelle walked beside them.

In the center of the community stood a large crowd of ants and roaches. Half of New South Dairy 50, all those not related to Henry, had come. Friends and co-workers of all Meadow Commonwealth's members were there, as well as most of Henry's clients.

Henry and Regina climbed out of their baskets, and walked together through the crowd to an open area in the center where a small surface had been set up. It was piled high with grassfrond seeds.

Henry turned and faced his Promised One. "My life was empty, plain and ugly, like this rock. But then you came." He struck the rock against another he had placed on the ground. It broke in two, revealing a center filled with sparkling crystals. He handed his symbolic gift to her. "I come to you now to give you myself and begin to fulfill our promise because you filled my emptiness and made my life beautiful again."

She accepted his gift and held out her own, a small sculpture she had made of the fertilizer basket. "My gift is from nature and from my own hands. It may not seem like a traditional mating gift, but it symbolizes how I feel. I come to you now to give you myself and begin to fulfill the promise we made, because I would do anything for you."

He smiled at the statue, set it down and took her front pods in his. They rose and spoke the words of the mating promise before all their friends. In Ant tradition, they dedicated themselves to each other, to their community, and the community promised to support them. They broke and shared the seeds with everyone, ant and roach alike, those who understood the meaning and those who were seeing it for the first time.

In accordance with Roach mating regulations, Henry signed the contract he had prepared, and handed it to Rick along with the mating cord.

"Wait, Henry," Rick said. "Look." He pointed to the path into the community.

Coming toward them was one lone roach, Master Robert. Henry took Regina's pod gently. They waited. The crowd moved apart and Robert walked up to them. He stooped low and spread his front pods out to the sides before Henry.

"I read all of it ... As you wanted. I didn't want to believe what you wrote ... I was escorted to the archives of the condemned. I read it. You were right about everything ... and I was wrong. You were ... kind ... actually ... in your portrayal of my great-uncle. I came today by my own choice."

Henry tipped his antennae in acknowledgment. He handed the cord and the mating contract to Robert. Robert reached for the ink pot on the surface where the grassfronds had been, dipped the tip of his pod and signed it. Then he made a loop in one end of the cord.

Regina held out her right-front pod. Robert slipped the loop around it and said, "You are no longer mine. You haven't been for quite a while. Perhaps you never were, but I give you to Henry, and I ask that you forgive me for what I did to you."

Regina whispered, "I forgive you."

Robert reached down to tie the other end of the cord to Henry's back left pod, as roach fathers had done for generations.

"Wait," Henry said, extending his front pod instead. "Not behind me, but beside me as my equal."

"As you wish. Have I your forgiveness as well?" Robert asked as he tied the bond.

"Yes."

Robert lifted their pods toward those assembled said, "I could not give my daughter to a better creature."

Pods drummed the ground in approval. When it grew quiet Robert spoke again. "One other thing. Rebecca, I miss you. I do care about you. I'll try to be different. Please, come home. You, too, Rochelle, it you want to live in my household."

Rebecca looked at him, at her daughter, and at Henry. Henry smiled at her. Then she walked forward and joined her mate.

Rochelle called out to Henry. "May I speak?"

He nodded.

She moved to the front and faced those assembled. "The Essence has preserved me to see this day. In Henry and Regina are all things made new in Roacheria. They are the nymphs of old wars, both real and symbolic. In their union, hatred has turned to caring. In the ideals of Meadow Commonwealth, all roaches will see a new way of life. Master Robert, you have set my heart free of a fear you never knew I had. I am Riley, daughter of Gabriel. I am your cousin, Gallo."

The joyous celebration that followed was unequaled for many season cycles. Even Henry and Regina lingered long after dark, dancing with their guests.

As the two swirled together, Regina said, "To think that all this time, Richard and Ginger, Ruth and her brothers, and Gallo, who treated me like family, truly were my family."

Henry held her close and looked at those dancing around them, ant and roach, thin, large, and mixed. He understood his dream. In another dimension beyond theirs, Old Rex had finally united with Henry's antcestors. In their time, Henry had helped Robert—and many others who thought as he did—become one with all of them.

*   *   *   *

Exactly two time frames after their mating day, Regina laid her first egg. Neither Henry nor Regina had any doubt about what name they would give their first-hatched. They only waited to see whether they would use the male or female version. She was Gabrielle.

Gallo and Rochelle/Riley both left the physical world later that season cycle, content to have known each other for a brief time.

Robert continued to change gradually. Ultimately, he provided free medical care to all the members of Meadow Commonwealth. He was instrumental in convincing his colleagues to do the same for other similar groups.

More and more commonwealths formed, often getting their initial funding from Roacheria's wealthiest families. In each case, the families granting starting funds divorced themselves from any power or control over the individuals in those groups. Although the shanties did not disappear, those who lived there did not stay because they were trapped in a dead system.

Ten season cycles later, shortly after the death of his father, Young Sir Reese initiated several changes in the S.E.R.C.B. as its new Supreme Executor. He came to Meadow Commonwealth personally with his eight-season-cycle-old son, and gave Henry parchments he called, "A belated mating gift—the restitution the Chief Enforcer could not authorize." The documents recanted Henry's banishment from South Dairy 50 and reunited him with his family. The event was celebrated by the building of a new bridge over the border stream at the place where Henry had sat so often and meditated.

Afterward—Gabrielle Roach

Throughout the many seventhdays my father sat with his grandnymphs, telling us the story of his early life, his health continued to decline. Some days, his joints were so stiff—the lasting result of his abuse at the hands of the Enforcers—that I had to carry him. He drank far more pain potion than was regarded as safe, but we never denied him when he asked for it. Toward the end, my mother related many parts of the story because the pain potion clouded his mind. But on the last day, when he told of their mating, it was as though he were young once more.

When he finished, he rose and slowly danced with my mother, pulling the little ones in with them. "Dad," I said, "are you sure you should do that?"

"I may not be able to move very well, but I will always dance with your mother," he replied.

After the dance, he limped into his sleep chamber and returned with a carton containing his journal and several other documents. "I give these to you for your safe keeping," he said. "As I waited for my grandfather to leave this world before I wrote his story, please do the same for me. When that time comes, ask permission from Sir Reese or his family. I owe him that."

I took the carton from him, set it down, and embraced him.

I wish my father had lived to see the day I was appointed to the S.E.R.C.B., as its first female member. I represented Meadow Commonwealth and several other commonwealths around it. When Sir Reese the Third hung the medal around my head, I thought of my namesake and what he had written in his journal so long ago. "If my fantasy of being the one to control things should ever come to pass, I vow I will treat those beneath me with the dignity I saw the Ant Council Chief give those refuse collectors in South Harvester 45."

I lifted up a silent thought in meditation. "I will do it for you, Gabriel."

APPENDIX

TIME LINE OF MAJOR EVENTS

<u>SEASON CYCLE</u>

Roach (O.R.)	Combined Colonies of Insectia (C.C.I.)	
1		Enslavement of border colonies by Roacheria
33	1	Beginning of Combined Colonies, violent conflict to free enslaved colonies
177	144	Rex hatches in Roacheria
198	165	Death of South Dairy 50; Antony Dairier hatches
201	168	Enslavement of Henry, Howard, and Herbert by Rex
212	179	Antony emerges from pupation as an adult
213	180	Sir Rodger banished from Roacheria
219	186	Beginning of Ant/Roach Archeological project, Henrietta's mentorship, murder of Antony's family and violent confict with Roacheria
221	188	Peace with Roacheria, mating of Antony and Henrietta
222	189	Establishment of New South Dairy 50
245	212	Death of Rex
257	224	Death of Heniretta, hatching of Henry Roach-Dairier
275	242	Death of Antony
279	246	Henry establishes Meadow Commonwealth

Genealogy Charts
The Ant Families

Gen.1 Howard

Gen. 2   David/Dorothy   **Henry/Adeline**   Herbert/Corina   Cort

Gen.3 Arthur, **Antony**,   **Henrietta,** Hilda, Annie   Corin   Art/Allie
    Drew, Arlene, Allen,   Andrew

Gen 4. **Rodger** /Genny Roach (sister of Rayanne)   Corina/Al
    (adopted by Antony and Henrietta)

Gen.5 David, Dorothy, Arthur, Drew,
        Henry/Regina   Adeline-**Dell**/Donald

Gen. 6   Gabrielle and sibblings

The Roach Families

Gen. 1 **Sir Rudy**/mate (brothers) Sir Royal/mate
                (numerous descendents not
                specifically mentioned)
Gen.2 **SirRex**, Rolinda   **Gabriel**/mate (brothers)   Griffin/mate
            Regina/mate
Gen. 3   Rudy/mate   Gabrielle-Genette, Rochelle-Riley   Gallo

Gen.4.   **Robert**/   Rebecca   Richard/Ginger
            (not aware of her relationship to Rochelle)
Gen. 5 **Regina**-mate of **Henry Roach-Dairier**   Ruth (mate of **Rundell)**
                                Gallo, Griffen

Gen. 6   Gabrielle

Gen. 1 **Sir Rodger**

Gen.   4 daughters of Sir Rodger, youngest mates Sir reginald
      Sir Reginald   **MaterRoland/Ralyn**   **Sir Ronald**/mate

Gen. 3 Sir Reginald   three sons,   daughter, **Geree'/George**
    (the Younger) late life son, **Rick/Genelle**   **Rodger/Ginny**
Gen. 4 various descendants
    not specifically mentioned

Gen. 5   Ray/Ramona   **Henry Roach-Dairier**
                                   And sibblings

Other Characters
not necessarily related to each other
included so the reader may relate to approximate age of contemporaries

Gen. 1 **Master Gerard**/mate   **Sir Rolo/Rachael**

Gen. 2.   **Master/Sir Raphael**   son   **Master Diandra**

Gen. 3 **Renee**/ Rita   **Gerry**/ Rayanne Gen.4 (Ginny's sister)

Gen. 4 3 nymphs   **Sir Reese**   son   Master Riedel Trainer Renard

Gen. 5.   **Reese** (book 3)   **Gatlin**   **Rusty**

Printed in the United States
116581LV00002B/127/A

9 780975 341032